COUNTS OF EIGHT

BRYNN FORD

For dark romance readers everywhere,
you are my people.

Thank you being unapologetically daring.

CONTENT WARNING

This is a dark romance series involving many triggering elements which may be upsetting for some readers. A complete list of tropes and triggers can be found on the author's website at brynnford.com/triggers.

SERIES NOTE

Counts of Eight is book 1 of 3 in a complete trilogy. It is not a standalone, and the books must be read in order.

BOOKS BY BRYNN FORD

THE FOUR FAMILIES
Counts of Eight

Dance with Death

Pas de Trois

THE FOUR FAMILIES SPIN-OFF
King of Masters

EMBER GLEN
Spark of Madness

Blaze of Misery

Embers of Mercy

STANDALONES
Sugar Wood

Jagged Line Paradise

LAWLESS
Coming Soon!

The Darkness We Hide

PROLOGUE

Anya

1 Week Ago

"COME WITH ME and do exactly as I say," Nikolai hisses into my ear.

My arm is already hooked through his at the four families' talent reception as he drags me away from the crowd and down an empty hallway. I always go with him and do exactly as he says because I have no choice in the matter.

We're following Vigo of the Vittori family down one of the many halls in the O'Shea family's ostentatious estate in Ireland. Nikolai steals surreptitious glances behind him to see if we're being followed. Everything about this screams *danger*, but as his slave, so does everything else in my life.

I'm practically jogging to keep up with him. His strides are too long and sharp for my petite height to match. My high heels click with every step along the hardwood floor as he drags me along, echoing in the empty hallway. Nikolai huffs out a low grunt of agitation and stops abruptly. I nearly topple as he whips around to face me. He bends, shoving his shoulder into my gut and wraps his arms around the backs of my knees. He stands, lifting me, hoisting me up over his shoulder with ease.

"Must you always draw so much fucking attention to yourself?" he growls.

Being swept up over his shoulder catches me off guard and I feel lightheaded for a moment as the top half of my body is flipped upside-down and dangles over his back.

He strides off faster than before, presumably still chasing after the Head of House for the Vittori family. We turn into a room and I hear the door click and lock shut behind us. Nikolai tosses me off his shoulder carelessly, as always, and I fall onto a plush chair.

The room we're in reeks of cigar smoke and my vision seems clouded. A fireplace burns bright orange in front of me and the air is warm. Nikolai doesn't sit and neither does Vigo. Both men square off with each other in front of the crackling flames. I look back and forth between them as they stand seething.

"So," Nikolai finally says, "what information do you have?"

"Information isn't free, Nikolai," Vigo Vittori replies in his heavy Italian accent with a sinful looking smirk.

Nikolai holds his hand out toward me. "You can take whatever payment you like from her as long as you return her alive and able to dance."

My heart sinks low in my gut, rolling a wave of anxious nausea through my entire body. My neck muscles tense up immediately with the knowledge that I'm about to be used.

I'm in shock.

I belong to Nikolai.

He's never shared me.

Vigo looks me up and down and nods his approval as Nikolai casually adjusts his cufflinks. "Deal. I'll take her for the night."

Nikolai laughs. "The night? I don't even know if I can trust your sources, Vigo. Particularly since all signs point to your family as the ones who brought down that plane and my entire family along with it."

"My sources? The information I have comes straight from

the horse's mouth. I have the recorded phone conversations to prove it."

"Give me the recordings," Nikolai demands.

Vigo laughs. A humorless smile twists his features into something that looks purely demonic. His deep, honey-brown eyes glow inhumanly with the reflection of firelight. Thick, jet-black hair frames his devious expression.

Black—a color that seems so fitting on him.

Dark and all-consuming.

"You think I'm just going to hand them over?"

"I've offered you payment. I'm no fool, Vigo. You've been pining over Anya for years. You should be grateful for five minutes with her," he sighs, pauses, then lets desperation lead him into concession, "but I'll grant you two hours."

Two hours with *me*.

I think my heart stops beating. I no longer feel the thrum of my pulse. My breath has been stolen from me. Nikolai is fiercely possessive and territorial. I could have never guessed he would offer me up for another man to use, especially not this one.

I wonder if rape from one man feels different than rape from another. I know it can't possibly be better. My instinct tells me that with Vigo, it will be worse.

My eyes burn a hole in Nikolai's black tuxedo jacket, seething with the wish that he had been killed along with his family last year in that plane crash. He made it crystal-clear that he would cut off my head and serve it on a platter if it ensured he got what he wanted—information on why that plane went down.

Vigo's aura suggests that decapitation might be preferred to letting him use me. At least then it would all end. At least then it would be quick, maybe even painless.

Considering the option, Vigo looks me over appraisingly.

"I'll take her for two, but I'm not giving you the recordings. I'll let you listen to them under my supervision once I'm satisfied with the payment I've received."

"If you're not handing over the recordings, then I'm not giving her up for two hours. *One* hour and you let me hear the recordings. And I supervise your use of my slave or no deal."

"Are you serious?"

"Do I look like I am anything other than serious?" Nikolai snarls.

I can only see the side of his face where his lip twitches upward in the corner. I can picture the look in his gray eyes without having to think about it. I know it all too well. I know how his skin wrinkles into crow's feet when he narrows his eyes. I know how his cheeks twitch as his nostrils flair in frustration.

My breath and my heartbeat kick-start in a rush as Nikolai's hand twitches at his side. My spine straightens instinctually, sitting up straighter, preparing for the inevitable urge to flee before his temper ticks.

Surely a demon must recognize the Devil—just as Vigo recognizes my master.

"Fine, fine," Vigo holds up his palms, "I don't care if you watch. Maybe she'll enjoy that."

Nikolai makes an amused sound. "She won't. But I don't care. I just want my information. Anya…" He holds out his hand as he says my name and I stand.

I reach out my trembling hand as my nerves run cold and make me shiver from head to toe. He pulls me to stand next to him, snaking his arm around my waist and holding me tightly to his side. His fingers dig into the side of my stomach and my muscles twitch beneath his rough touch.

"Before I hand her over, tell me which of the four families were responsible for the death of mine? Tell me, and then I'll give you the hour before we listen to the recordings."

Vigo waits a dramatic beat, though none of this matters to me at all. "The Campbells."

Nikolai's lip twitches as it twists into a sneer. "The fucking Americans. I knew it."

His hand slips from my side to my back and shoves me forward. I stumble on my heels, but Vigo's arms reach out and snatch me. I feel sick, nauseous, not just in my stomach, but throughout my entire body.

"Don't worry, beautiful, I've got you," he croons in his overbearing accent.

I shove at his chest, managing to push him away one step, but he rushes me. I wouldn't stand a chance getting away as Nikolai remains a brick wall behind me. Trying to back away, I bounce off his chest and fall right into Vigo's arms again.

Nikolai steps up behind me and pulls the zipper on the back of my black evening gown. He tugs at the straps and they fall down my arms, the entire sweeping, sequined dress slipping off in one swift motion. I tug and pull backward, trying to break free from Vigo's hold, but Nikolai stops me. He grabs my long brown hair, twists it around his fist, and yanks hard. I gasp with the sharp sting of it.

His breath is warm against my ear. "If you fight him again, I will hurt you, *rabynya*."

I swallow hard, pressing my eyes shut to center myself. I reach deep down within my soul to find the blizzard that's always lying in wait. I let the storm blow in around my heart and freeze it, making me cold and hard against the oncoming assault.

Nikolai's hand skims up from the back of my thigh to my ass and squeezes tight, bruising me with his fingertips. "You may use her ass and her mouth, Vigo, but her cunt is off limits.

That belongs to me and me alone. You may give her pain, but you will not harm her in such a way that will prevent her from dancing. No broken bones, no sprains. She is a talent slave, after all, not one of your broken dolls to toss around. I need her strong enough for her new dance partner who is arriving next week. Do you understand?"

I have a new partner arriving next week?

Another stolen boy to help me entertain *moy khozyain. My master.*

My heart races, thumping painfully behind my ribs and tears rush to glass over my eyes. I blink them away, refusing to let them fall, letting them freeze inside my internal snowstorm instead.

"Oh, yes, I understand," Vigo says. "Now hand her over and start your clock, Mr. Mikhailov. I'm eager to take my payment for your information."

Nikolai releases me with a hard shove forward and I let Vigo drag me away to the bed in the far corner of the room. With the blizzard snow falling over my soul, my emotions are hidden behind a layer of ice. The ice protects me from the pain of being present in this moment that reminds me that I am a slave to the Mikhailov family.

I am Nikolai's belonging.

CHAPTER 1

Ezra

Present

ONE HEAVY BLOW to the side of my head knocks me sideways. I drop to my knees from the force of it, which is exactly what they want from me. An aura of pain whips around my head, pulsing an ache inside my skull. If I was able to see, I imagine there would be flashes in my vision—dark spots of pain as it throbs. The black hood they put over my head hours ago prevents me from seeing anything at all.

I grunt, planting my right boot firmly on the hard ground beneath me, straining against the pain in a vain attempt to push to my feet. I stumble, unbalanced with my wrists zip-tied behind my back.

Someone grabs me at the elbow and I act on impulse, pushing myself full force against the touch. I use my weight to barrel into them, but it's no use. Three other hands are on me in an instant—grasping me, pushing me, forcing me down to the ground. There are voices all around me, some shouting, some ordering, all in a language I don't understand.

When they get me to my knees for a second time, they keep me there. Powerful hands press down on my shoulders as I try to shake them off.

"Get off me!" I shout, though I don't know who I'm

shouting at.

"Stop fighting them. It will only delay the inevitable."

I freeze at the unexpected croon of a strong female voice. I had heard only men since I was captured, and the change surprises me, though the sound is muffled through the fabric hood.

"Good," the woman says once I stop struggling.

"I suppose you wish to know why you're here," she says.

She speaks in English, but there's a hint of an accent there. She speaks fluently, but it's clear English isn't her native language. The clipped syllables and rushed flow of her words hint at something Slavic.

Am I still in the Ukraine?

I know that can't be right. I was in Kyiv for a performance yesterday when I was taken. I woke up on a plane and had to have spent hours there. After we landed we traveled by car for another two, maybe three hours before I landed on my knees here.

My breaths are heavy, agitated from the fighting. It's hot behind the hood, each exhale adding fresh heat. It feels like a slow suffocation. I want this damn thing off my head, not just so I can take a clean breath, but so I can see the fuckers who are holding me down.

"Where is *here*?" I demand.

"*Here* is home," the woman tells me. "That's all you need to know for now."

I laugh humorlessly. "Home?"

"Take that thing off his head. Let me see him."

There's a whoosh of air as my face is freed from the obstructive barrier. I squint as bright, fluorescent lights overwhelm my vision. I blink rapidly, determined to get my eyes to adjust quickly so I can assess my surroundings. I was under that hood for so long that it's nearly painful to open my eyes.

I flinch as fingers wrap around my chin. They're delicate

and soft as they tilt my head to the side. The odd touch ignites a brief, electric spark that puts me off my game enough to hate it. I jerk my head to the side, forcing the hand that touches me to fall away.

I force myself to look up, though the light burns behind my irises, and take in the sight of the woman standing before me. She's petite, her dark brown hair tightly pulled back into a low bun, and thick, matching eyebrows spread broad across her wide eyes.

Blue.

Clear, crystal blue eyes.

Cold as ice blue eyes that cut into mine like a spiked icicle falling from a rooftop gutter above my head.

She looks young and old at the same time, and she doesn't smile. Subtle frown lines along the sides of her mouth indicate a prolonged season of displeasure.

She appraises me sourly, then lifts her head to look beyond me and speak to someone somewhere behind me in the room.

"*Moy khozyain.*" The foreign words are forced from between her plump lips in what I finally work out to be a Russian accent. "Another hip-hop dancer? Is this the best you could give me?"

I study her face as she speaks. She looks disappointed, humbled, frustrated, and terrified all in one expression. Her eyes blink and she flinches at the same time I do. A forceful voice booms from somewhere behind my head with an accent that matches hers.

"How dare you ask me that? Remember your place, *rabynya.*" His tone is gruff, insistent. "I will expect your apology for questioning me later this evening."

The woman's eyes drop to the floor, darting quickly away at the command. "*Da, khozyain.*"

I turn my head, craning my neck to see the man with

the forceful voice, but I only catch a glimpse of him exiting the room before cold skin lands on mine again. The woman's hand comes down hard across my cheek, slapping me to get my attention. I sneer, lifting my head to look at her.

"Who the fuck are you?" I demand.

"I am your master. You are my slave. The sooner you accept this, the easier it will be for you."

Her insinuation that I should just accept whatever fucked up situation I've been forced into pisses me off, fueling the flame of my instinct to fight. I find myself faltering as I feel the surge of adrenaline to attack this small, likely fragile woman in front of me. But I need to take her down to distract the men on either side of me, each holding one of my shoulders, just long enough so I can take them out and get the fuck out of this place.

It's a place that looks so safe and comforting and familiar with its pristinely kept hardwood floors, mirrored walls, and bright lighting.

It's a dance studio large enough for thirty world-class dancers to practice in. It doesn't matter if the space feels comfortable to me, there's danger here. I shove down all the warm feelings it threatens to bring to the surface and let the rage take over.

One and then the other, I plant each foot firmly onto the floor as I lift to my feet without warning. I rush the girl, lunging after her with a guttural groan of determination. She expects my attack, shifting and side-stepping in an attempt to get out of the way. All she manages to do is lessen the force of my blow as I duck to ram my shoulder into her gut. It knocks her to the floor, and she lands with a thud as I fall on top of her.

For a beat, a mere nanosecond of time, our eyes connect. Hers soften for the briefest moment of vulnerability before they immediately freeze over again into glacial blue.

She's stronger than I had anticipated for such a tiny thing. Before I can get off her and back onto my feet, her hands grip my shoulders with deadly intensity and her fingertips curl, digging in deep as she pushes back.

She rolls me onto my back and climbs on top of me, settling her weight against my hips, which press my hands painfully into the hardwood floors beneath my ass. They're still zip-tied, crossed at the wrists which are sore and raw from the way the plastic cuts in, deeper and deeper every time I struggle to break free.

Though her weight is minimal, it's still existent, still forces my knuckles to grind against the cold floor, causing them to bruise and ache.

It's not long before the two other men who had been holding me on my knees reappear, coming up on either side of me to help her hold me down.

Are these really the best henchman they could find?

Each man places a hand on either shoulder, grinding me down to the ground as the woman lets anger cloud her features.

The man with the real muscle looks down at me with his teeth bared as he pushes down on my shoulder, his white snarl adding a little brightness to his five o'clock shadow. His dark brown eyes flicker with determination. I can sense he's annoyed with the way this has ruined the careful, modern styling he's done to his ashen-hued, thick, light-brown hair.

Satisfied that I'm properly subdued, the woman nods to the men and slowly stands. "This is the last time you will behave like this, *mal'chik.*"

"Fuck off."

She steps up to my side and lifts her right foot. This is the first time I notice she's wearing pointe shoes.

It's a goddamn ballerina holding me hostage.

I laugh at how ridiculous this whole situation has become.

She lowers the point of her slipper to the hollow of my throat and I swallow as she presses down. I can't help but notice the graceful curve of her foot as she points it with the ease of a natural-born dancer.

"I'm capable of balancing on nearly anything, *mal'chik*. I could rise here against your throat, shift my weight onto your windpipe, and crush it underneath the pressure. I suggest you choose to behave if you wish to live. Death in this place has little meaning. That's a lesson I intend to teach you quickly."

I fight the urge to cough as she shifts, her knee bending as she moves more of her weight onto the foot that slowly suffocates me.

Death by ballerina.

There's a pathetic way to die, though it makes for a killer headline.

With my hands pinned painfully beneath me to the hardwood floor, my shoulders forced down, and this fucking ballerina's hard-tipped pointe slipper on the vulnerable hollow of my throat, I feel completely powerless.

Pathetically, embarrassingly powerless.

I try to speak, to use my voice to get her to stop, but it just comes out as a croak as she presses harder. The side of her lip curls up and it makes me want to wrap my hand around her throat and choke the look out of her myself. I stop my struggle, conceding with stillness and gradually, she lessens the pressure on my neck. When she lifts her foot away, I cough and clear my throat and cough again.

She tilts her head to the side as she looks down at me. "Would you like a drink of water, *mal'chik*?"

"My name…" I huff out a sharp breath, "my name is Ezra. I don't know who the fuck this *mal'chik* is, but you've got the wrong guy."

She shakes her head and clicks her tongue. "No. You are *mal'chik*. It means *boy* and that's all you are to me."

I cough again. "I'm no boy."

"You're wrong. You're a boy and a slave and that's all. You will call me master and you will do as told."

"Like fuck I will."

"Get him up," she tells the men holding me down as she walks to the center of the room. "String him up in the corner and leave us."

Together, they lift me, hoisting me up from beneath the elbows as I get my feet beneath me. Exhaustion from my ordeal over the last twenty-four hours is starting to sneak in as my most recent burst of adrenaline rapidly recedes.

The recent blow to my head teams up with the brief deprivation of oxygen to gang up on me, forcing my body to truly feel the effects of it all for the first time.

The fight in me drains as moments pass. I try to tap into my reserves, but they're practically depleted. I'm unable to stop them as the men drag me to a far corner of the room. They cut the zip-ties from my wrists and trade it for rope, wrapping it around and around my wrists, now in front of me. I try to hide my intent as I lift my hands to swipe across my face, something I've been itching to do since my nose started to bleed from a hit an hour or so ago. There's still some fresh blood resting inside my nostril.

I try to catch them off guard, taking a swing at the man to my right, but I'm weak. Instead of getting the upper hand, I get hit once, twice, three times in the side of my stomach, aching pain shooting up my side with each strike. My body folds around the area of attack as I grunt in yielding.

They attach the free end of the rope around my wrists to

a pulley system suspended from the high ceiling. I look up as my arms are dragged high above my head to see several of these suspension systems peppered across the ceiling.

By the time my arms are settled in place, stretched far above my head, I know I'm trapped. I yank down, twisting my arms against the binding, but it's useless.

Satisfied with their work, the men casually saunter out of the room, walking away as if what they'd just done was perfectly normal.

Just another Tuesday at the office.

Music jolts me back into defensive mode as it rings out over a speaker system in the studio. My head whips around, searching for the source of the classical piano music that starts to play. I catch a glimpse of myself in the mirrored wall to my right.

I look like hell.

My dirty blond hair looks particularly dirty, falling in grungy pieces around the crown of my head. There are dark circles under my normally bright and well-rested green eyes and my sandy skin is brushed with smudges of dirt.

My jeans look like they've been drug through the mud, the pre-manufactured tear near the knee of the right leg is ripped open into a gaping hole. The collar of my T-shirt is stretched out and uneven from someone hoisting me up by the fabric. There's dried blood on my face and hands from wiping at my bloody nose.

My whole body aches from hours of fighting.

My eyes catch her movement in the reflection from the mirror first, a graceful line of a woman sweeping her arms and stretching her legs. I turn my head to watch her as she begins to dance.

As much as I already hate this bitch, I still can't tear my eyes away from her. Her movements are precise perfection.

She's a frozen heart that melts to music and dissolves to dance.

Fuck her.

As she lifts to the tips of her toes and stretches her arms high above her head in a way that mirrors my own captive position, I can make out the full shape of her. She's slender, like every other ballerina I've ever met, yet has a touch more curve in places that draw curiosity to see what's beneath the stretched-out fabric of her black leotard.

This woman wishes to own me, to do me harm, for what reason, I still don't know. But the sight of her talent in motion gives me goosebumps, makes my heart thump and my thigh muscles twitch to be in motion with her on the dance floor.

A dancer always dances.

The song comes to an end and so does her movement. Her eyes immediately lock onto mine and again comes the glacier from the icy blue, scraping slowly but steadily across the space between us.

She strides across the floor toward me with all the poise of a dancer exiting the stage after a performance.

She sighs. "I wasn't expecting you today. You've interrupted my rehearsal."

"I hate to break it to you, princess, but this has interrupted my whole life. So why don't we just cut ties now and get out of each other's hair?"

"No one leaves once they're brought here." Her eyes shift away, then back to pierce mine again.

I let my tired head fall over onto my arm. "Please spare me the cryptic bullshit. What am I doing here?"

"You're here to dance."

"To dance?"

"I require a partner for our annual performance. My last didn't live up to my master's expectations..." She steps closer, invading my personal space. "That partner is gone now, and you are here to replace him."

"Gone?"

"Yes, that's what I said. Why do you keep repeating me? My English is excellent, can you not understand me through my accent? I lived in New York since I was eleven. Perhaps I've developed another accent that you have trouble understanding." She tilts her head as her words drip with sarcasm.

The side of my mouth curls up. I might have found her interesting if it weren't for the circumstances.

"I understand your words, but it doesn't help me understand why I'm here."

Her eyebrows knit together. "I told you, *mal'chik*, you're here to dance. All you need to do is accept that and obey me and we will get along fine. Continue to fight and there will be consequences," she turns her head toward the door, "for the both of us."

"What consequences?"

She circles and disappears behind me. I turn my head as far as I can, feeling the need to keep my eyes on her every move. I can only see the shadow of her movement in my peripheral vision, but I hear the clunk of something hard thud against the floor.

Thud, thud, thud, with every other step she takes, moving to stand beside me. I crane my neck to look around the back of my arm and see her there at my side, a black cane in hand. I watch her eyes as they rake across my body, surveying me with an appraising look.

"You look strong, though you're nearly too tall for me." The end of her cane taps against the heel of my boot. "Yellow boots, jeans, T-shirt. Has my master brought me another beat-boy? A hip-hop dancer? If that's the case, I may as well sign both of our death certificates now." I feel the heat of her breath as she sighs against my side.

"Looks can be deceiving," I reply.

She makes a sound of agreement. "True. So, which is it? What style do you dance?"

I swallow as she steps closer. "Contemporary."

She laughs, though it's without humor. "Of course. You'll have the worst habits of all."

I jump as her hand falls upon my shoulder and my head turns instinctively to look at the source of the touch. Her hand is small, like her, with delicate, slender fingers. Her nails are bitten to the quick and unpolished, the skin around them torn and red in places.

When she speaks again, her voice is smaller, quieter than before, and holds a secret plea that I don't think she wanted me to hear. "I think you're the last, *mal'chik*. I need you to submit to me. I need you to learn the rules quickly, and I need you to follow my instructions carefully."

Her fingers drag across my upper back, tracing an invisible line between my shoulder blades. My muscles jerk at the tickle of her soft touch along my spine as her fingers travel down, her hand stopping at the small of my back.

My chest tightens.

My breaths quicken.

This woman is powerful, there is no doubt about that with the way her touch electrifies me. It pisses me off to react that way to someone who holds me hostage, someone who thinks she has the upper hand, someone who wants me to follow the rules.

"I don't follow the fucking rules."

She lifts the cane and holds it perpendicular to the floor. She swings it to land with a light thwack, flat against my abs, and my muscles jerk as I suck in my gut, flinching away from the black rod. She moves to stand behind me, pressing in closer, reaching around me to grab the other end of the cane with her free hand, pulling both ends back hard. It digs into my torso, creating a line of pressure right across my belly button. I curl around the ache with a low grunt.

"That may have been true before, but it's not true now. You can give me your submission freely or it can be forced from you."

Her body molds to mine along my back as she yanks, tightening her grip with the cane, using her strong body against mine for leverage to dig into me.

"You'll have to force it," I growl.

"That's fine," she breathes, releasing the cane in an instant, and moves away. "I always get what I want."

I open my mouth to bite back, but clamp it shut again when pain shoots through my backside. She strikes me with the cane, right across my ass. I groan. The pain is sharp and ebbs quickly, striking up my agitation.

"That one doesn't count," she says.

I could see her now, standing by my side. My breath hisses through my teeth as I blow out the literal pain in my ass.

"What's your name?" I ask.

"It doesn't matter."

"What's your name?" I demand more forcefully the second time. I'm punished for my insistence with another strike that forces a groan.

"I'll tell you my name when you've earned it with your submission. When I can trust you to obey me, when I can trust you to dance with me, then you'll know my name."

"I'd prefer to know now so I can personalize my hatred of you."

I can see her head dip. "The others hated me at first, too. It won't stop me from breaking you. I have to break you, *mal'chik*. It's a simple matter of life-and-death."

"You won't break me."

"I will." Her head lifts and her arm pulls back. "It's time for you to learn your first count of eight."

I chuckle and hear how tired my voice sounds with the low rumble of it. "Do you really think I'm going to dance for you right now? The moment you untie me, I'm knocking you on your ass and getting the hell out of here."

"You misunderstand me," she says. "I don't mean for you to dance. You're not ready to be unshackled, to be free with me just yet. I don't trust you, and you don't have respect for the situation you've been forced into. The first count of eight you will learn is pain. Pain is what you get when you refuse, when you deny, when you disobey. You'll count as I strike, *mal'chik*. If you refuse or miscount, I'll start again."

She swings hard and the cane collides with my flesh, slicing an even sharper pain than the last through my cheeks, rippling down the backs of my thighs. I try to hide that it hurts, but hell, it stings.

"Count, *mal'chik*. That was *one*."

I purse my lips in refusal.

She sighs. "Fine, we'll start again."

She swings and strikes again, landing with precision over the thickest part of my ass. My thighs clench against the shooting pain that runs right down the back of my legs. It's clear she's practiced at this. She must be, given how much it hurts for such a petite young woman to be swinging that thing at me.

Without warning and without giving me time to choose, she hits me again, but this swing lands across the back of my thighs. I cry out involuntarily and my knees buckle, forcing me to sway in my suspension. She hits me in the same spot, one, two, three more times, each sting more painful than the last.

"Fuck, stop!" I yell at her.

She tries to flatten her tone, but I hear the hint of trepidation. "Now count, *mal'chik*."

As the cane lands against my ass again, I weaken.

Like a fucking coward, I weaken.

"One," I force myself to say.

Her hand softly touches the middle of my back but drops away almost immediately. "Good. Again."

She strikes.

"Two," I say.

I'm rewarded again by the softness of her fingers drawing low on my back, stopping just above my belt buckle before falling away again.

She strikes.

I groan, "Three."

"Very good."

This time, a gentle grazing along my side that makes me flinch.

She strikes.

"Four."

Again.

"Five."

Another.

"Six."

"Good, *mal'chik*. Only two more."

If her goal is to convince me that she gives a shit about the pain I'm feeling right now, she's doing a damn good job. She could make me believe she didn't really want to do it, but I know that would be naïve of me to think.

The woman is beating me, holding me against my will. She would be stupid to think I won't fight her again when my hands are freed and my energy is restored.

"Seven," I manage to say as she hits me, and I hardly have time to blink before the final strikes falls. "Eight."

The cane clatters as she drops it to the floor and circles around in front of me. She stands still, watching me, her chest rising and falling as harshly as mine. She looks the same as she did before, but her face droops with contradiction.

Her blue eyes slice into mine and it shoots through me, just the way the pain shot through me when she struck me with the cane.

"I don't enjoy punishing my partners," she says quietly. "It's simply what I must do to survive. You'll understand that soon enough."

I lift my head to meet her eyes. "Tell me your name."

Her chin rises with dignity, her eyes narrow, her lips purse together. I see a flicker of warmth pass across the cold blue of her eyes like a lightning strike. As quickly as it appears, it's gone.

"You will call me master."

CHAPTER 2
Ezra

THE GIRL WHO thinks she's my master walks in front of me as I'm half-dragged behind her by the same men who first brought me to her.

I can walk, but I'm tired and sore.

My wrists burn from the cable ties and the rope.

My throat aches from the pressure of her pointe shoe.

My gut throbs from punches thrown.

My ass stings from being beaten by her cane.

Apparently, my pace isn't good enough to keep up with Her Majesty, so the men pull me along by the elbows. My hands are tied in front of me with the rope that suspended me in the dance studio.

She glides ahead of us with a dangerous kind of swagger. Her steps are commanding and intentional, yet lack a certain sense of conviction.

I take in my surroundings as I'm led through an audacious mansion estate. The dance studio is on the ground level and leaving that space is like crossing into another world entirely. While the studio had been modern, sleek, and simple, the manor it's attached to is traditional, dark, and cold.

From the west wing, we move toward the center of the

home. The hallway we follow surrounds me with burgundy-colored walls decorated with ostentatious gold portraits of people who were more than likely dead. It opens onto a grand entrance, a vast space which allows the ceiling to stretch high above me, two stories high.

To the right is what I assume is the main entrance of the home. The tall, wooden doors have intricate designs carved into long, etched-out rectangles that stretch from nearly the bottom to the top. To my left is a grand staircase, the ends of which curl out at the bottom landing, opening wide across the marbled floors, beckoning us forward to climb the steps.

She takes us toward it and as we ascend, the image of it makes me think we're crossing the tongue of some ancient monster. We scrape its taste buds as we walk up each step and tempt it to swallow us whole.

God, I'm fucking tired.

We turn right at the top of the staircase and follow another long hallway, this one just as dark and looming as the one downstairs. I'm taken all the way to the end, to the very last room in the dead end hallway.

The blue-eyed girl unlocks the door with two different keys in two different keyholes. It's a simple barrier, but an extra step to delay my escape when I attempt it at the first reasonable opportunity. I watch as closely as I can manage from several strides behind but my eyelids droop from sheer exhaustion.

She steps inside, holding the door open for us, pressing her back against it and holding out an arm as if I'm a guest in her medieval castle turned gothic tourist destination hotel.

"This is your room," she says.

The guards give me a good shove and I land on the floor with a thud. I grunt and wince, feeling all of my various pains roar to life at the same time. I swiftly roll onto my back and rise to a sitting position, grimacing from the burn across my backside where the cane struck me the hardest. It's the best I can do to put myself in any form of defensive position when my body and brain are screaming at me to rest.

"Is there room service?" I do my best to play it cool. "I'd love a steak right now."

The side of her mouth twitches and I nearly think she's going to smile. It turns into a sneer instead.

"Your confident charm will be gone within days. If I had any feelings left, I might think I'll mourn the loss. But I don't. And I won't." She blinks, and her eyes stay closed a beat too long as she sucks in a deep breath.

"If you think beating me on the ass with a cane is going to break me, then you're going to be disappointed," I tell her.

"I know that won't break you. What will break you is yet to come."

She looks down at her hands, which are now raised in front of her stomach. Her fingers clutch together and she wrings her hands around the keys she holds. My eyes narrow, zeroing in on the anxiety that she seems to be washing her hands with.

She's still looking down at them when she speaks again, "I think my master will come to see you tonight. I expect you to be on your best behavior," her head lifts, turns toward me, "for both our sakes."

I glance down at my own bound hands before looking back up at her. She's moving toward the exit.

My tone is gruff with irritation, but I try to sound patient because, for some reason, I feel compelled to be. "Are you ever going to tell me your name?"

She halts and turns back to face me. Her eyes rake over me, scraping across my form from my tied wrists up to my face and I shiver.

"Yes, *mal'chik*. When it's been earned. I've already told you that, so quit asking."

My eyes manage to catch hers just before she slams the door shut between us. I hear her turning the two locks on the door before she leaves.

I let my head fall back, though there's nothing behind me to catch it like I wish there were. Instead, I tilt it side to side, stretching my aching muscles before deciding I need to get on my feet. I shuffle them beneath me and steady myself with my fastened hands, pushing my fists down into the cushioned seat of a cream-colored armchair. Dust and flecks of dried blood from my knuckles smear the sheen of the embossed fabric.

I spin and take stock of my room.

Ugly forest-green walls with the same over-the-top gold picture frames and crown molding as the rest of the mansion make the oversized room feel like close quarters. There's a king-sized bed next to the door with a headboard carved as intricately as the front doors in the grand entrance. The pristine white comforter looks untouched, as if it was just freshly laundered, or perhaps, brand-new. I swallow, remembering what the blue-eyed girl told me—that I wasn't her first partner here.

There are no windows.

It's just a cleaner, more comfortable prison cell.

Wandering around the space, I find a small bathroom on the opposite side of the bed and I'm thankful for that, at least. It's bright white inside and it smells of bleach.

I swallow, feeling an odd pang in my gut at the smell.

I walk back into the bedroom and pull open the drawers of the old, sturdy furniture that probably costs more than a year's worth of my New York studio apartment rent. The first four I pull from the bottom of the double dresser are empty. Only the top two drawers have something inside, but the contents are of no use to me for defense or escape. The drawer on the left contains an extra set of clean, white bedsheets. The drawer on the right surprises me.

I find neatly folded T-shirts which, on first glance, wouldn't have made me bat an eye, except that a closer inspection reveals that they're *my* T-shirts. They're T-shirts from the luggage I had packed when I traveled from New York to Kyiv five days ago.

"Shit," I mutter to no one.

I turn, frantically scanning the space for the simple black suitcase and I spot it, sitting in the far corner behind the armchair I'd smudged when I got to my feet.

I rush to it, tossing it down and tearing into it as quickly as I can with my hands tied together. I pull at the zippers, dig into pockets, hoping foolishly that I'll find my pocketknife. I search the whole damn suitcase as if some magical pocket will appear and give me what I need to escape, to defend myself, to help me in any way at all.

But the luggage is completely emptied.

Why did they even bring it here if they've already emptied it?

To taunt me, of course.

I sit back on my heels, letting out a frustrated breath and wishing I could at least run my hands through my grungy hair. I wonder how long I'll have to wait in this room with my hands tied together. The more I think about it, the more I realize how uncomfortable it is for my wrists to be forced so tightly together and it makes me squirm.

I grab the side of my suitcase and shove it hard into the corner wall with a grunt, "Fuck!" I shout. "Fuck, fuck, fuck!"

I jolt, whipping around to look behind me at the door when I hear the locks unlatching. At first, I think the blue-eyed girl who won't tell me her name has returned, but then I wonder if it's someone else. She told me that her master would be visiting me tonight, and I wonder if her master is the same man I caught a glimpse of in the dance studio.

I know I'll find out soon enough as the door creeps open. It's pushed just hard enough to swing wide without bouncing against the wall and swinging back to closed. Instead, it's more like a curtain being drawn, revealing the villain to the captive audience for the first time.

The man stands in the doorway, legs planted strongly, about shoulder-width apart. His eyes are narrowed on me, as if he's agitated by my very presence.

"My name is Nikolai Mikhailov. I'm your new owner." He shares the same accent as the blue-eyed girl.

I push off the floor and get to my feet, trying to do it as steadily as I can so I don't come off as weak. "As I told the girl, nobody owns me."

He steps across the threshold into the bedroom. I feel the force of him moving toward me and I take an automatic step back. I immediately realize what I've done, giving him some semblance of power over me by my instinct to move away. I step forward again, twice, making up for the lost distance.

He stops once he reaches the end of the bed, tilting his head toward it. "Sit. Let's talk."

Without waiting to watch for my compliance, he reaches for the door, pushing it shut. I haven't moved yet when he turns back around to face me. He doesn't speak, just lifts a thick eyebrow, and the corner of my mouth lifts the same way in challenge.

He crosses his arms over his broad chest and cocks his head, and I literally feel the violent vibration of his soul slice through the space between us like a dagger. If the blue-eyed girl is winter, then this man is the fucking arctic circle. I strain every muscle in my body against the eerie feeling his presence imposes. My pride begs me to hold, to stay, to passively resist by remaining in place. But my instinct tells me to obey for now to spare my skin.

I leave the defiant smirk on my face while I slowly move toward the edge of the bed. I don't let my eyes leave him for a second as I lower to sit, perched at the very end. Nikolai shifts to stand in front of me.

He reaches into his pocket and I shift backward as he flicks open a switchblade and moves toward me.

"Hold out your hands," he says with no expression on his face.

"I don't trust you with that thing," I say honestly.

"Hold out your hands, *mal'chik*. I won't ask you again."

I believe him.

I slowly push my hands forward and he reaches out to snatch me, gripping the ropes that bind me where they wrap around my wrists and yanking my arms toward him. I flinch as he starts to saw away at the rope, but I don't dare pull my hands away for fear his blade may slip and injure me.

"If you fight me, you will lose," he tells me with a flick of his gray eyes from his blade to mine. "I'd hate to have to purchase a new comforter for your bed again. Anya's last partner bled all over the last one before his time with us ended."

My heart hesitates a little longer between beats before thumping painfully back into order.

Anya.

Is that her name?

The blue-eyed girl?

I dare to ask the question, "What happened to him?"

The rope separates and falls free and I rub my sore, chaffed skin.

Nikolai folds the blade and pockets it in his tan trousers, taking a slight step backward. "It's of no matter to you. He's gone and you're here to replace him."

With my hands freed, my fight reflex jumpstarts a new rush of adrenaline that forces my instincts to kick in. My head jerks back to look in the direction of the door. I immediately realize that I could slide off the side of the bed, throw the unlocked door open, and make a run for it. But some smarter, saner part of me wonders what the fuck I would do then.

I don't know where I am.

I don't know what or who might be in the hallway.

I haven't assessed this man's physical capabilities, though it's obvious his intentions are nefarious and it's unlikely he possesses an ounce of empathy.

I'm itching to jump and run, the urge to do it literally burns under my skin. My knees jerk up, ready to run and I clamp my palms down over them to hide my intentions. It's too late, though, because this guy already knows what I'm thinking. In a flash, he's got his switchblade out and open again, at the same moment my muscles flex to pull me upright off the bed. I've hardly moved toward the door before he comes after me.

He grabs me by the back of my shirt, tossing me backward and throwing me onto the floor with strength and ease. I'm strong, I have endurance, but the way he flings me with such a simple flick of his wrist puts me in check immediately.

I jump back up off the floor, ready to fight. But looking at his cold face, the same heartless expression he held from the moment he walked through the door, I hesitate. There's no passionate fury, no violent rage, just cool, collected indifference and somehow, that's more frightening.

"I told you," he says, flipping the blade in his hand. "Fight me and you'll lose."

I'm taking in heavy breaths as my adrenaline crests over the peak and starts to fall. "Just tell me what the fuck you want from me. Why am I here?"

"Sit and we'll discuss. Your incivility is unbecoming. It makes me want to shove this blade in the side of your neck and I just might if you don't sit, *mal'chik.*"

I lock my fingers behind my head, stretching back before letting them drop with a thud against my sides. "Fuck, fine."

Once again, I'm moving toward the bed, forcing myself to relax enough to sit, though I'm agitated, twitchy, fidgety. It's not easy with him standing there between me and my freedom, threatening to stab me.

I'm not gonna die in this place.

As I lower to sit, he hovers above me. He smells like cigar smoke and whiskey. His prominent brow line shadows his gray eyes, emphasizing his permanently narrowed eyes.

"You are here for one reason and one reason only. I've brought you here to serve Anya, to perform with her."

"Perform for who?"

"Mostly for me. You'll learn more in time. Right now, all I want from you is to understand your place. You are in my home. It's belonged to my family for four generations. You will respect me here as the Head of House. You know my name, but you will call me master. Anya calls me the same as you are both my belongings. But she will also be your master, and you'll refer to her in whatever manner she deems respectable. You will obey her. You will follow her rules. You will not question or fight her. When she asks you to dance, you will dance and you will get it right. If you don't, she may punish you and I will support it. If she can't control you, I will punish her, so know that your actions will impact the entire household. Now, kindly remove your socks and shoes."

"What?" I stare up at him like he's just grown a second head.

He sucks in a breath and his lips flatten into a straight line. "Don't make me ask you again." His wrist ticks and light bounces off the blade, reminding me it's still in his hand.

I shake my head in frustration, but bend all the same, untying the laces of my boots. I kick them off and pull off my socks. I sit back up and plant my hands on my knees, looking up at him with a sneer.

Nikolai side-steps and bends to one knee near the bedpost to my left. My brow furrows with concern as he reaches beneath the bed and I'm twitching to run again. He grabs something that clanks, the sound of metal against metal and I can't sit still. I pounce to my feet and step away, but he's quick.

His hand clamps around my ankle, pulling hard and I nearly lose my balance. I naturally try to kick him off, but he's quick, latching a metal cuff around my right ankle.

"What the fuck?" I shout at him, but it's already locked in place.

I look down to see the cuff attached to a length of metal chain and I don't know how I missed seeing it there before, attached to the bottom of the bedpost beneath the frame. It's cold and oppressive against my skin and immediately, I bend to claw at it.

Nikolai stands and places his switchblade back in his pocket, satisfied with his safety now. I crouch and shove at the bedframe, trying to move the post, but it's solid as a rock, bolted down to the fucking floor.

"I would have given you freedom in your own room with just a locked door, but you've proven you're impulsive and can't be trusted. You're lucky I've seen your talent firsthand, otherwise, I'd end you now and find another to replace you.

Anya will struggle with you. I can already sense it. But it will be all that much more satisfying to watch you break, comply, and still fail to satisfy me in the end. Your chains will reach as far as the toilet, but you'll be confined here until I decide to release you. I'll send her for you when I'm satisfied you've had enough time to know your place."

"Fuck you. Both of you."

The corners of his lips curve up ever so slightly and somehow, it makes his look even harsher, his nose more pointed, his jaw more angled and sharper. With his nearly chin-length, ash-brown hair slicked back and deliberately styled, the overall appearance of him screams wolf, predator.

"Get some rest, Mr. Bell. You have some trying times ahead of you."

He slices out of the room, sharp and severe like the blade he carries, and the door falls shuts behind him. I chase forward after him, but my chains stop me before I can even reach the door to bang on it and beg to be let out. I hear the locks turn and I still.

I look up to the ceiling, lacing my fingers behind my neck, and huff out a heavy breath full of anguish, the angsty groan of a caged animal. Rabid vexation rips through me with the jolt of pain that reminds me of my injuries. I shout out my distress to the ugly forest-green walls when the realization finally hits that I am well and truly fucked.

CHAPTER 3
Anya

MY NEW PARTNER'S name is Ezra, though of course I call him *mal'chik*. Not because I want to, but because I know it's what Nikolai will call him and he will insist I do the same— just as he insisted with the other men who came before him.

I despise my native language for no reason other than the fact that it has been used to degrade me for the past three years. I was born in Russia, raised there by my single mother until I was eleven years old before I was shipped off to New York and immersed in training to become a ballerina.

I was happy in that life, but I was stolen away from it three years ago, just after my twenty-first birthday.

I force thoughts of that life away, back into the dark corner of my mind, seal it, and wrap it shut in a black box that reads *do not open* on the side. My eyes narrow at the thought that I had opened it at all today. It was dangerous to remember life when I was free because I knew I would never have that life back.

The lid of the box had cracked open when my eyes fell upon Ezra in the dance studio for the first time. I think it was the emerald-green of his captivating eyes that did it. It reminded me of the fresh and bright green plants I kept in the two-bedroom apartment I shared with a roommate in New

York. I had always surrounded myself with shrubs and greenery. I took pride in tending to them as they brought me a sense of brightness, of happiness, of life.

I haven't seen such bright green life in years. Though a vast forest surrounds the estate, it's full of dead trees in the cold of winter that never seems to come to an end. Life is shrouded forever now in cold, lifeless gray.

But Ezra's green eyes brought back the reminder of vibrant life against this cold, ongoing death march. It was as if he reached inside me and pulled out the dusty box of remembrance and hope that I had kept safely tucked away.

Nikolai had given me three dance partners before Ezra. Three men who hadn't met his expectations in performance for the Mikhailov family's turn to host the quarterly meeting for the four families.

Thus, the men before Ezra had disappeared. I presume they are dead. I can't afford myself the luxury of hoping they made it out alive because that would give me hope that I might someday do the same.

Hope is a dangerous thing and Ezra's spirit still thrums with that electric spark of lightness. I could feel it when I touched him. I could sense it pulsing from his soul. But because I'm forced to dance, I have to force Ezra to dance with me. That means I need to control him, and not just because Nikolai expects it.

I have to control him to protect myself. If he can't dance to my master's expectations, then this may be it for me. I've felt Nikolai's patience with me waning, his frustrations growing, and he takes it out on me.

I will remain in control.

I will make Ezra submit.

I will train Ezra to perform with me in the perfection that

Master requires.

I will do this by being the woman to strip his hope from him piece by tiny piece until he has none left. Only then can I control him, use him. Only then could I even consider the possibility of a predictable, complacent survival in this nightmare life. I don't even consider the possibility of escape anymore. I don't believe it's possible outside of death.

I swallow and pinch my eyes shut, steeling myself as I approach Nikolai's master suite. The door is open because he's waiting for me.

It's been hours since I brought Ezra to his new room and I know Nikolai has been there as well. I've since showered, styled my long, dark chocolate colored hair so that it tumbles in wavy tresses, reaching down to the middle of my back. My master prefers it down when we're alone.

I wear a simple, black silk chemise for him under the long oriental-style robe that covers me. I've tied the robe shut tightly around my waist, double knotting the bow. I know it will prove to be no barrier for Nikolai because he takes what he wants but it makes me feel better all the same.

The silky floral fabric feels soft against my arms and I make a useless wish that it will remain on my body tonight. The softness of it is a comforting embrace that, once removed, will expose me to be used.

I cross my arms over my body, stepping over the threshold into his suite, shielding myself from what is to come.

Nikolai is sitting on one of the two oversized armchairs in front of the fireplace, his back to the door. The fire burns orange and bright, and I can feel the heat of it from where I'm standing. I can see he's still dressed in his usual attire—a button-down rolled up at the sleeves and open at the collar, covered by a tweed vest, tan slacks, and sleek dress shoes. There's a glass of whiskey in his hand and one ankle is crossed over his knee.

With a soft voice, I announce my arrival, "*Moy khozyain.*"

My master, in Russian.

I hate the words and it feels so much worse to say it in his language than in mine. I'm fluent in both, but I was building an American life when I was taken and forced to live in his world.

He allows me to speak with him in English, a small grace he granted me after my first year of obedience. It's something so simple, but it gives me a small amount of power. I refuse to let go of it and choose to speak English whenever I can. Still, I am required to address Nikolai in his native tongue, though he's fluent in both languages as well.

"Close the door and sit beside me, *moya rabynya*."

Moya rabynya.

My slave girl.

"*Da, khozyain*," I say, pressing the door shut behind me and crossing the room.

I walk around the armchair beside him. It angles toward him, facing the fire, and I slowly lower to sit.

He takes a sip of whiskey from his glass and speaks without looking at me, "Ezra Bell is impulsive and reckless. He's overly confident and sarcastic. But I've watched him perform, and I know he is more talented than the other partners I've given you."

His head turns slowly, and I lower my gaze toward the floor before he can make eye contact. I haven't yet determined his mood tonight and know it's better safe than sorry.

He prefers my submission.

Perhaps that's why I'm so insistent on maintaining control over my dance partners. One of the many reasons among simple survival.

He continues and I can feel his eyes take me in. "If you can break him, he will be a good partner for you. If you train him well, you may win back my favor this year."

I knew his enchantment with me was fading, but the way he reminds me makes me feel cold inside.

"*Da, khozyain.*"

"Look at me, Anya."

I lift my chin and meet his gray eyes. The side of his mouth twitches, attempting to form a small smile.

Happiness isn't a feeling he's accustomed to.

"Come here and let me look at you," he says.

He has trained me not to hesitate, so I don't. I come to stand in front of him and he nods his head toward the floor, so I fall to my knees as he uncrosses his leg and sets his whiskey on the side table. He spreads his legs apart and leans forward, reaching out with both hands to hold my face, his fingers landing softly against my cheeks.

"You look beautiful, Anya."

"Thank you."

Nikolai sighs on a low growl as he shifts closer in his seat. "What do you think of Ezra?"

I try to breathe deeply, but the air catches in my throat. I swallow and harden my exterior shell before responding, "If you've selected him for me, I'm sure he'll make a fine partner."

"That's not what I'm asking you." His grip tightens against my jawline. "Do you find him attractive?"

With a flip of a switch my shields are up, armor on. This little game of entrapment is a favorite of his when he's feeling particularly brutal, when he's feeling particularly weak.

"I'm not concerned with his appearance, only in his ability to perform."

His right hand slides back along my jawline and his fingers dig into my hair. "Answer me truthfully. Do you find him more attractive than the others?" His jaw clenches and his eyes narrow in on mine, digging deep.

He'll know if I'm lying so I have no choice but to answer truthfully, "*Da, khozyain.* But I belong to you."

He bends, leaning in close. His lips are a mere inch from mine, his breath hot against my face. When he exhales, I smell his whiskey.

"Prove it to me."

I close my eyes, but only for a moment. "Tell me how and I will."

His fingers curl into a fist around my hair at the side of my head. Nikolai bares his teeth at me as he yanks my head sideways, growling out a command, "Take off your robe."

I inhale a breath of courage and reach down to loosen the knot. It slips apart, removing the barrier of my armor.

It already feels like defeat.

It *always* feels like defeat.

I remain strong, though, because I won't give him the satisfaction of knowing that.

I let the silk glide down my arms and it falls to the floor, encircling me as though it knows it's my only protection. One of the thin straps of the barely-there chemise has fallen, and Nikolai's eyes are drawn to it. His head dips and he presses his lips to my bare shoulder before sinking his teeth in.

He is the predator and I am his prey.

Always.

The bite makes me flinch and groan, and he mistakes the noise for wanting. Nikolai hears what he wants to. He wants me to want him, so I let him believe it if it keeps the peace.

I have the scars to remind me why that peace must be kept.

He pulls back and moves his hands to grip my shoulders and starts to push me sideways. "Get on your hands and knees, *rabynya.*"

I turn and fall on my hands as he's forcing me to the ground. I'm on all fours beside the crackling fire with only the small sheath of silky fabric to hide me. He drops to his knees and climbs up behind me. He grips my hips with both hands, fingers digging into my sides as he slides up behind me. His knees are inside my legs, nudging my thighs, encouraging them to spread wider for him.

I let my head fall forward in defeat as one of his hands trails up the back of my thigh, creeping over my rounded backside to lift the hem of the short nightgown. Internally, I whimper at the touch, knowing the pain that's to come from this position, knowing which part of me will be violated tonight in front of the fire.

He reaches out to fist my hair behind my neck and pull my head upright. His hips thrust against my bottom and I feel the bulge of his erection through his trousers.

"I wanted to give you pleasure tonight, but you were disrespectful to me when I brought you a new partner, questioning my choice. So, instead, I'll take my pleasure from you and fuck you until you bleed for me. I want your tears tonight, Anya. Give them to me and I'll spare you the pain of being burned."

He holds my hair so tightly that I can't turn my head, but my eyes flicker over to the flames burning beside me. My eyes burn just as hot, and though the determined woman inside wishes to deny him those tears in favor of flames, I can't, and he knows it.

This has happened a thousand times before and it will happen a thousand more before I'm given the gift of freedom or death and it damages me still.

When he fucks me in that forbidden entrance from behind, it always hurts and it always brings me tears and it always gives him power.

"Tell me who you are," he growls.

I struggle to keep my voice steady. "I am slave to the Mikhailov family. I am your belonging."

He suddenly lets go of my hair and my head jerks forward. I don't look over my shoulder when I feel his hands move between me and him, his buckle coming undone, his zipper being pulled. I retreat inward and try not to think too much. I try to listen only enough to follow his commands and move on from this vile moment as he's sliding my underwear down to expose me.

Nikolai reaches around me and his fingers graze over my lower belly. "I need you wet for me if you want to lessen the pain."

My stomach rolls in nausea.

His hand moves lower and his fingers glide across my sex, finding the spot that he knows will trigger my arousal.

My body always betrays my mind and my heart in these moments. Nikolai is talented in touch, an experienced, older man—fifteen years my senior. Though his soul is filthy with violence and coldness and brutality, he is still a physically attractive man. I hate him almost as much for being beautiful on the outside as I do for being so disgusting on the inside.

Though it sickens me that my body reacts to him at all, it's a good thing that I do because it lessens the pain of his intrusion.

There was a time once when I felt something more for him, early in my captivity when I felt starved by loneliness and was desperate for human connection beyond his violence and hatred and the torment he caused me. It was a day when I was emotionally vulnerable and pathetically needy.

That day, I had come to him, sought him out in hope of comfort from my master. I came into his room as he was taking a shower. In my naïve despair, I went to him in the bathroom and stood waiting in the doorway. He saw me standing there through his glass shower door and watched me as he finished bathing. The room had filled with steam by the time he got out. I saw something different in his beauty that day, and I haven't seen it since. I saw something raw, exposed, as broken as I felt.

He came to me, glistening with droplets of water. His damp hair, which he normally straightens and slicks back, was wavy around the edges in the steam, softening the severe lines of his predatorial features. He stood in front of me that day, his presence quiet and unassuming for the first and last time. He watched me and waited for me, and it was only moments before I bared myself to him.

I pulled off my clothes, piece by piece, revealing my body to him willingly, bit by bit ceding control in foolish wanting. I'd let down my guard, weakened my defenses, and opened myself to him. He kissed me sweetly, touched me softly.

He backed me up against the countertop and fell to his knees for me. That day, he made me come with his fingers. He studied me with attentive eyes, watching as I became aroused for him, watching my wetness shine as it slicked his fingers, exploring all my most private places. It was the first and only time I felt so connected to Nikolai that I felt like I wanted him.

I held onto that time he made me feel so good because it was the only recent memory I had of feeling worthy and worshipped. I pretended that's all it was during moments like the one I'm experiencing with him now. I have to remember the way he touched me then, the way he made me feel, I have to think of it to become aroused for him now.

His touch is the same now as it had been then, but it doesn't make me feel the same. This touch is different because it's a lie, a manipulation of the truths he discovered that day when he made me come so completely undone for him. That day for me was a connection, but for him, it was a mere study and he uses his knowledge against me now.

I let him touch me, forcing my body to react, obliging him with the physical reaction he wants as he spreads my wetness all across me, dragging it along my crack, to the place he wishes to defile me.

He's already pressing his erection against me, eager to force his way inside. I scream when he finally does, showing me no gentleness, no time for adjustment, no mercy. He buries himself to the hilt and I feel like I'm being ripped in two. Nikolai folds his body over mine and pushes me down to my elbows, forcing my ass higher into the air.

I'm enveloped by him, consumed by him, oppressed by him.

"Tell me how much I hurt you, *rabynya*. Give me your tears and tell me of your pain."

"You hurt me more than anyone ever could, *moy khozyain*," I say truthfully as tears slip from my eyes.

He will never understand how true that is. I might have found a way to love him if he hadn't abandoned his humanity.

I could have loved a monster.

But I could never love the Devil.

CHAPTER 4
Ezra

THE SKIN AROUND my fingertips is raw and peeling from my useless attempts to pry the metal cuff from my ankle. I'm weak, starving, lost inside the dark spaces of my mind.

"Nikolai Mikhailov," I say into the desolate space of my room.

I won't forget the name of the man who chained me to this bed and left me here alone. I've been without food, without sunlight, without company for a long damn time. I picture myself as a wilting leaf on a flower that is slowly wasting away and dying in a cold, dark space.

I'm losing my fucking mind.

There's no clock and I don't wear a watch, so I have to guess at how long I've been locked in this room. It feels like it's been a week, but in reality, it's probably been a little over two days.

For the first time in my life, my fight has drained out of me. I'm slumped on the floor with my back against the bed, my head dropped onto my arms that rest on my knees. My anger has been replaced by need, basic need.

All I want right now is food, a proper shower, a full fucking glass of water. All I can do right now is drink from the bathroom faucet and it runs slow with low pressure. I can reach the toilet, but I can't even get to the shower with the chain shackling me in place.

I slept the first night, though the fight in me still existed, jerking me awake every now and then. I'm more tired than I've ever been, and I've had nothing but time to sit and wait. It's an agitated rest to be shackled, locked in a room with nothing to do but stare at the ugly walls and talk to myself.

And I've decided that I'm not that great of company.

Surprisingly, I've been thinking about the blue-eyed girl. She seems familiar to me, but I've been struggling to place her. For a while, I wonder if she just seems familiar because she's the only person besides Nikolai Mikhailov that I've had any contact with in days.

The more I try to connect my memory of her in my brain, the more I wish I could see her face. I think if I could look at her again after all this time spent trying to place her, that I'd know.

It was something about her presence, the way she holds herself, the way she dances. Maybe I've seen her perform somewhere. More likely, she just reminds me of any number of dancers I've seen before.

I know it's more than that, though.

It's something in those sapphire eyes.

Fuck.

I'm grasping at straws, trying to remember things, to make connections that aren't really there. It must be my brain's way of staying active and keeping me sane.

I laugh out loud at the thought of sanity. I feel like it's right on the brink because at this point, I don't know whether anyone is coming back for me.

When will I eat?

Will I starve to death in here?

Is Nikolai Mikhailov's the last face I'll ever see?

Fuck, I hope not.

I don't think it would bother me so much if the blue-eyed girl's face is the last I see.

He called her Anya.

I suppose I should stop thinking of her as the gorgeous blue-eyed girl with the grace of an angel, but at least the thought of a beautiful face somewhere out there helps me feel a little less alone.

I hear the locks on the bedroom door turn, but I don't turn to look. I know I'm just hearing things because I thought I heard them before. A couple of times, actually, but no one was there.

"*Mal'chik.*" The voice slices into the room and I spin to see her at the door, the blue-eyed girl.

She comes into the room and sets a tray on the side table next to the armchair. I've stilled and I blink at her, unmoving because I don't believe she's actually there.

Her hair is down and I can see how long it is, tumbling in perfect, coffee-colored waves down her back. Her eyes seem even bluer than I remember and her features softer. Perhaps I'm just happy to see another human because I recall hating her so fervently when I arrived, but at this moment, she's truly stunning to look at.

A sight to behold.

An angel swooping down into my hell.

I'm losing. My fucking. Mind.

"Is your name Anya?" I ask.

Her eyes narrow. She steps back and reaches up to tuck a strand of hair behind her ear.

"It's *master* to you, and I command you to eat."

The muscles in her neck move as she swallows, and I think I see hesitation before she leaves the room. As the door shuts behind her, I finally come back to life. I spring to my feet, but my chain prevents me from reaching the door before she turns the first lock, then the second.

For a moment I'm pissed at myself for being so slow to act. But I forget quickly about the fact that I'm alone again when the smell of fresh, warm stew fills my nostrils. I go and lift the tray that Master left for me and sit on the edge of the bed.

I flinch before I pick up the silver spoon with the intricately carved swirling design on the handle.

I called her Master in my own damn mind.

"She's not my master," I say out loud to remind myself that these people don't own me, but it doesn't come out very convincingly, so I say it again, "She's *not* my *master*."

I have a fleeting moment where I think I should refuse the food and go on a hunger strike. After all, they want me to dance with her. I won't be able to if I'm starved and malnourished.

My mouth curls up sideways in the corner as I say to nobody, "That will show them."

But the smell of the soup is nearly intoxicating after being denied nourishment for so long. Steam curls as it rises from the dark broth. I dip my spoon into it and stir, noting the colors of the vegetables.

Fresh orange carrots.

Precisely green peas.

Flawless white chunks of potato.

Perfectly tender chunks of beef.

It all looks freshly made and my mouth is watering.

I scoop and lift the spoon to my lips and eagerly take a bite, hunger strike and scalding broth be damned. I devour the entire bowl before I even notice the warm bread and scoop of butter beside it, and I scarf that down, too.

Now that I've eaten, I feel refreshed, renewed, hopeful I can survive this ordeal long enough to escape. I stand and set the tray back on the side table by the armchair and hesitate.

I've already scoured the parts of the room I can reach. All the drawers and built-in cabinets are empty. Anything I could potentially use as a weapon or tool has been removed from the room.

I'm still cuffed.

I'm still locked in.

I'm still captive.

I look down at the empty soup bowl and suddenly feel deceived by the brief jolt of energy it's nourishment gave me.

I feel fucking betrayed by it.

I reach down and snatch the bowl from the tray and hurl it across the room. It slams with a thud and bounces off the far wall, entirely intact.

It doesn't even give me the satisfaction of shattering for me.

I think another day has gone by when the door finally opens again. This time, I jump up the moment I hear it, eager more than before to eat with the tease of food I was given yesterday. I spin to face the door and the blue-eyed girl enters the room.

Her hands are empty and my stomach grumbles in disappointment. She's hard and cold again, not the way she looked when she brought me the soup.

"On your knees," she commands, closing the door behind her.

I waver.

Her eyes pierce into mine and though no part of my psyche wants to bend for my captor, my knees fold all the same. I lower to the floor, but I keep my eyes on hers, my expression dark with the anger I feel at myself for obeying so quickly. I don't even know why I did.

"Good," she says with narrowed eyes as she moves closer. "Eyes on the floor."

"I'm not taking my eyes off you," I growl.

"I'm flattered, really, but you will obey if you want to eat."

Her challenge ignites my stubbornness. "Then I guess I won't eat."

Her eyebrows slant down toward her tiny, round nose and she tilts her head as she regards me. A curious look spreads across her rosy cheeks. Boldly, she walks to stand right in front of me. I could reach out and grab her, tackle her to the floor, hold her hostage until Nikolai Mikhailov returns.

If he ever returns.

And what the hell would I do when he does?

My heartbeat surges with the urge to do it—to toss her to the ground and pin her beneath me and force her into this captivity along with me. It burns heat inside my chest that coils and festers.

She hovers above me and her chest rises and falls sharply with a quick breath. I can nearly feel the air rush out of her on the exhale, and I breathe it in. The cool, wintry breeze of her breath melts over the fire burning in my chest. It drips like a waterfall into my stomach, tugging unnecessary need into my belly. The feeling persists when her icy fingers touch my chin, grip me firmly, and pull my head up higher to look at her.

Her voice is a low whisper. "Remember this while you sleep tonight, *mal'chik*. You made the choice not to eat."

I open my mouth to clap back at her with a snarky reply, but I don't even get the chance. With a graceful spin, she releases me and turns, striding with sure steps to the door.

She's gone before I can even blink.

It's fuck all o'clock on the forty-second day of December in the grand old year of two thousand thirty-seven or some bullshit.

I don't know whether it's night or day anymore.

I've been fed three times since they brought me here and my interactions have been limited to brief exchanges with the blue-eyed girl. Each meeting ends with me frustrated in my stubbornness and inexplicably more desperate to obey her, though I fight it.

I don't think I'm going to fight it when she comes back.

If she comes back.

God, I hope she fucking comes back.

CHAPTER 5

Anya

KEEPING MY INTERACTIONS with Ezra brief and cold has been more challenging than it was with any of the others. He was broody and sullen with me—understandably so—and it should have put me off.

It *does* put me off, but in a fiery sort of way that makes me *want* him to keep fighting me for control.

Of course, I don't want that—my survival depends on his submission. I need his submission to be able to train him, but he hasn't given it to me yet.

He's been locked in his room for five days, has earned meals only three times, and I'm concerned because I need him to be strong enough for the way I manage my rehearsals. Time is wasting away while I wait for him to cave and concede control, and I've finally come to my wits' end. He's not pliable and easily manipulated like the others had been.

In my life before, I might have enjoyed that quality about him, but now, I find it infuriating. As I approach his room, I place a hand over my belly and take in a deep, steadying breath. The way he regards me whenever I enter his room is unsettling in a way that makes my pulse race. He's not aware of his effect on me, or at least, I don't think he is, but I have to be careful with my reactions.

I meet his snarky tone with a snarky tone of my own.

I meet the intensity of his eyes with my own piercing gaze.

I meet his fire with my inferno.

I know I must be careful not to fan the flame too high, though.

Everything must be carefully controlled with him.

I unlock the door and open it carefully, stepping inside and shutting it behind me. Ezra has just risen to his feet from sitting on the edge of the bed and whips around to face me. His shirt is off, though his jeans remain intact. I catch a glimpse of his defined torso at the moment his eyes narrow on mine and my fingers twitch at my side.

I think with certainty he's going to be difficult today, but then his face droops in defeat. He circles to the stand in front of the end of the bed as I walk across the floor to meet him and, without my directive, he lowers to his knees.

I take in a sharp breath of surprise as he sits back on his heels and places his palms on his thighs, lowering his eyes to the floor. He is the chiseled statue of a man kneeling in worship and I am the object of his adoration.

The part of me desperate for some semblance of control in this tortured life aches for him to be mine completely, hopeful that this submission is given beyond his desperation for food and comfort and connection. I know that kind of submission as I give it daily in exchange for the things I need for survival. For the first time, I want more than that from this partner. I just don't know exactly why.

I stand in front of him, close enough for him to reach out and touch. I stand there waiting, wondering if he is trying to trick me into complacency so he can attack, but he doesn't move. I decide to test his obedience.

I walk backward a few steps and stop. "Crawl to me."

His shoulders slump as he sighs, but he drops down and crawls to me all the same. My stomach clenches at the vision of his shoulder muscles flexing with the slow, crawling movement. My attention is drawn to his ankle when the metal chain clanks its insistence that he does not go any farther.

I shudder, remembering the ache and irritation of the hard metal cuff. Mine was on for two weeks when I first arrived here years ago. It always bothered me to see my partners wearing it when they first arrived. But the reminder of it now, on this partner, triggers something more visceral within me. I can feel it on my ankle as though I am wearing it myself.

"If I remove the chain, what will you do?" I ask him.

He lifts his head, but he's too close to me on his hands and knees and our eyes don't meet. He doesn't reply.

"Will you obey me if I remove the chain? I'm not interested in being attacked. If Master finds me here injured or dead or held as your hostage, he will slice you open and mercilessly rip out your organs. So, if I remove the chain as a reward for your submission, what will you do?"

He shifts to sit back on his heels. "I'll obey."

"Look at me and tell me again."

Ezra tilts his chin upward, meeting my eyes with that sparkling green that reminds me of life and sunlight. "I'll obey. Please, just take it off."

I sigh. "Go sit on the bed and wait. I'm going to leave to get you food. If I come back and you've moved from that spot, the chain will stay and you'll remain is this room for another night. Do you understand?"

His eyes narrow with a flicker of hope, immediately replaced with fear.

The fear is what I want, what I need to keep him under

my thumb.

I should be happy to have seen it cross the vibrant green, but it makes my stomach roil with nausea instead. I don't understand the feeling because he's just given me the obedience I need to control him.

Watching me, he rises to his feet in front of me, and as he comes to his full height—probably a good six inches above me—I feel an urge to step back. I won't step back, but regardless, the urge is there. The way he holds me with his eyes, the way his presence pushes heavy against my chest, my heart… it frightens me.

I'm thankful when Ezra nods slowly and steps backward, watching me for two steps before he turns and lowers to the bed. I let out a breath of relief when he finally lets go of my gaze, letting his head drop as he rubs his palms nervously against his jeans.

"Good, *mal'chik*," I tell him, then clear my throat. "I'll return within the hour."

His head snaps up to look at me again and I'm caught up in the fear his features hold. I feel a need to reassure him like I've never felt before.

"I'll return, Ezra. My word is good. I don't have any reason to lie to you. I promise." I leave the room and lock the door before he can respond.

Why did I make a promise?

I know better than to make promises here. Though it's a promise I intend to keep, I know Nikolai could call for me and force me to break it by no fault of my own. I've never promised anything to any of my partners before and my forehead wrinkles at the thought that I've just done it now.

I walk briskly to the kitchen on the ground floor, all the time wondering how I could do such a stupid thing. But more importantly, I wonder *why*.

I make a quick lunch for Ezra.

Mal'chik, I remind myself.

I hurry because suddenly I'm terrified that Nikolai will show up and demand my time. It's been years since I've made a promise to anyone and the thought of breaking it makes me want to cry. I have no right to make promises to anyone when my life is not my own. I feel tears well behind my eyes as I put his food on a tray and lift it from the butcher block island.

I turn and a fresh kind of panic I haven't felt since my first weeks here at Mikhailov Manor rushes inside me. I expect to see Nikolai standing there, but he isn't. Still, the panic that he could have been ignites my anxiety all the same.

It was always terrifying to turn and find him waiting for me when I didn't expect it, but now I've gone and made a promise.

A promise to be somewhere.

To be there for someone else.

And I can't stomach the thought of breaking it.

My chest tightens as all the air rushes out of my lungs. I take two steps forward but then halt because painful sobs stop me dead in my tracks.

I spin back toward the counter, setting the tray down with a clatter, but at least I manage not to drop it to the floor. I grip the counter's edge, lean forward, and sob over Ezra's meal.

It's been so long since I've felt so much that I don't even know how to handle my own outburst. I have no choice but to let it overcome me. I let go and let it grip me and it's painful to relinquish control. My body trembles with the purge of emotions that I don't understand.

When I finally decide I've had enough of this bullshit, I stop.

I stop crying.

I stop wallowing.

I stop fearing.

I take back control, harden my heart, let ice freeze over the bits of my soul that just thought they could melt. I grab the tray and march back toward Ezra's room before emotion can stop me again.

I stop at Kostya's door in the same hallway first. Kostya is one of the men Nikolai pays to protect me, or so he says. Really, Kostya is an escort, following me and my partner during the day, ensuring we don't attempt escape or suicide or murder. He's a distant cousin of the Mikhailovs, but that means nothing. At the end of the day, he's just one of the hired help.

Kostya is younger than Nikolai, but older than me. He told me he was twenty-eight when I was first brought here three years ago, when I was twenty-one. He opens the door after I knock, dressed for the day in a plain black suit and tie, as always. He's starting to grow out his ash-colored facial hair, and it's just a hint longer than his usual five o'clock shadow. His hair is styled nicely, thick strands that wave to one side from where they are parted.

The cut on his cheek from wrestling with Ezra when he was first brought in seems to be healing nicely, but I don't tell him that.

I don't talk to Kostya.

I don't think I can trust him.

He comes with me and opens Ezra's door. I don't have to give him my keys because he has a set of his own.

I walk in and my heart thumps hard once, twice, to find that Ezra has obeyed. He remains motionless as I bring the tray into the room and set it on the table beside the armchair.

"Eat first," I tell him, "and I'll remove your chain before I go."

"Before you go?"

"No talking," I snap. "Eat and listen."

He stands to grab the tray and sits back down on the bed, digging in without hesitation.

I speak slowly and cautiously, aware that my emotions just got the best of me and I will *not* let that happen again. "After you eat, *mal'chik,* I want you to take a shower and get dressed. I'd like to take you to the dance studio today."

His head snaps up. "You mean, leave the room?"

"Only so long as you are obedient. There is a man who serves Master to protect me. You've met him. That's Kostya by the door." I nod toward him in the doorway. "He brought you here."

He scoffs, "Like I could forget."

"He will hurt you if you try to hurt me. And then I will hurt you."

"And then your master will hurt you for failing to break me?" he says it so plainly that it gives me pause.

I don't respond to his question. I don't want him to think I'm weak or that I'm afraid of my master.

I can't show that I am.

"If you behave, you might get to dance for me today."

He drops the spoon he was holding onto the tray, some of his fire returning as he stares up at me with narrowed eyes. "And if I don't?"

I step forward into his space, looking down at him where he sits on the bed. "Then you'll remain here, shackled and alone, wondering when your next meal will come. Does that seem like the more appealing option to you, Ezra?"

Ezra.

Shit.

I shouldn't have said his name.

He tilts his head at me, and I know he knows I've slipped

up. "No, it doesn't."

I straighten, lifting my chin. "Then you'll obey."

It's a command, not a question.

He lifts an eyebrow and begins to eat slowly, so I step back. Several quiet moments pass in awkward silence before he speaks to me.

"Am I allowed to talk to you?"

I tilt my head, noticing the loneliness in his features. It's a look that's hard to recognize unless you've experienced it yourself.

And I have, in spades.

I tuck a strand of hair behind my ear, thinking I should have pulled it back in a bun before coming in here. I look older, more serious with my hair pulled back tight.

"Yes, you're allowed."

"I know I'm supposed to call you master, but can you just tell me…is your name Anya?"

"Yes."

"Nikolai is your master?"

"And yours."

"Why? Why are we here? And why am I bound and mistreated while you have free range to go wherever you want?"

I chuckle, crossing my arms over my chest. "You haven't even begun to understand mistreatment. I've earned certain freedoms and it's taken me years of trust-building with my master. You should start by giving me your full submission and perhaps you'll get lucky with similar freedoms."

"I don't believe in luck."

"Neither do I."

There was a pulse, a beat of connection and immediately, I knew I shouldn't have allowed a concession in the form of agreement. All the same, I didn't regret it. Especially when the corner of his lip ticked upward in an almost grin.

I need to get out of here.

"Do as you're told, *mal'chik*. I'll leave you to eat and shower."

I reach into my pocket to pull out the small key that releases the latch of the metal cuff. I bend at the knees, lowering in front of him. I have to lift the hem of his jeans, sliding them up his leg to reveal the hidden latch of the cuff. My fingers graze his skin in the process and he jumps at my touch.

"Hold still," I warn with a cold look. "If Kostya thinks you're about to harm me, he may come after you and the result would be less than ideal."

"Sorry, it was just…" he hesitates. "Your fingers are cold."

I insert the key and twist it, relieving Ezra of the burden of being shackled. "Cold like my heart." I stand. "Don't mistake my conversation for connection, *mal'chik*. I'll rip your heart in two if you make the mistake of thinking you and I are anything more than master and slave."

"I wouldn't dream of it, *Master*." Sarcasm seeps from his pores like sweat, a natural response for him.

He angers me.

He lights a fire in my chest and it burns in my belly.

The almost welcome heat overwhelms me, and I reach out and slap him just to put out the fire. His head falls to the side, but before he can reach up to touch the spot where I hit him, I grab his chin and yank his head back to me. I sense Kostya moving in closer, on the defensive.

I bend and put my face close to Ezra's, giving him all the coldness I can muster from deep within my wintery soul. "This is not a joke, *mal'chik*. If you had any idea what Nikolai is capable of, then you would cut the bullshit right now. I suggest you forget connection and conversation and get used to loneliness.

It may save you in the end."

Before I can read into the look of softness and sympathy behind his lively green eyes, I turn on my heel and storm out of the room. Kostya exits behind me and I lock the door as swiftly as I can manage. I dismiss Kostya, asking him to bring Ezra to me in the studio in an hour.

Emotion is welling again, and it threatens to break me entirely. As I rush off down the hallway, crossing the estate to the far end of the west wing to my room, I repeat my own words in my head, giving myself the same advice I've given to Ezra.

Embrace loneliness, Anya.

It will save you in the end.

CHAPTER 6

Anya

I'M ROTATING THROUGH a turn when I catch a glimpse of someone entering the studio. At first, I think it's Kostya and Ezra, and I feel content with that, but as I land coming out of a second and third rotation, posing my arms gracefully, I see that's its Nikolai.

He claps for me, the sound of it echoing in the expansive, open space of my dance studio. I take a bow in curtsy out of politeness—because he won't tolerate otherwise—and he shoves his hands in his pockets, leaning his shoulder against the door frame.

I cross the room to stand in front of him and bow my head, waiting for him to speak or command.

"Is he ready to dance?" Nikolai asks.

"*Da, khozyain.* He kneeled for me today and obeyed my command. Kostya should be bringing him to me soon."

"Good, I'll stay and watch."

My head whips up and I catch his gray eyes. "Why?"

I regret speaking almost as immediately as his cruel demeanor returns. Nikolai reaches out, grabs me by the back of my neck, and spins me. He whips me around with ease and slams me face-first into the mirrored wall beside the door. My hands come up to catch myself, palms flattening against the cold surface and I turn my head to the side just in time to avoid my nose crashing into it. It didn't heal right the last time he broke it, and I don't want to risk going through that again.

His body pins me to the mirror from behind as he curls around me, fingers digging into the side of my neck.

"Are you questioning me again, *rabynya?* I thought you learned your lesson the other night. Or are you just begging for a repeat?"

I keep my voice and my breath steady. "I'm sorry."

"For?"

"For questioning you."

I'm not allowed to ask questions.

I'm not allowed to misunderstand directions and ask for clarification.

I'm expected to know and obey.

Nikolai steps back but doesn't let me go. Instead, he spins me around to face him before pressing his body into mine. His breath is on my face. It's warm and smells of cigar smoke. He strokes the back of his hand gently down my cheek and I fight the urge to recoil, leaning into it to placate him instead of following my instinct to slap it away and run.

"Beautiful girl," he croons, "I nearly miss the fight in you."

He contradicts himself constantly.

Why should he miss the fight in me when he wants my constant and consistent obedience?

"Maybe one day I will set you free in the forest..." He bends to whisper against my ear, "Chase after you, see which hunter finds you first this time, hmm? Will it be me or the wolves that prowl the tree line?"

I'm tempted to sneer at him and ask him what the difference would be, but I don't. I know better than that. I swallow, considering that Ezra might've responded the way I wanted to given the manner in which I've witnessed him communicate with a sardonic temper.

I don't like that Ezra has popped into my head again. It's dangerous to think of the boy when Nikolai has a hold of me.

He'll sense it.

Finally, I respond, "I'm certain it would be you."

He presses a soft kiss to my lips then pauses as he pulls back to look at me. "Yes, I imagine it would. Just as it was when you tried to escape the first time. And aren't you lucky I found you first?"

No.

"*Da, moy khozyain.*"

A throat is cleared nearby and we both look to see Kostya standing in the doorway. Nikolai lets me go and walks away to the far corner of the studio.

There's a black, grand piano there, though I'm never granted the privilege of a live player. I think its presence speaks to Nikolai's self-aggrandization. He fills his home with the appearance of culture and refinement, though he possesses none naturally.

He sits on the bench and waits for me to welcome Ezra to the studio, to direct him, to command him. He's never come in this early to view me with another partner and the thought of it makes my nerves pulse with anxiety. I clench my hands into fists to hide the way they tremble.

Why is he here?

Nikolai could easily just watch from the security camera. There are only two inside Mikhailov Manor and one of them is here, inside the dance studio. The other is just outside the boardroom, near Nikolai's home office. The rest are on the exterior grounds to monitor for escapees or unwanted guests—

as if anyone could find the manor if they didn't know exactly where it was.

It was curious to me early in my captivity that there weren't more cameras inside the manor to monitor my behavior, but I quickly learned that secret-keeping is taken rather seriously by the four families.

There are secrets no family wants on camera.

Kostya grabs Ezra by the shoulder, nudging him into the room before pressing his hand between his shoulder blades and shoving. Ezra stumbles but recovers, shooting daggers at Kostya as he looks back at him over his shoulder.

I move to the center of the room and turn to face Ezra. "Come. Kneel."

His forehead wrinkles as he surveys the space, noting Nikolai in the corner. Ezra's eyes linger on Nikolai as he slowly makes his way toward me. When Ezra decides to give me his attention, our eyes connect, blue meeting green, and I feel a pause.

I don't know how else to think of it.

It's a pause in existence.

Briefer than a moment, a quick beat of calmness, nothingness.

It's pleasant.

He lowers to his knees in front of me and I gasp because I truly expected his fight to return the moment Kostya brought him out of his room. His eyes are still locked on mine and when I go to look for it, I see it there, the fight in him. It hasn't gone completely, he's just hiding it away, biding his time.

That should scare me to know he's still got that hope that the fight is worthwhile because it means I'll struggle to control him. Instead, I find that I'm glad it's still there, that *he's* still there.

I'm thinking about him as if I know him.

We don't know each other.

"Eyes on the floor, *mal'chik,*" I command and I'm grateful that he obeys. "I want to see you dance today. I want you to show me your best solo, let me get a sense of what you can do."

"Okay," he says slowly, and I can see his brow wrinkling in consideration.

"Can you dance in what you're wearing?"

I rake my eyes over the outfit he's chosen, unsurprisingly similar to what he wore when I first saw him a week ago. Ripped, faded, well-worn jeans and a simple black T-shirt with a logo for a band or something that I don't recognize. I want to ask him about it, though I'm not sure why. I have no idea what bands or movies or books are popular now. Three years is a long time, and I'm sure much of the outside world has changed, gone on without me.

He nods and mutters, "Yes."

"What kind of music do you need?"

He shrugs. "Anything is fine. I'll freestyle."

I scoff, "I want to see your best, not some random contemporary bullshit."

His head whips up to look at me. "It's not random bullshit, I know what the fuck I'm—"

I slap him.

Not because I want to.

Not because I would if we were alone together, though I certainly would have given him a verbal lashing all the same.

I hit him because Nikolai is watching, and he expects it.

Ezra's hand touches his cheek and his eyes burn green fire to ignite the air between us. My breath catches at the look, but I maintain my composure.

"If you're so sure of yourself, then I expect you to blow me away. Stand up and get ready. You dance when the music starts."

I steal a quick glance at Nikolai—a quick look for reassurance that he is pleased with my outburst to discipline. He tilts his head down, a subtle nod of approval, and I exhale.

I catch Ezra glaring at Nikolai when I look back down at him. But then he looks up at me. A shimmer of understanding dances between us and I feel it stir a long-forgotten feeling of connection, of attachment.

Though I wish I could explore this look a little longer, I know I can't.

I whip around Ezra and march across the dance floor, hoping my face isn't as visibly flushed as it feels. I cross to where Nikolai is perched on the piano bench. The stereo system is behind him, nestled into the wall.

I scroll through the selection of songs on the touchscreen to find something slow, dramatic, emotional. Something that will be fitting for him as a contemporary dancer.

Though I never cared to showcase my other partners in their own style, I feel a misplaced need to ensure I give Ezra the best shot to impress Nikolai.

I shouldn't care.

He'll be dancing in my style anyway. Ballet is what I've trained to dance since childhood and it's what Nikolai stole me away to do—to be his own personal ballerina. It's my job to train my partners to be the perfect complement for me in *my* style.

I don't understand the anxiety that overcomes me in hopes that Ezra isn't too weak to perform spectacularly, especially when I don't even know whether he is a spectacular dancer.

I find the song I'm looking for and turn back to see if Ezra is ready. He's standing, though he bends to remove his socks and shoes and moves to place them against the back wall of the room, beneath the barre. He blows out a shaky breath with his lips formed in an "O" shape.

He tilts his head from side to side, stretching his neck, and shakes out his hands and legs. A piece of dirty blonde hair from the longer strands on top of his head falls across his forehead. He brushes it out of his eyes with a flick of his wrist as he lifts his head, searching the room to find me.

I could never miss that green fervor from his eyes shining across the room at me. He gives me a small nod to indicate that he is ready for the music. It's such a normal look, a simple nonverbal communication, the most basic thing…yet it feels so profound.

I nod and he stills. Without looking away, I tap the screen where my finger hovers over the play button and the music gradually rolls in.

He's still looking at me.

He grasps the hem of his shirt and lifts, peeling it up and over his torso, exposing his chest.

And he's still looking at me.

He sways, a soft movement, a gentle rocking from side to side as he stands in the center of the dance floor, bare-chested, bare-footed, wearing only the jeans that are torn and frayed over one knee.

And he's still looking at me.

I shudder when he takes a step and glides right into a coupé turn, spinning three, four, five times with the toe of his left foot resting against his right ankle to form a triangle through his rotations. His balance is impeccable as he leaps out from the turn with impressive strength and height.

I'm already speechless with the first count of eight, and I can't tear my eyes away.

I've never enjoyed contemporary dance. It doesn't follow the strict rules of classical ballet that I thrive on. It takes liberties, breaks contracts, defies conventions.

But Ezra.

Ezra is…a word I can't think of.

Perhaps there isn't a single word for the way he dances.

Perhaps there are too many.

Powerful, graceful, dangerous, beautiful, reckless.

His use of the floor is brilliant. He alternates through turns and remarkable leaps, drawing a large oval around the room with the trail of his movement.

His leaps are the most impressive thing of all. I've seen dancers who can leap gracefully, and I've seen dancers who can leap powerfully. I've never seen one who could do both so exquisitely as this.

The way he twists and turns his lean muscle, dipping to the floor, tumbling over his shoulder, rising again only to spin and push out into another extraordinary leap.

I can't speak.

The song ends long before I think it should, though it still takes me too long to realize it. Ezra has ended his improvised performance like a warrior, kneeling on one knee, fist to the floor, chest heaving as he catches his breath, looking like Superman himself has fallen to the Earth. Every muscle in his chiseled frame is rigid in the picturesque pose.

He tosses his hair out of his face as he lifts his head and looks up. Sweat gives his skin a glossy sheen which emphasizes the enormity of the work he's just accomplished.

I'm stilled, astounded by his talent, and I feel something I haven't in a very long time.

Pure and simple attraction.

Nikolai pulls me from my daze as he rises to his feet from the bench in front of me. "Ezra Bell," his tone is light, unusually jovial, "you are truly incredible." He turns back to look at me.

"Isn't he incredible, Anya?"

I swallow and clear my throat. "Yes. Yes, he is."

Ezra stands and he is fury wrapped in grace.

Nikolai claps twice as he walks to meet him on the dance floor. He stands beside Ezra, reaching one arm across his back to hold his shoulders in both hands as he guides him to walk over to where I stand.

I cross my arms over my chest as Nikolai moves him to stand directly in front of me. Ezra looks near hyperventilating with the way his chest heaves, but I can sense it's not from exhaustion from the dance. It's anger, it's defense, it's the spike of adrenaline that I've felt so many times myself when Nikolai comes too close.

"Your new partner is more talented than you," Nikolai says to me with a smile.

A sinful, horrid smile that stabs me in the heart.

My head tilts and my eyes narrow, but I immediately soften my expression, hoping Nikolai didn't see it falter.

"I think you will learn his style, Anya."

I swallow the line of questioning that claws its way up my throat, remembering being slammed into the mirror when I questioned him earlier.

I try to rephrase my questions in a manner of acceptance, but it comes out as utterances and stuttering. "I'm not…I'm not sure I understand…"

It's cold between us in a flash as Nikolai releases Ezra and takes a step toward me. Instinctively, I step back.

"Hey," Ezra shouts as Nikolai closes in on me.

"What don't you understand?" Nikolai asks as he steps in close, looming above me.

"It's always been ballet," I state boldly.

He reaches out to snatch me by the throat, yanking me

toward him, and I whimper. "And your ballet performances have always failed to please me."

I can't look at Nikolai and it's not because it's terrifying to watch the evil wash over his face before he hurts me. I'm used to that. It's because I can see Ezra behind him, his eyes wide, nostrils flaring. His fingers flex and bend into tight fists at his sides and he sways in agitation. I try to command him with my eyes to back down. I shake my head to tell him no, but he can't see me through the flash of lightning that ignites his outrage.

I quickly make the leap from nonverbal signals to outright shouting as Ezra lunges for Nikolai.

"No!" I scream.

Ezra grabs Nikolai by his shoulders and pulls back hard. Thankfully, Nikolai releases me before Ezra whips him around and tosses him onto the floor. I jump away, moving my back against the wall, pressing against it as Ezra goes after him swinging. Nikolai turns his head just in time to avoid being punched. Ezra's fist lands hard on the floor beside Nikolai's head and he roars out a groan of frustration.

Nikolai rolls to the side, but Ezra manages to get on top of him and lands a punch to his gut before strong arms lift him away. Kostya is there, yanking Ezra back, who is still kicking and swinging. Seconds later, Ezra's body goes rigid, twitching and trembling from the electric shock of Kostya's stun gun that he's jammed into his side.

As Ezra falls to the ground, Nikolai rolls and jumps to his feet, walking in quick, long strides across the dance floor, his dress shoes clacking and reverberating off the walls, mixing with the sound of Ezra's groans.

He gathers a length of rope that we use with the pulley system on the ceiling, twisting one end around his open hand before grasping it tightly within his fist, a devilish sneer spread across his cheeks.

He comes up behind where Ezra has fallen and crouches down to his haunches above his head, leaning over him and placing the rope across his throat. Ezra coughs as Nikolai pulls the ends around behind his neck, twisting them together.

I squeak as I try to clamp down the scream rising through my chest, knowing that no matter what, I can't let Nikolai know that this affects me.

Nikolai cannot know that my insides are coiling and burning with the fear I feel, knowing that punishment is to come for Ezra.

I've never feared like this before, and I don't even fear for me.

Ezra's hands fly to his neck, clawing at the rope with wide eyes as Nikolai tugs, heaving him backward, dragging him across the dance floor and toward the door.

I freeze, watching Ezra kick, listening to his strangled screams as he fights to get free. They disappear through the doorway and my heart kickstarts a new rhythm with the need to chase after him.

Not to chase after Nikolai.

To chase after Ezra.

I follow them out of the studio, watching as Nikolai wrenches Ezra by the rope around his throat in starts and stops, one long drag after the other. He does this all the way down the hall to the grand staircase.

I think that's when he'll stop, but he doesn't.

Nikolai steps backward onto the first step, then the second, and lifts on the coiled rope.

Ezra's eyes dart desperately around the room, but he knows he's helpless. He's already overexerted himself with the dance, given how little he's eaten over the past week, and that he's only just been removed from his room for the first time.

Nikolai makes it to the fifth step before he realizes he doesn't care to exert the effort it takes to drag him all the way up. He lets up on the rope enough to allow some slack.

"Roll over and crawl," he commands Ezra.

Ezra rolls to his side, flipping onto his hands and knees and crawls up the steps slowly, panting and breathless. Nikolai still holds the rope around his neck but pulls it from the side as if he was taking his dog for a walk on a leash. Ezra's chest heaves as he struggles to catch his breath.

My eyes burn hot as I follow behind Kostya, who follows behind Ezra with his stun gun out and ready.

It feels like it takes hours to ascend, watching the pain and struggle that Ezra faces in this maddening journey.

I don't know why it bothers me so.

Nikolai has treated all my partners this way. He's treated *me* this way for even longer. I've endured untold pain and punishment at his hand for years.

And still, this bothers me in a whole new way.

He forces Ezra to crawl all the way back to his room like this as he hisses and jeers at him. When we've all crossed the threshold into the bedroom, Nikolai clamps the metal cuff to Ezra's ankle once again, solidly securing him.

As Ezra sits on the floor, leaning his back against the bedside, huffing and puffing and fighting to catch his breath, Nikolai lets loose.

CHAPTER 7
Anya

NIKOLAI WHIPS THE back of his hand and it lands with a solid thwack to Ezra's cheek. "You clearly don't know your place yet, *mal'chik*. Is this Anya's fault? Has she not done well enough to train you in your submission?"

Truthfully, I hadn't done anything to train him to submit to me. I had hoped leaving him locked up and alone, deprived of light and company and sustenance would be enough to gain his submission. It had worked well enough with the other boys.

Though I had been crueler to them, I suppose.

I didn't want to be as cruel to Ezra.

Mal'chik.

He's the boy.

Just the boy.

"No, no, no," Ezra holds up a palm to Nikolai. "She trained me," he lies. "She trained me well, it's not—"

Nikolai's body freezes in contempt. "Are you lying for her? For *her*?"

"I'm not, it's not her—" Ezra stammers

"Anya," Nikolai points to a spot on the floor beside where he stands, hovering over Ezra, "come."

I lengthen my neck and lift my chin, putting on an air of

confidence that I don't feel an ounce of internally. I move to stand where he wants me.

A line slowly creeps along Nikolai's face as his lips stretch at one corner, tilting at the side to form a smirk that makes tingles crawl like spiders along my soul. I shudder from head to toe because I know the look. It's a look that only the Devil himself could make.

"Kostya, you may go," Nikolai commands and Kostya leaves us, shutting the door behind.

Oh, no.

No, no, no, no, no.

"*Moya rabynya,* look what you've done." Nikolai stands beside me and slides his hand up my spine until he catches the back of my neck, gripping me firmly.

"I've done only what is expected of me, *khozyain.* I promise you."

I dare a glance down at Ezra and immediately wish I hadn't. The look he gives me with fearful, wide eyes chisels away at the ice around my heart.

Nikolai is boiling in his hateful violence and its evaporating into rage-fueled lust. He is deviant in his desires, and I can see it happening now in the way it hazes over his features.

"You've made this man want to protect you. And he's only been here a week. How did you do this, Anya?" He laughs. "I know it's not your charm and gentle smile."

You made me charmless and joyless.

I don't respond as he presses his nose into my hair, dragging it upward along my cheek as he inhales me.

"You're foolish if you think making him fall for you will do you a service. He can't win with me. No one can. You know that better than anyone," he whispers against my cheek, his voice low and husky.

"I do know that," I assure him. "I'm not foolish."

"Perhaps not. Perhaps you've found a more effective and entertaining way to get him to obey you."

Entertaining?

"I don't mind his concern for you," he goes on. "It will make him more obedient, a more trustworthy partner, and it will make you a stronger dancer. Because of that, I will finally have the most talented slave."

Nikolai shifts to stand behind me, one large hand flattening against my belly. "I'm going to reward you for this, Anya. And I'm going to do it here so he understands that you are *mine*."

I press my eyes shut and breathe deeply. "I don't require a reward for doing my work."

"Don't be so humble. Besides, the reward isn't entirely for you. It's for him. To show him who you belong to. Now, tell him who you are."

"I am slave to the Mikhailov family. I am your belonging."

His hand slips upward and captures my breast, digging in with his fingers over my black leotard, making me whimper. Ezra jolts and manages to get to his knees but stops abruptly when Nikolai slaps my breast in response.

I flinch and lean back, away from his hand, but I can't move because he's right behind me, holding me in place. He grabs my nipple through the fabric and pinches me violently. My face scrunches against the ache and I hold back the groan that threatens to escape.

"Stop, *mal'chik*," I tell Ezra with as much level insistence as I can muster. "You will obey, you will *not* interfere. He is my master and he may do as he pleases with me."

I don't want Ezra to see this, I don't want to dampen his urge to fight, but I do want him to obey for my sake. I know better than to think that what Nikolai is about to do is a reward.

It's manipulation.

It's abuse.

I have to endure it and I will, but Ezra must obey and stay still. All he has to do is watch my torture, feign his submission to my will, and all will be well.

"Good," Nikolai encourages my mastery over Ezra and runs his free hand down the side of my hair, petting me, stroking down my side, down my belly, lower and lower. "Move the fabric aside for me."

The air shakes its way out of my lungs as I reach between my legs, catching the strip of fabric of my leotard that covers my sex and tugging it to the side beneath my wraparound skirt.

He widens his stance behind me to sink down as he dips his fingers between my legs. He curls around my back, a hot breath of filthy lust rushing out against my neck as he buries his face in the crook.

"Don't—" Ezra begins.

"Shut up, *mal'chik*. Be quiet and be still," I tell him.

My voice is sharp, but my eyes are soft as I silently plead with him not to say another word, not to move unless asked to, to obey without question or hesitation.

Because it will only hurt me more if he doesn't.

"You're going to come for me, *rabynya*," Nikolai demands and there's no air left in the room. "I'm not going to stop until you do, so make it happen if you don't want to be left raw and aching."

"*Da, khozyain.*"

I don't dare steal a glance at Ezra now. It's not the first time my master has violated me in the presence of a partner. But it's the first time I've felt so ashamed by it.

He toys with me, his fingers doing a dance along my entrance to find me dry as the desert. I close my eyes and try to remember the time in the bathroom, the time I came to Nikolai willingly, when he gave me pleasure without pain. I always cling to that memory when he wants me wet and ready for him. But it's not working, and I don't know why. My forehead pinches, straining against the new kind of shame I feel standing here like this in a way I've never felt before.

I can't fail now.

I can't fail at this.

I force myself to recall the way Nikolai kissed me in that memory, the way he held my face with need and devoured me with passion and humility. I tried to remember the way I felt after being lonely and finally connecting with him in a way that wasn't pain or torture, just pure pleasure.

Still, nothing.

"Get wet for me," he hisses against my ear and I hear the hint of frustration building.

The memory dissipates as panic rises up to erase it, hitting me hard over my heart. I put my hand there to feel it beating wildly with anxiety. My fingers brush Nikolai's still on my breast and when this happens, he mistakes it for wanting. His erection presses against my lower back and he hisses before forcing his fingers past the opening.

I whimper at the harshness of his calloused fingers forcing their way inside me dry, and I buck backward against him.

"Come on, Anya," he kisses along my neck, "get wet for me. Show this boy how you respond to me, show this boy what it takes a man to do."

My eyes flutter open in frustration as I try to rationalize my way through my sudden lack of response. I want this to be over, but it won't end until I come. I don't want to look, I try not to look at Ezra, but I know he's looking at me. I can feel his eyes on me, though I had hoped he would look away. I had hoped he would be too horrified or disgusted to look at me.

But I feel his stare.

My gaze slips and his eyes catch mine and I'm locked in beyond choice or reason. There's fear behind the green—and hatred, and shock, and even something more.

I think it's need.

I'm sure it's need when his bottom lip falls open and his breath catches.

"Oh," I breathe out.

I've found my desire in Ezra's green gaze.

Nikolai pulls his fingers back at my reaction, swirling around my clit, completely unaware that I'm watching Ezra watching me. As Ezra shifts uncomfortably, something stirs inside me, swirling with the touch of confident fingers, and somehow manages to turn me on.

I allow a small smile to touch the corners of my lips, so slight I imagine it's hardly perceptible as Nikolai draws arousal from me.

No, it's not Nikolai who draws it from me.

It's Ezra.

But it can't be Ezra.

He's my slave and my partner and nothing more.

I know nothing about this cocky, sarcastic, reckless boy who holds me in his stare.

But if that's true, then why does my body swell as he leans forward while he watches me?

Nikolai toys with me with his expert hands, circling around and around, and actually makes me feel…good.

The scene and the circumstance is lewd, my devilish master with his arms wrapped around me from behind, tugging down on the top of my leotard to expose my breast. He touches me until I'm sinking at the core, folding around his fingers as my body desperately urges me to seek release—whether I want it or not.

Inconceivably, I want it.

Nikolai leans me forward, bending me down to the bed beside Ezra's head and I put my hands down on the comforter to hold myself up. He holds my hip in one hand while the other continues its assault.

It's the same contradiction of feelings I always have with him. I want his fingers inside me, but I don't. I want to let go, for just that moment to feel like I don't have to be in complete control, but I don't. I want the pleasure, but I don't.

My arm blocks my face, breaking my eye contact with Ezra, but it doesn't feel broken, not entirely. I can still feel his stare burning into my skin, threatening to melt my icy core.

Nikolai hooks his fingers inside me, stroking against the spot that's sure to make me lose control. I'm overcome by the urge to fall into Ezra's lap, to unbutton his jeans, expose him, impale myself on him, and rock until I come undone.

Why Ezra?

Why is he in my mind?

The fantasy of him beneath me, still, quiet, letting me use him to get myself off swirls in my belly, clenching through my core, threatening to send me leaping off the edge. I'm panting and writhing against Nikolai's hand, feeling shameful, yet somehow powerful that he doesn't know I'm thinking of the boy beside me and not him.

Pleasure swells and I'm ready for it in a way I didn't even know was possible.

I want it.

I need it.

I'm just about to crest as I hear Ezra exhale beside me.

I whimper out a sound in my heated need.

But I don't peak.

Nikolai rips his fingers out, lets me go, slaps my ass, and sends me wobbling forward. I bend at the knees, falling to kneel beside Ezra on the floor as I whip my head to look at Nikolai over my shoulder.

"I didn't—"

"I know you didn't come. And you're not going to. Learn to control him without gaining his sympathy. You don't deserve any."

CHAPTER 8
Anya

MY HEART SINKS.

My breath catches in my throat.

A sob overcomes me, but I pull it back inside, swallowing it down.

Nikolai leaves us alone in Ezra's room and it takes me moments to catch my breath and regain control of myself.

Silent, sickening moments pass before I lift my forehead from the bed and sit back on my heels. I look down at the floor between my knees and the bed and place my palms flat against my thighs. I breathe in deeply through my nose, pushing air out through my mouth, over and over as I try to shake off the aching need between my legs.

If I were cruel, I could become a master like Nikolai. I could use the slave boy beside me and make him finish what Nikolai had started. But even the thought of such a thing makes me sick to my stomach. It puts perspective back into focus. Nikolai hadn't just brought me to the brink of pleasure, he used and abused me to make a point.

"Hey," Ezra says softly at my side.

I turn my head to look at him. "Don't," I say. "Don't speak. There's nothing you can say right now that will make things any better."

I get up off the floor and reach between my legs to adjust the fabric of my leotard to cover me again. I look over at Ezra and catch his eyes, looking where I'm exposed, then darting away quickly as I cover myself.

"Don't worry," I tell him. "I won't use you in that way."

He looks taken aback. "I wasn't thinking that."

I look at the bulge that's straining against his jeans and he shifts, trying to hide it. He pushes off the floor and moves to sit on the edge of the bed. It's curious that he's aroused, though I suppose it's not all that surprising. Perhaps all men are the same in their violent tastes.

I'm slowly shielding myself with each breath I draw, steeling myself to protect against further emotional pain. "I trust you understand your place now."

I untie, adjust, and rewrap the black chiffon dance skirt around my waist, taking a step back as Ezra climbs to his feet.

I don't fear him, but my eyes narrow, considering that Nikolai left me alone with an impulsive slave who hasn't been properly broken in enough to behave. He attacked Nikolai, after all, and I'm perplexed that Nikolai hasn't taken more care with my safety, at least in sending Kostya back to the room. Once my skirt is straight, I shake my head slowly and straighten to my full height.

"I remember who you are," Ezra says.

"Excuse me?"

"I remember you now. I've been trying to figure out where I know you from and I think I remember. You're Anya Antonov, the soloist from the New York City Ballet that went missing a few years ago."

I lift an eyebrow. "And what difference does it make?"

He shrugs. "It doesn't. It's just interesting."

"Interesting? Well, I'm glad my disappearance serves as entertainment for you."

"You were slated to be a principal dancer before you were twenty-five."

"I was, though that's not my life anymore."

"They called you a legendary talent in the news when you went missing." He pauses. "He kidnapped you?"

"Do you think I came here of my own free will?"

I feel like a liar when I say that. I didn't choose to come here, to be his slave, but I did get on that plane with him all the same when he offered an opportunity to excel in my craft.

How could I have known his intentions then?

"Jesus." He puts his hands behind his neck and the stretch of it emphasizes the broadness of his chest. "How long have you been here?"

"Three years," I tell him and wonder why I'm still here, rooted to the spot, having any sort of conversation with him.

I cross my arms over my chest when I should simply leave the room.

"Have you tried to escape?"

My head falls to the side and incredulity mars my tone. "Is that a serious question?"

A small smile tugs at his lips, though he's trying to hide it. I wonder what it is about me that amuses him so much.

"Where the hell are we?"

I sigh, thinking again that I should leave. Instead, I move backward and lower slowly to perch on the edge of the armchair. I need a moment to come down from this spoiled high anyway.

"I don't know exactly," I tell him honestly. "Somewhere in Russia, but nowhere near civilization."

"Russia." His brow wrinkles as he sits on the edge of the bed. "How have you survived here this long? With him?"

I look at him squarely. "All of my choices have been stripped from me except for one. Dance or die. I choose to dance. That's how I survive."

"He's impatient with you."

"He demands perfection and obedience. When he doesn't get it, it's my fault."

His head snaps sideways to look at me with narrowed eyes. "It's not your fault."

"Of course, it's not my fault. I'm not delusional, *mal'chik*. He hasn't brainwashed me." I narrow my eyes at him as I push to my feet. "I'm a slave. And so are you. Master is right, you need to learn your place."

"Do I?"

I march over and slap him without any conviction at all. "Get on your knees."

He places his hand on his cheek and looks up at me. "What will you do if I don't, Anya? Will you call him back in here? Tell him you can't train your slave? The slave who, in his own words, is more talented than you?"

I latch my small hand around the side of his neck and dig my fingers in before tugging him forward. He could easily pull out of my grip if he wanted to. My hands are tiny in comparison to his neck and broad shoulders. I consider it a win when he lets me drag him forward off the bed and he falls to his knees.

"You're in over your head here," I tell him. "You haven't even begun to comprehend how deep in shit you are."

His eyes are hard and soft all at once as he pleads, "Then *tell* me."

I don't want to tell him everything. It's too much and I don't trust him yet. I need to trust in his submission before I can tell him everything, before we can really begin to rehearse for our performance at the quarterly event. And we need to do that soon.

My shoulders slump and I try to breathe out some of the tension that's straining between us in favor of earning his understanding.

"I will tell you everything. Not now, not yet. First, I need to know that I have your submission, I need to see it."

"I'm literally on my knees in front of you. What the fuck else do you need to see?"

I lift an eyebrow. "I need to see that sarcastic attitude roll off your fucking shoulders. That would be a start."

He gives a gruff sigh. "Okay, *Master*."

Now he's just being an asshole.

I step away from him and stride toward the door.

He calls after me, "Wait, don't leave me in here, please."

That simple plea tells me what I need to continue to do to break him into submission.

Isolation.

He wants to talk, to interact, to connect, so I'll put an end to that and go right back to the beginning.

"Enjoy your time alone, Ezra," I say.

I walk out, shut the door behind me, and lock it.

A few more days in isolation with minimal sustenance ought to do it.

I hope.

CHAPTER 9
Ezra

IT'S ONLY WHEN I feel like I'm starting to get used to the isolation that I start to fear I'm going insane. It feels like a century has gone by in this fucking awful green room, but I know it's only been a week. I know this because Anya brings me one meal each day and each tray has had a small torn piece of parchment with a number scribbled on it.

The first day there was a one, the second day a two, and so on.

The last meal was day seven.

Seven days with nothing more than a girl walking into my room, setting down a tray, and leaving me alone again.

The only connection I got from her was the scribbled numbers and some small gesture that reminded me of her humanity. Sometimes it was a look or the demure tuck of a strand of hair behind her ear. I think I even got a small smile of reassurance once, but I know I must have been dreaming it.

I actually *had* dreamt it one night, the first night she left me here alone. I felt shame at the dream because it was sexual in nature. My fucked-up brain had memorized the look on her face when she granted the smallest smile the day Nikolai fingered her right in front of me.

What Nikolai had done to her was a violation that made my shoulders tense and my muscles flex with the urge to hurt him. But whatever reaction her body was having to it was undeniably beautiful. And I felt sick for thinking that for even a moment. I felt even worse for dreaming about her pleasure. At least it was consensual in the dream. And it was with me.

I hear the locks turn the day after note number seven.

I climb off the bed where I'd been lying, looking up at the ceiling, and drop to my knees at the foot of the bed. I do this because it seems to please her. I do this because she wants my submission and my trust. I do this because I can't stand the isolation anymore, and I'm nearly willing to do anything for her just so she'll grant me the kindness of taking me out of this fucking room.

Maybe, just maybe, some part of me just wants to please her because I crave her approval in some fucked up way.

She enters and sees me there and though my head is bowed for her, I can see from my peripheral that she's pleased. Warmth spreads across my chest at the thought. As usual, she brings in the tray and sets it on the side table next to the armchair. I expect her to leave immediately, as she has been doing, but she surprises me this time.

Crossing the room, she comes to stand in front of me, then bends and lowers to her knees, mirroring my position. She puts soft fingertips under my chin and lifts my head so that we're nearly eye to eye. I'm taller than her so she's looking up at me.

I think I could deep dive in her blue eyes, get swept away in the hurricane. Her plump, pink lips curve into a smile and I can't help but smile back.

"Your submission pleases me, Ezra," she says.

I feel like I've just reincarnated from the life of a dog back to humanity.

She slowly leans forward. Her cheek grazes my cheek as she seeks my ear to share a whisper, a secret. I want to throw my arms around her and hold on for dear life when her touch ignites my need for connection, for affection.

"Just be sure the cuff goes back on before Nikolai comes into the room."

She stands as swiftly and as gracefully as she kneeled and walks to the door. She pulls it open but hesitates before she leaves. She turns her head over her shoulder and gives me a look. I don't really understand her expression, but her eyes meet mine and I feel relief for the brief moment of interaction in our gaze.

Goddamn, she's a beautiful powerhouse.

She leaves without another word and I'm held in place by that look.

After a minute, I remember how fucking hungry I am and go to the tray she left me. I sit on the floor with it and immediately look for the paper I expect to have the number eight on it, but it's not there.

Disappointment sinks my insides.

I pick up my spoon—she never gives me a fork or knife, regardless of the meal—and it hovers over the plate as frustration sets in.

How can I be so frustrated over a piece of paper with a number?

I know it's because that piece of paper with the number was the only real form of communication I've had over the past week. Its absence rips a weird sort of panic through my chest.

What if seven was the last note?

How will I track how long I've been here?

I search the tray again, frantic to know if perhaps I just missed it. I pick up the plate to look beneath it and my hands freeze mid-air, holding it above the tray. I blink and pause with what I find.

Beneath the plate is a small key.

'Just be sure the cuff goes back on,' she had said to me.

"Fuck," I mutter as I set the plate on the ground beside me and pick up the key.

I don't even take a second to think as I shift my cuffed leg out in front of me. I know right where the keyhole is. I've clawed at the damn thing often enough, trying to find a way to get it off me. I insert the key and twist it. It takes me a few tries, but eventually, it clicks and the cuff falls open.

"Holy shit," I say, jumping up off the floor.

My blood spikes with adrenaline as I run both my hands through the hair on top of my head. I spin with the energy it gives me and try to make sense of this.

She gave me a key.

A fucking key.

'Just be sure the cuff goes back on before Nikolai comes into the room.'

I bend down and pick up the key where I dropped it on the beige carpet. I look at it in my hand, then look at the door, wondering if it's the same key.

I rush to the door and insert the key in the bottom lock, turning it in a hurry. I nearly collapse when I turn it and it clicks. I quickly slide it into the next keyhole just above the first but when I try to turn it, my heart sinks.

It won't turn.

"Shit," I say into the void that is my room.

I try again, but it won't turn.

I try again.

Again.

Again.

And I'm gonna lose my shit if this fucking door won't open.

What is this?

Part of me thinks she's trying to give me hope just so she can yank the rug from beneath my feet. Perhaps the key really was just meant to free me from the bed chain and nothing more. She had told me to put it back on before Nikolai comes, though I have no idea when he's coming.

But why would she do that?

I'm so agitated from the adrenaline and the hope I had that I decide I'm getting this fucking door open. Without thinking, I grasp the doorknob and turn, ready to pull with all my might. I yank back hard and tumble backward onto my ass.

It opened.

The door opened.

The second lock wasn't latched in the first place.

I'm so shocked that I immediately jump up and push it closed again. Then I realize what I've done, worried it will somehow lock automatically, and I quickly yank it open again.

Sweet baby Jesus.

The door is open and I'm not chained. I can leave this stupid room.

I lean my head around the doorframe to peek out into the hallway and find that it's empty. I reluctantly pull myself back inside the room and take a deep breath, knowing that I should take a beat to think this through. My muscles are twitching and jumping, pulsing with each heartbeat with the message to run, run, *run*.

I don't think about an escape plan, I just move.

I creep out into the hallway, tiptoeing past the rows of closed doors. When I come to the end of the hallway, I stop. I can see outward toward the edge of the grand staircase and clearly see all the way across its vast opening to the opposite side of the manor and to a hallway beyond it. I prepare myself with a deep breath and then stealthily move toward the staircase.

I stay alert, looking everywhere, all around me, watching for movement and ready to pounce on the defensive if anyone comes after me.

I have to get the fuck out of here.

No matter what I have to do.

I reach the top of the staircase and I'm about to take off down it, intent for the exit. But when my foot lands on the first step, I'm halted as the memory of soft fingers lifting my chin and sapphire eyes meeting mine floods my sensibility.

I can't leave her here.

She's as much a victim as I am.

She's more of a victim really.

I need to rescue her.

But where the fuck do I find her?

This estate is huge and I've only been in two rooms. Mine and the dance studio.

I step backward, back onto the landing, thinking her room must be somewhere on this level, perhaps on the opposite side. Bravely—or perhaps, stupidly—I head toward the far hallway, opposite the way I came.

I creep down the hall, walking softly, staying close to one side of the wall. I have no idea what the fuck I'm doing or why I'm going to find this girl instead of getting the fuck out of here.

I just know I can't leave without her.

CHAPTER 10
Ezra

"*MAL'CHIK*," ANYA'S VOICE comes from behind me in a sharp whisper.

I'm startled, nearly jumping out of my skin. I unintentionally take a swing at her as I spin to face her, but thankfully, she ducks just in time.

"Jesus," I say quickly. "Come on, come with me, let's get the fuck out of here."

Her forehead is wrinkled, her blue eyes piercing. She looks down and reaches forward to grasp my hand. Her touch is ice melting my fire.

"Come with me," she demands, spinning me back around and pulling me after her down the hallway.

We pass two doors and come upon a third. She pushes it open, pulling me inside. She releases me just beyond the threshold and slams the door shut behind us.

"What the fuck are you doing?" she demands. "How did you get out of the room?"

"How did I get out of the…" I'm confused. "I found the key you left me. I came to find you so I can get us the hell out of here."

Her expression is taut and she bites her lip in agitation.

"The key was for the cuff and I told you to put it back on before Nikolai comes to your room. How the hell did you get out of the room?"

I tilt my head. "I used the key. How the fuck do you think I got out?"

"But it only unlocks the…" Her eyebrows lift suddenly, widening her eyes, and her hand slaps over her mouth. "Oh, my God. I didn't lock it." She spins away and paces a few steps before whipping back around to look at me pointedly. "I forgot to lock the door."

Anya's hand drops to her chest and she swallows hard. "You forgot?"

"I forgot. Oh, God. Ezra, I'm—"

Her voice catches and I see her chest rise and fall rapidly. In my adrenaline-spiked state, I'm tuned in and aware, and I can practically hear the air going in and out of her mouth as she slumps backward against the closed door.

She didn't mean for me to escape.

She was just trying to give me the comfort of removing my ankle cuff.

I should be angry at the realization but seeing her panic over a mistake that could be costly to her softens me. It slows my rushing pulse. It makes me step back from the ledge. It makes me feel overcome with the need to comfort her.

"Hey," I say, taking a slow step toward her.

She slides down the door gradually until she's slumped on the floor.

"Anya, it's okay. Listen. I'm out now and I can get you out of here, okay?" I try to reassure her. "I wasn't going to leave without you."

She looks up at me with a furrowed brow. "You came for me?"

There's so much confusion and misunderstanding behind her blue eyes and all I want to do is make sure she knows I'm telling the truth. I should be getting her ass up and dragging her out of here before someone realizes I'm gone, but the privilege of staring into the haunting clarity of her eyes is challenging all my instincts.

I nod. "Of course I came for you. We've got a better chance together than we do alone."

That's when she blinks and turns her head away, hiding behind her icy shell. She pushes to her feet.

"I need to take you back to your room. Before Nikolai knows what happened. And you can't tell him about this. Do you understand? You can't ever tell him."

I snap, "Anya. Are you out of your fucking mind? I'm not going back in there. We're getting the fuck out of here. *Now.*" I grab her hand and then the doorknob.

She leaps in front of me, slamming her back against the door between us to keep it shut. I let go of the doorknob, but her hand is still in mine.

"*No,*" she insists. "There is no getting the fuck out of here."

I step toward her. "What the hell do you mean? Let's *go.*"

We're chest to chest against the door and she's not budging. "Ezra, listen to me. There is no escape. You can walk out the front door right now if you want, but you won't make it a mile past the tree line."

I huff, looking down at her.

"There are wolves in the forest. He feeds them, draws them closer to the manor. Even if that wasn't a concern, the forest stretches for God knows how far, and it's dense. Overwhelming and disorienting. I know because I escaped once. I was lucky that Nikolai came after me. I wouldn't have survived another hour lost in that freezing forest if he hadn't found me. There is *no escape.*"

That's enough to give me pause and the pause makes me realize how close we're standing to one another. I take a small step back as the realization makes my ab muscles clench in a way that I don't want them to clench for her. I drop her hand and turn, pacing away from her a few steps.

"So, you've escaped before and didn't make it."

"It was a hopeless, useless attempt. I just didn't know better. I don't want you to make the same mistake of thinking there's any hope at all of making it out of here alive."

I whip around to look at her. "That's bullshit. There's always hope."

"You're wrong. Here, there's only survival and you have to follow the rules if you want that. I spent a lot of time and energy trying to believe something different."

She pushes away from the door and steps forward, brushing past me to cross to an ornate dresser against the far wall, on the opposite side of her meticulously made bed. She bends to pull open a drawer at the bottom. She takes out a small cardboard box, about the size of a shoebox, though it's covered in a pink and green floral print. Soft pink roses, I notice, and think it seems so perfectly fitting for her.

Soft and pretty and blooming, protected by unyielding thorns.

She turns to face me, holding it in her arms as though it's a puppy or a child that needs to be tended to with care. We both walk toward one another and meet at the end of her queen-sized bed. She lifts the lid, flipping it over onto the mattress.

"Photos?"

She nods, carefully pulling the photo at the very end of the neatly lined row out of the box. She holds it up to me, showing me a picture of a young girl, probably in her early teens. She's sitting on a city stoop, looking down at a cell phone in her hands. I realize her features are similar to Anya's as I look up at her face then back down at the photo. The girl's hair is brown, but a little more golden than Anya's, and shorter.

"Is she family?" I ask and she nods.

"My sister. Lidia. She was fourteen here. Turn it over."

I flip the photo over and find scribbling on the back.

Two numbers.

Fourteen and thirty-five.

"This is the first picture Nikolai brought me when I arrived here at Mikhailov Manor. Lidia was fourteen years old at the time. I had only just turned twenty-one."

"What's thirty-five?"

"Thirty-five yards," she says.

She takes the picture from me and puts it back inside the box. She plucks the photo from the front end of the row and shows it to me.

"This is from last week. She's seventeen now. Her eighteenth birthday will be in a few months."

I look over at Anya and see the small curve of a smile on her lips. But then she frowns as she flips it over.

Again, two numbers.

Seventeen and fifty.

"Fifty yards. It's the scope measurement from a rifle trained on her when they took the photograph. I get one picture a week. Every year for the past three years."

I'm speechless.

She hands me the photograph and paces away, crossing her arms over her chest. I briefly thumb through some of the other photographs in the large stack, careful not to disturb her carefully ordered row.

"Nikolai's reach is vast, Ezra." She lowers to sit on a cream-colored ottoman near the corner window and I'm momentarily distracted by the sunlight behind her. "If I could somehow even manage to survive the wilderness and find a way back to the real world, it wouldn't matter. She'd be dead within the week. Or worse."

"What's worse than death?"

She lifts her head and meets my eyes. "This."

An eerie prickle creeps along my spine in understanding. What I've endured over the past couple of weeks pales in comparison to the hell she's been put through. I saw first-hand what Nikolai has done to her, the violation of his fingers twisting inside her. There's no telling what he had to do before that to break her, to break a woman like Anya, who is obviously so strong.

The thought of it nauseates me and provokes some weird caveman compulsion that makes me feel fiercely protective of her. I set down the photo and go to her, crouching on my haunches in front of her. Her eyes widen at my bold presence and she sits a bit straighter to pull away from me, though I don't budge.

"We have to work together, okay? If we work together, we can figure a way out of this."

"You're not hearing me. There is no way out of this. It's not just Nikolai. It's an entire empire that reaches across the globe."

"What kind of empire?"

She sighs. "The Mikhailovs are in the business of stealing and selling."

"What, like drugs? Weapons?"

She shakes her head. "No. People."

"You're telling me they're selling people?"

"Yes." She nods. "He knows what he's doing. He knows how to keep us here. He knows how to control us."

I give her a small, tilted smile. "Well, the joke's on him. I don't have any family he can hold me hostage with."

She sighs and her shoulders slump, the movement swaying her toward me. I swear I can feel her soul push against mine.

"It doesn't matter. You can't leave. Neither can I. All we can do is survive."

"And how do we do that? Play by his stupid fucking rules?"

"Yes."

I shake my head. "I don't think I can do that."

She leans all the way forward and grabs my face in both hands. "You have to, Ezra. You *have* to."

I know just how fucked I am when she touches me, when I see the tears of desperation glass over her eyes as she pleads with me. She's the kind of girl a guy like me has a hard time saying no to. I don't want to say no to her. I have the fleeting thought that I wish I knew what she was like in the real world, and I feel my heart tug tight against my chest.

"Okay," I say. "Okay, I get it. But if I put my trust in you that this is what we need to do, I want you to know that puts you on the line. That makes you responsible for my well-being."

A flicker of acknowledgement then acceptance crosses her eyes, and I know she understands me with the way it twists in my gut.

"I know. I just need you to follow the rules. It's less painful for me when you do." She lets her hands fall away from my face and they briefly land on my knees before falling away entirely. "I have to take you back to your room. I have to lock you in before he finds you. You're not allowed to be here, especially without Kostya."

I shake my head. "I can't. I can't go back there."

"You have to. There's no other choice. But I swear, I won't leave you there, okay? We just need to convince Nikolai that I've broken you. That you kneel for me now. If we can convince him of that, then you'll have more freedom in the house."

I put my hands on my knees and push up to stand, lacing my fingers together on the top of my head as I spin and pace. I feel her coming up behind me and I drop my hands to my sides, spinning to face her. Her fingers graze mine as she reaches to hold my hand and I snatch both of hers in mine, desperately craving the small moment of affection.

"I know it's hard," she says softly, "I know. He kept me in isolation for months when he brought me here."

She survived this for months?

If she could get through it for months, I could certainly manage a little while longer.

I sigh and before I even understand why I'm doing it, I step forward and wrap my arms around her petite frame, pulling her into a hug. She doesn't recoil and I'm thankful for that, though I can sense she doesn't know how to respond.

I'm immediately aware of the fact that I haven't showered in a week, other than to splash some water on the most important parts of my body from the faucet in my bathroom. I wish I smelled better for her, and that seems like a petty fucking thought in all this.

I inhale the scent at the top of her head. It's floral and fragrant and bursting with life. It's the scent of fresh cut roses and I can't stop myself from kissing the top of her head. That chaste kiss is what melts her and she presses into me, slipping her arms through mine to wrap around my waist. She lets her head rest against my chest and all I can think of is standing here and holding her.

I really, honestly don't want to let her go.

But the startling sound of the door clicking open kickstarts my heart to get ready to fight for my life, to fight for her life, to fight for *our* lives.

CHAPTER 11
Anya

ONE MOMENT WARM arms encapsulate me, and the next, they're shoving me away. The click of the door startles us both. Just when I think things are going to be okay, that I've gotten through to Ezra, that he understands why we have to play by the rules and submit to survive, it all comes crashing heavy upon our heads.

I fully expect that Ezra will jump into action and rush the door, but I hadn't expected him to do this. He pushes me out of his embrace, farther back into the room, then spins lightning fast and steps forward toward the door, standing protectively between me and the oncoming threat.

I have a moment of hope, dangerous flashing hope, that it's only Kostya coming into my room. But Kostya always knocks and he only comes to collect me when Nikolai calls for me. I know it's Nikolai before I even see him.

"Ezra," I warn, fully expecting to see him launch himself at Nikolai on the attack.

Instead, Ezra steps backward, holding a hand behind him, as if the palm of his outstretched arm could form a protective shield around me. No one, not one of the three men before him, would have done that for me.

My heart skips across an unwilling beat.

Nikolai is seething at the door, though he has yet to cross the threshold. His fingers roll methodically into fists at his sides.

What do I do?

What the hell do I do?

There's only one thing I can think of.

"On your knees, *mal'chik,*" I say to Ezra, hoping he'll know, praying he'll understand.

He glances back at me, but it's quick, and then he's watching Nikolai again, bouncing with feral energy.

"*Mal'chik,*" I snap at him through gnashed teeth.

He looks at me and I think he sees the meaning in my stare. I think he understands that we have to pretend this is nothing more than me training my slave.

I'll be punished for this regardless.

Nikolai has found me alone in my room with the boy.

But I may be able to lessen the severity of the consequence—at the very least, for Ezra's sake—if we can convince him that this is nothing but bad judgment on my part.

Gradually, thankfully, Ezra comes into understanding. There's a slight bob to his head and he nods to me, lowering to his knees. It's slow movement, his body is rigid with tension and ready to jump back up on a dime if this turns into a fight.

I need him to see that it can't always be a fight.

It only makes things worse.

It only gives Nikolai a reason to punish us.

I slip deep within the borders of my soul to guard myself as I find my shield and step forward courageously, moving in between Ezra and Nikolai. Ezra's agitation is so visceral, it's as if I can feel his pulse through my own, and that connection is unnerving, unsteadying.

I lower to kneel in front of Nikolai, bowing my head in

contrition.

"I'm sorry. I know I'm not supposed to bring him to my room. I wanted to show him the photographs of Lidia. I wanted to make him understand."

"Quiet, *rabynya*," he snaps, "Come with me, both of you."

He's growling, practically salivating in territorial possession, reminiscent of the night I once tried to escape and found myself face to face with a snarling gray wolf.

There are wolves outside but an equally dangerous one within, and I'm currently his prey.

I rise to my feet. "*Da, khozyain*," I turn my head toward Ezra. "Come, *mal'chik.*"

His brow furrows, but somehow, he manages to get control of his questioning expression. With a shake of his head, he gets to his feet with a clenched jaw.

Nikolai leads us both out of the room, down the hall toward the grand staircase. My heart thumps wildly against my ribs as I open my stride to keep up with his long steps.

I don't know what he's thinking.

He's silent as we walk, and that's more terrifying to me than if he were to yell and scream and throw me against the wall and hurt me.

There's feral, male energy all around me, one pulsing with ill-intent, the other with ferocious goodness. It's overwhelming the way that it ropes its way around and tugs at me from both sides.

Nikolai nearly runs down the grand staircase and I quickly follow behind, not looking back, simply hoping that Ezra is keeping up and following as he's supposed to. Any step out of line from Ezra right now will only make whatever the hell we're heading toward worse, likely for me.

Nikolai reaches the bottom of the staircase several steps

ahead and stops beside Kostya, who is already standing there in wait. He spins around to face us as we chase toward him.

When my foot falls onto the landing, Nikolai snaps, grabbing me by the scruff of my neck. I shriek and my shoulders instantly tense as his heavy hand pushes down on the back of my neck. I know immediately he wants me on the ground, but my body still pushes back against the force.

He bends down as he pushes harder, hissing against my ear, "Crawl, *rabynya.*"

I respond to his command and slump to my knees on the hard marble, catching myself on my hands as he releases me with a flick of his wrist that tosses my weight forward. Nikolai walks again, striding forward with the confident steps of a shrewd businessman on his way to roll heads. The click of his sleek dress shoes across the marble reverberates in my bones as I follow him on my hands and knees.

I feel Ezra moving faster toward me and I see him coming up along my side.

"Behind me," I insist. "Don't make this worse."

"Fuck!" The tremble in his voice ripples over my skin.

His voice is tinged with agitation and fear. Thankfully, he falls back in line, though I can see him twitch with frantic, nervous energy.

I know Ezra isn't accustomed to this sort of behavior, but I wish he would come to terms with our circumstances faster. His concern makes this feel so much worse, in a truly unique and thoroughly revolting manner.

Nikolai has already traversed the small hallway that leads to the dance studio and stands in the doorway, glaring at me. I move across the floor as swiftly as I can, flinching at the way the unforgiving marble slams into my kneecaps with every motion.

All I'm wearing are cotton shorts and a well-worn, off the

shoulder sweatshirt. Because my legs are bare, the coldness and the hardness of the floor is jarring as my bones knock against it, one knee, then the other, over and over.

Nikolai has moved well inside the studio by the time I make it to the threshold. I keep going, wondering if Ezra might actually explode from the pent-up rage he's barely keeping under wraps. He's practically dancing with the constant movement, with the jolts and twitches that scream so loudly that he wants to fight.

Once I reach the center of the dance floor where Nikolai stands waiting, his foot comes down on the small of my back and slams me down flat to the floor. I turn my head just in time for my cheek to press into the cold floor, my arms and legs sprawling, as the air is forced out of me in a rushed groan.

"You fucker!" Ezra screams. "Get off me!" And I know Kostya is holding him back.

"*Mal'chik*. Please," I barely whisper, filled with sadness, a quiet plea into the empty space and I don't even know if he can hear me.

"You're failing, Anya," Nikolai says to me. "I don't believe for a second you brought him to your room just to show him photographs. You like him. You want him. You're trying to use him for yourself and neglecting your task of training him to perform for *me*."

"No, I swear…I promise you, I was just trying to show him why…why he can't keep fighting me, trying to escape."

His foot abruptly lifts. "Get up."

I jump to my feet in a hurry and turn to face him.

"Get rope. Tie his hands together."

"*Khozyain*, please, it's not his—"

I stop myself from finishing that sentence.

Why am I defending Ezra?

It's his fault we're in this mess in the first place.

Except…I forgot to lock the door.

It's my *fault.*

Nikolai's head cocks to the side. "Are you trying to prove my point? You never hesitated to bind a partner in the past."

I shake my head quickly and take a step back. "No, I'm sorry."

I turn and rush off to the corner to gather a length of rope. I take it to where Ezra stands, now with Kostya forming a human barrier between him and Nikolai. His legs are wide, his hands clenching and unclenching, chest pumping with rapid breaths. I slip between Ezra and Kostya and stand in front of him.

"Put your hands in front of you, *mal'chik*," I tell him.

He huffs, overwhelming me with the runoff stream of his adrenaline sweeping all around me. He does as he's told, but his arms twitch and his hands shake. As I start to wind the length of coarse rope around his wrists, I intentionally let my fingers graze his knuckles, praying he can feel my regret for stamping down his hope so effectively.

I twist and turn and coil and bind with practiced mastery. Nikolai is an expert in the art of binding, and he's passed all his knowledge on to me. It's knowledge I wish I didn't possess. When I'm convinced that Ezra is bound to Nikolai's satisfaction, that he's bound in a way that he won't be able to escape without assistance, I step back, bow my head, and wait.

The *click, click, click* of Nikolai's shoes across the dance floor is like a slow ticking clock, counting down the seconds of the oncoming punishment. When I finally feel Nikolai's presence at my back, like a whoosh of arctic air through a door being thrown open during a winter storm, I shiver from head to toe.

"Put your arms behind your back," he says.

No.

No.

No, no, no.

"Please, no, please," I beg unashamedly because I know what he's going to do.

He fists my hair and yanks my head back harshly, forcing me to stare up at the ceiling.

"I'm not asking, *rabynya*, I'm telling."

I swallow and breathe, in and out, closing my eyes to try to find my center. It's shifting and wobbling off course. I bring my shaking hands behind me and try to convince myself that everything is going to be okay.

Nothing is okay, but I have to pretend in order to survive.

Nikolai releases my hair and my head drops forward. I'm caught by green before me. Green eyes that remind me of thriving, vibrant life. Green eyes that throb with radiant energy.

As Nikolai secures my wrists behind my back, I let myself live there in the green because it's the only color that I have to cling to in this overcast, gray, shadow-filled, onrushing punishment.

Nikolai moves to our sides and looks back and forth between the two of us.

"You are both heading for a world of pain if you continue to misbehave like this. You have one job and one job only and that is to fucking dance."

"I think there's a problem then, boss. I haven't gotten paid for this job yet," Ezra says, his voice is flowing magma, hot and wild.

He turns his head, disrupting his eye contact with me in favor of squaring off with Nikolai. "And your benefits plan really fucking sucks."

I sigh and the exhale is filled with a mixture of exasperation, dread, pride, and perhaps, a bit of humor.

Nikolai takes a step toward him, his chest nearly pressed

into Ezra's shoulder at his side. "I'm curious…" he begins with a smirk. "How is it possible that Anya has yet to wipe you clean of your arrogance? Her own should have outmatched yours by now."

"I'm not arrogant," Ezra insists, and I wish he would just shut the fuck up.

Every word he utters will add time to the punishment to come.

"Oh, yes, you are. I'm just surprised she hasn't crushed your spirit yet. She did so well with the others."

I see Ezra's face tick at this remark, as if considering something he hadn't before.

"I'm unbreakable," Ezra replies.

Oh, God.

I wish he hadn't said that.

I wish, I wish, I wish he hadn't said that.

Nikolai speaks low and harshly, "Perhaps you are. But I know she is not. Come."

He turns on the spot and walks briskly out of the room. I shake my head at Ezra and his face drops, probably at the recognition of surging fear in my expression. He doesn't know what is to come, but I do. I know and I wish I didn't because knowing makes it that much worse.

I don't wait to make sure Ezra follows behind me as I trail after Nikolai. Kostya will drag him along with the threat of his stun gun if he doesn't cooperate.

Two-and-a-half years ago was the second time I received this punishment. I remember freezing in fear the moment he tied my hands behind my back just like this. I was unwilling and unable to move when he told me to follow after him because I'd experienced this punishment for the first time just weeks before.

I had known the horror that was coming and the fear of it rooted me to the spot. My stubbornness and fear had ultimately only made the second punishment worse—he kept me in longer and it took longer to bring me back. So now, I follow him immediately, hoping my acceptance will make it easier.

If only Ezra will keep his mouth shut, then maybe it won't be so bad.

I look down at the floor as we walk, crossing the estate to the east wing, still on the first level. Walking past the grand staircase, we enter the garden corridor. We're still indoors, but tall, rectangular windows are carved into the dark stone walls every few feet, reaching high above us, the stone curving above to form an archway overhead.

If there was sunlight and life at Mikhailov Manor, it would shine through here, it would bring light into this dark, dark residence. But its perpetual winter, perpetual gray, perpetual cold, perpetual darkness.

We pass through the corridor and veer left, walking down two steps that fall onto a cracked stone-paved landing. This area of the home is a more recent addition, more modern than some of the other parts of the manor which still held their historical décor.

We're standing in an alcove that feels more like a cave, intentionally designed that way. The light from the garden corridor fades back into darkness here, save for the recessed lighting in the stone overhead. The walls are rough, made to look like the rocky interior of a grand cavern, and it's humid, surrounding us with an overwhelming dampness. To me, it's a stony secret passage, a hidden gate that leads to the depths of the underworld.

This alcove serves as the gateway to a steam room that no one uses anymore toward our right. But we'll be going left, in through the single glass door cut into the cave-like wall that leads to the indoor pool.

This is where reality strikes.

This is where my body reacts.

This is where I step backward, lose control, and tell him no.

"No, no, please, *moy khozyain*, I can't…"

"Anya." Ezra sounds as though fear has washed away his reckless energy.

Nikolai comes after me. "Yes, *rabynya*, yes." He snatches me by the elbow, dragging me forward.

I don't fight him, but I resist. I know it's going to happen whether I want it to or not, and though I wish I could be more dignified, more graceful about accepting my fate, my human instinct refuses to let me.

A stirring panic swirls in my chest, pulling into a dense ball that rolls around my ribcage as it lights on fire. It's like a dense star burning bright in a flash of light, then dying, collapsing, becoming a black hole that pulls my entire life force into that single dark space.

Nikolai pulls the glass door open with one hand, dragging me from the elbow with the other as I try to pull away from him.

"No! No, no, no. *Moy khozyain*…" I beg. "*Moy khozyain*, please. I'm sorry, I'll do better. I'll be better, I promise."

I hear how pathetic I sound, yet I'm powerless to stop it—that black hole in my chest is pulling and changing me, taking away my control, altering the way I react.

He shoves me past the door, then Kostya forces Ezra behind me before letting it drift shut. I back away until I hit the side wall and can't go any farther. I keep my eyes locked on Nikolai, suddenly instinctive and defensive like the prey he's made me become.

I can feel Ezra's eyes on me.

I can hear him yelling.

I can sense him struggling.

I can see Kostya tying Ezra's bound hands to a towel bar that's bolted into the sturdy wall.

I know all these things are happening, but my conscious is shutting down in my panic. My lungs are working double time, my breaths quickening, and tears singe my eyes, knowing that soon I won't be able to breathe at all.

Nikolai is coming after me now.

I'll be under the water soon.

I'll be entirely breathless soon.

I'll be dead soon.

CHAPTER 12
Anya

NIKOLAI'S HAND FIRMLY wraps around my upper arm and I scream. I scream so loudly and so sharply that everything else in the room stills.

Nikolai stills.

Kostya stills.

Ezra stills.

The smell of the chlorine wafting in the air even feels exceptionally stagnant for an extra beat.

But when that beat passes, everything shifts back into focus. It's a new tilted perspective, but a true one. I can see all too clearly what's happening to me.

Nikolai walks, pulling me along, moving us both toward the rectangular pool. He stops us at the steps, using his toes to kick off his shoes but doesn't dare let go of me.

If he let go of me, I would crumble.

Everything in my body is telling me to fall, to crumple to the floor, curl up into a tiny ball, a tiny, nonexistent ball that evades all attention. I wish to be as small and unremarkable as a stone on a walkway, something Nikolai could walk right past and forget about.

Instead, I feel like a boulder he's stubbed his toe on, the

boulder he's now kicking back at in useless frustration, as if kicking me will ease his annoyance.

Kicking me isn't enough to satisfy him, though. He wants to roll me off the cliff's edge, drop me into the ocean, and watch me sink heavily to the bottom.

He drags me to the stairs that descend into the shallow end of the pool and we both step down. My sneakers soak up the water, making my feet instantly feel heavier. He fists the railing with his free hand, using it to pull himself. His other hand pulls me, while I pull back.

I'm facing away from him, jerking in the opposite direction with all my might. His hand slips purposefully down my arm, falling to the rope that binds my wrists at my back and grasps it tightly, using it to keep a firm grip on me. I'm still fighting him on the second step down as he drops onto the pool floor. With one sharp tug, he heaves me backward and I slip into the water, nearly drifting onto my back as it catches my fall from the steps.

I right myself quickly, springing up to press my feet against the blue, mosaic-tiled floor. My hair is heavy at my back, dipped wet at the ends.

Every scream and shout I make in protest echoes off the walls, bouncing back in a haunting chant as if a dozen of me were yelling out their torment all at once.

Nikolai pulls me in front of him and our eyes catch. I beg him with mine, but his are unyielding. He's intent on punishing me. I hardly even remember what for now.

It doesn't matter.

He wants to hurt me and so he will.

My soggy clothes hang heavy on my body. The off-shoulder gray sweatshirt pulls me, drags me, encourages me to succumb to the water and sink to relieve the weight of it.

My whole body is trembling uncontrollably now. My bones feel like they've been wrapped in winter air and every part of me shakes.

Nikolai grips both of my shoulders painfully, his fingers bruising. His head snaps up to look behind me just before he spins me around, forcing me to face Ezra. He stands poolside above us with his arms secured to a towel bar on the wall that's level with his chest.

I make a mistake.

I look at Ezra.

I see his horrified expression and I *feel* it inside my chest.

I feel his fear, his pain, his terror swirling with mine, and it's more painful than any feeling of horror Nikolai has ever managed to pluck out of me himself.

"This is what you need to understand, Mr. Bell," Nikolai's voice bellows, echoing in the wide, open space. "Anya is mine. If you try to win her heart, play on her sympathies, you both will lose. This is what you will get."

I feel the curl of his fingertips around my shoulders, the grip of his hands as he tightens his hold. My pulse quickens, knowing it's happening before I can react to it consciously, logically. All reason slips my mind in fear as Nikolai's weight shifts over my shoulders. I open my mouth to scream instead of taking a breath like I should have and then he's pushing me down.

Ezra strangles out a horrified scream and then his sound fades into a whoosh, a rumbling void that soaks up our shouting and washes them away. Tepid water rushes into my nostrils and I snap my mouth shut to create a barrier the only way I can.

I'm buried beneath the surface now, only its water that holds me in my grave instead of soil.

I don't immediately fight. Although I knew it was coming, it still takes me by surprise. The shift from air to water is entirely bewildering. It takes me a few seconds after the initial shock to remember what's happening, where I am, who's holding me down.

My knees are on the tile floor. All I want is to break free from Nikolai and get to the surface. I lean forward and drop my body down to the pool floor, using the way he pushes down on me as leverage to go deeper. I flatten my body and roll, facing the surface above me. Nikolai's hands have lost their grip and fallen away.

I thrash and kick and rise above the break as Nikolai rushes for me. I manage to stand, but it's only just long enough to take in a deep breath, only just long enough to hear the echoes of Ezra's distress for me bouncing off the walls.

Nikolai wraps his arms around my midsection and my soaked, heavy hair whips around my face, strands covering my mouth and nose. He spins me fast in his hold, this time grabbing the ropes around my wrists with one hand and grasping the back of my neck painfully tight with the other.

He bends me forward at the waist, forcing my face into the water, pushing me down beneath the surface, drowning me again. I squirm, throwing every ounce of energy I have into fighting him.

But I'm failing.

He's got a hold on me and no matter what I do, there is no getting away from him now.

The adrenaline in my body fights with my experience. It tells my brain to fight, though experience knows there is no point. Experience knows that Nikolai won't let up. Experience knows that I've drowned in this pool before. Experience knows I'm going to die here again.

Going against every physical instinct, I force myself to still. I let him hold me under the water and I start to count.

One. Two. Three. Four. Five. Six. Seven. Eight.

One. Two. Three. Four. Five. Six. Seven. Eight

One. Two. Three. Four. Five. Six. Seven. Eight.

I know—because I've been here before—that I can make it to twelve counts of eight.

Nikolai's grip on me hasn't lessened, though I've essentially stopped fighting him. My body still ticks and thrashes every few moments, a natural physical reflex to get me out of harm's way, but I'm aware that's not possible.

I open my eyes as I continue to count. My hair floats and drifts around me in waves that look nearly black in their saturated state. As the water stills around me, I can almost make out the words being spoken and shouted above the surface, though not quite. I hear shouting, yelling. I think I hear a clanging sound, and I wonder if Ezra is strong enough to rip the towel bar out of the wall.

He probably is.

It won't be long now though.

My chest aches. My lungs are strained and desperate for air. Against my will, I inhale, and water rushes into my nose. It burns as it fills my airways and naturally, I attempt to cough it out. But opening my mouth only fills me with more chlorinated water.

I pinch my eyes shut.

One. Two. Three. Four. Five. Six. Seven. Eight.

One. Two. Three. Four. Five. Six. Seven. Eight.

I try to remember it's almost done, it's almost over. Consciousness will soon fade and turn into peaceful darkness. The counting gives me something other than the ache and fear of drowning to focus on.

One. Two. Three. Four. Five. Six. Seven. Eight.

I'm tiring, though my body tries to gasp in air. The time

between my unintentional twitches and muscle jerks lengthens and everything slows.

Everything slows.

Except for Ezra. There's the muffled rumble of Ezra's screaming and the echoing, muted *thump, thump* that I can only assume is the sound of him pulling against his bindings.

I think the vibration of his last scream sounds like my name, as if he's yelling my name, yelling for me.

Part of me wishes this is truly the end, not just a false end as Nikola intends it to be. He intends to kill me but bring me back to life. He's done it twice, and this will be the third time. Part of me prays this is it, that he won't be able to revive me this time because I'm tired of the fight.

So, so tired.

I hardly think fighting is worth it anymore.

There is *nothing* for me in this life.

There's no happiness, only pain and torture. There's no end to it in sight, nothing to look forward to.

As blackness creeps around my vision, as I'm starting to slip into unconsciousness, there's a bewildering flash of something bright. An image of green, vibrant emerald green eyes looking at me as if I'm worth something more than this life. As I begin to drift into that unwilling sleep, I see him as a vision, a dream, but it's clear as day who I'm imagining.

It's Ezra Bell and his crooked, sarcastic, entirely charming smile.

I've never had a vision drift into unconsciousness before, and this one is so pleasant, so calming, that I actually wish I could wrap my arms around it and bring it with me into the underworld.

No. Not it, but him.

If this is the end for me, I selfishly want to drag this man down with me, not to hurt him, but to comfort me. Some part of me already knows that if I asked Ezra to chase me into death, just so that I wouldn't be alone, he would.

What a ridiculous thing to think.

That's the last thought I have before the sweet slumber of death engulfs me in darkness and takes me away.

CHAPTER 13
Ezra

ANYA'S DEAD.

She's dead.

He killed her.

That motherfucking piece of shit just drowned her in the pool.

I'm not even aware of what I'm doing, I just know that I'm thrashing and pulling against this bar I'm bound to and I'm shouting. I don't even know what I'm shouting, but words of desperation and anger and fear are spewing out of me like lava from an erupting volcano.

Anya has gone still in the water, yet he continues to hold her there. Her hair floats all around her head, dark brown waves stretch out in strands all around her face. Nikolai has the audacity to breathe heavily with shallow, rapid breaths, as if killing her is an unwelcome exertion of his energy.

"Get her out!" I scream. "Get her out, get her out! Please, you're fucking killing her!"

She's already dead.

I know she is because I felt it the moment it happened. It was a snap inside my chest, an abnormal beat in my heart rhythm that happened the moment her body stopped jerking.

Finally, Nikolai rolls her body over in the water. She's completely limp, lifeless. For a moment, I think he's going to leave her there, but then I see him look down at her. His eyes are satisfied with what he's done, but there's also some sense of urgency behind his movements as he drags her to the edge of the pool.

He walks backward up the pool steps, pulling her with him, and when he gets out, he carefully lifts her and places her on the pool's edge, half on her side because her arms are still tied behind her back.

Nikolai kneels behind her, pulling his switchblade from his pocket, and saws at the ropes that bind her until they break free. Kostya snatches a red bag from inside a small, white box that I hadn't noticed hanging on the wall and ambles back to where Anya lays.

Nikolai rolls her onto her back and leans to place his ear over her heart.

Everything is still.

I'm still and I'm never fucking still.

I don't dare make a sound as Nikolai listens for the beating of her heart. He looks up after a minute and nods to Kostya, then they both stand and back away. Kostya returns the red bag to the wall and I realize then it's a defibrillator.

Oh, fuck.

Oh, fuck, oh, fuck, oh, fuck.

I had hope.

For a brief, shining moment, I had hope and now, it's slipping away from me. They're both just standing there, staring down at her.

Waiting.

"What the fuck are you waiting for? Fucking *save* her!" I scream and Nikolai looks at me sharply.

He cocks his head to the side. "Wait."

I can't wait, I need to get to her. I start pulling harder than before, as hard as I fucking can, and it doesn't matter to me that I already know this bar is not budging from the goddamn wall.

"Untie him."

Nikolai hands his blade to Kostya and I take the first breath of relief since the moment Nikolai caught me and Anya in her room.

I'm impatient as Kostya cuts me free and I run to her the instant the ropes fall away. I don't wait for anyone to give me permission, I slam to my knees next to her and lean down over her, looking for signs of life.

I don't know what's come over me. I don't know why the thought of losing her is too painful for me to bear. I hardly know this woman, and I'm only drawn to her for the simple fact that she's the only person I have in this captivity.

That's all it is.

She's my only potential companion and it's nothing more than that.

Yet somehow, I still feel my heart thudding hard against my ribcage as I watch and wait, hoping she's going to cough that water out of her lungs and start breathing again. Regardless of the reason I'm drawn to her, I know I cannot survive this without her.

Without Anya, I've got nothing to fight for, no reason to fight to survive this bullshit captivity. I just want to see her open her eyes.

"Open your eyes, Anya…Come on…open your eyes."

I've got to see that sapphire sparkle again.

There's a twitch.

Another.

Then she coughs and coughs and water spills from the

corners of her lips. She's naturally rolling to the side, so I lift under her shoulder, helping her roll as she continues to cough the water from her lungs. Then she's gasping and shaking and reaching, trying to find something solid to hold onto to. I reach over her and grab both of her small hands in one of mine, squeezing tightly.

"Ez…Ezra," she calls out before her eyes have even opened.

My heart stops.

I immediately feel the icy burn of Nikolai's eyes on my back, but I ignore it.

"Hey, it's me. I'm here." I sigh in relief. "You're okay. You're okay. It's fine now."

She blinks a couple of times before her eyes fully open and they dart around the room. She hasn't realized where she is or what's happened. But she called out my name and my pulse quickens impossibly faster than before.

In this moment of relief after such terror, I realize that she's under my skin. I don't know how or why, but she is.

There's something that connects us.

It's not just the captivity, though I want to believe that's all it is. If it were just the captivity and our circumstance, this wouldn't affect me so profoundly. It wouldn't make my heart beat frantically enough to set off warning bells that I'm at risk of stressing myself into a heart attack, into a tragic and unexpected death of my own.

I know there's something more to our connection when I feel it snap again in my chest, the same snap I felt when she died in the water.

"I expect you are capable of carrying her, hmm?" Nikolai says from behind me.

My eyes are on Anya, watching the pain of her gasping,

shaking breaths, looking over every inch of her body as if scanning her with my eyes can somehow heal her.

"*Mal'chik*," he bites.

I growl, "Give her a fucking minute, you sick piece of shit."

Anya's voice is a hoarse whisper, but it still possesses the strength to move a mountain, "No, Ezra. No. Do as you're told."

Her head turns toward me and she blinks. I'm so inexplicably relieved and elated to see that perfect shade of blue again that I immediately comply. My attitude isn't going to help her. I just want to get her out of this echoing, chlorine-saturated torture chamber.

"Yeah," I finally say to Nikolai, "I can carry her."

"Let's go then. Move."

"I can walk," she says, attempting to push to a sitting position with her trembling hands.

I shake my head in disbelief. Before she can move an inch farther, I scoop my hands beneath her body and lift her from the slick ground, cradling her in my arms as her soaked hair spills water on the floor beneath us.

I don't know if it's the sudden movement, but as I sweep her up, she loses consciousness again. Her right arm flops down freely, reaching for the floor in a swaying motion, and her left arm falls limply across her chest. Her head drops back with a jerk, her hair swinging.

"Shit," I grunt, hoisting her up higher in my arms, twisting her body toward me to cradle into my chest.

Nikolai and Kostya are already at the door, waiting impatiently like the pieces of shit they are. I walk, carrying her close against my body as she starts to wake again.

I turn sideways to get through the door that leads us back to the cave-like alcove. As we walk back through the arched hallway with its high windows, Anya finds enough strength to open her eyes again. I make sure mine are right there to meet hers as she looks up at me.

"I've got you," I tell her, and she looks like she believes me.

I hope she believes me.

She shuts her eyes.

"Anya?" I say, worried she's passed out again.

She hasn't.

I know she hasn't because her right-hand reaches up, slipping across the top of my chest and around to grip the side of my neck. Her head turns and she presses her face to my shoulder. The simple action shows me that, on some level, she trusts me. If she knew me at all, she'd know how important that is to me.

I think she must know me because I think I know her.

I know it's a dangerous concession for her to give away her trust.

Normally, it wouldn't be so hard to carry her as far as we have to walk, but I'm weak from malnourishment and tired from the adrenaline repeatedly ebbing and flowing. I hesitate at the bottom of the grand staircase, just for moment to readjust and make sure I don't drop her.

A good partner doesn't drop and as long as she's my partner, I'm not letting her hit that floor.

I'm careful carrying her back up the steps. We turn left at the top of the stairs, the opposite direction of my room. I follow Nikolai as he strides to sweep around the banister, past the hallway where I'd found Anya's room before, and continue going straight. A few more steps leads us to another hallway to our right and we follow it to the end.

Nikolai flings open a door and stands beside it, arms crossed, impatience all over his wicked face.

Reluctantly, I pass him and enter the room with Anya in

my arms, making sure to hold her away from him when I turn sideways to get her through the door.

As soon as I'm inside, Nikolai comes in after us and slams the door shut, leaving Kostya in the hallway.

"Is she awake?" he asks.

Anya rolls her head slowly away from my shoulder, turning her face toward the ceiling. "*Da, khozyain*," she answers, though she hasn't opened her eyes.

I can feel how her body tenses in response to him. It makes me want to hurt him in a hateful way I've never felt before.

"Set her on her feet," Nikolai demands as he brushes past us, walking around the four-post bed to what I assume is an en suite bathroom.

This must be his bedroom.

I lower her feet gradually to the floor and her hands find their way to my shoulders. She holds onto me for stability, but she doesn't have to. It's not like I'm going to take my hands off her while she's so unsteady.

"Take off her wet clothes," I hear Nikolai call from the bathroom.

Her drooping head lifts and she looks up at me, though I can see how the small movement makes her dizzy. She needs to rest. She needs a fucking doctor, but I don't suppose Nikolai is going to get her one.

"Go ahead," she tells me softly, giving me permission to strip her.

I suck in a breath and lift the heavy hem of her wet sweatshirt, pulling up from her waist and working to pull it up over her body. It wants to cling to her, and I have to tug as I peel it up over her head. She lifts her arms to help me and the movement nearly knocks her backward. I quickly snake one arm around her waist and lasso her against my chest. I hold her like that as I tug the sweatshirt, attempting to untangle it from her sopping wet hair which coils through the collar. Somehow, I manage to pull it off the rest of the way and toss it onto the floor.

"I've got you," I tell her.

"You keep saying that," she says sleepily.

"It's true."

Nikolai comes out of the bathroom and I step back from her, just enough to make this embrace look more innocent. And only because I wish to spare her more harm from this abusive son of a bitch who owns us.

He fucking owns *us.*

He comes over to where we're standing, holding out a bleached white towel to me. I take it and he steals Anya from my hold.

My jaw clenches.

But what the fuck am I supposed to do about it?

There's nothing I can fucking do that won't hurt her more in the end.

Without waiting for her okay, he peels the black sports bra from her body, tossing it aside, then shoves at her cotton shorts. He pushes them and her underwear down to the floor, helping her step out of her clothes.

Just like that, like nothing at all, she's been stripped bare.

Nikolai Mikhailov has stripped every barrier from this blue-eyed girl and exposed her naked and vulnerable to the world. What's worse is that it doesn't even seem to faze her. He's held every part of her hostage for so long that she no longer has any insecurity about being bare so long as he is happy with her behavior.

"Take her." He shoves Anya back into my grip and she curls against my chest as I grip her by both arms. "Dry her off while I get her something to wear."

I nearly slip.

I nearly say, "*How kind of you,*" in my normal, sarcastic way.

But with this girl in my arms—barely alive, weak, and vulnerable—I find some strength I didn't know I had to keep my smart mouth shut despite the way my lips twitch to speak.

She leans into me and I shake out the towel with one hand, wrapping it around her shoulders. I can feel her tremble against my torso and I reach around her back, rubbing over the towel with both my hands, hoping to create some friction to help warm her up.

"I'm freezing," she mutters.

"I know."

I take a breath and pull back a bit so I can move the towel to dry her. I have no choice but to look at her. She seems to sense my hesitation.

"It's okay, Ezra."

I nod, though she can't see it. She can't see it because her head is drooping from fatigue. I slide the towel down her backside and crouch to dry her legs. I work fast, coming back up her front and quickly draping the towel across her breasts before I can look for a moment longer than necessary.

I'm a gentleman, but I'm not blind.

I looked.

Of course, I did.

She's slender and toned and gorgeous beneath her clothes, but she also looks like she's been used as a goddamn whipping post.

Black and blue and yellow bruises mar the otherwise flawless honey color of her skin.

"Come here," Nikolai says, returning to slip a plain, white T-shirt over her naked body. "Bedtime, *moya rabynya.*"

She nods and shuffles as he takes her from me and guides her to the bed, *his* bed. He's actually careful with her now, pulling back the covers and tucking her in. It's messing with my head to see him act as if he gives a shit about her comfort or care.

He starts taking off his clothes. "You can go now, Mr. Bell. Frankly, I don't give a shit if you go back to your room, roam the manor, try to escape in the forest…It's not as if you're going to succeed in getting off the grounds anyway."

I scoff, "So all that time I've spent shackled to a bedpost, locked in a room with two different keys. That was just a fun experiment for you?"

He's down to his boxer briefs and I'm beyond fucking uncomfortable.

"Fun is a subjective term," he says as he walks around the bed.

He climbs under the covers and slides in behind Anya where she lays facing me. She's already asleep. Or she's passed out again.

"Get out, *mal'chik*," he says.

It feels wrong that he's using that word. I know it's meant to be a dig at me when it's used, to put me in my place, but it somehow feels okay when Anya says it.

It feels like something else he's taken from her.

"I hope you've learned your lesson," he adds, just as I reluctantly turn to walk toward the door.

I stop and swing back around to face him. "Lesson?"

"Anya is mine. You are hers, but she will never be *yours*. It's undeniable she has a soft spot for you. She's impressed by your talent and that's all it is. You'll be disappointed if you read further into it than that. You are her dance partner and nothing else. Make sure that remains so, *mal'chik*. It doesn't faze me to hurt her in order to control you. I would sooner kill her before letting her fall for a boy like you. Now you've seen the proof."

"Why the fuck am I here?" I turn my palms up. "Why do you even need me?"

An evil smile spreads wide across his face as he latches an arm around Anya's waist. I know she's passed out again because her body is limp as he pulls her back against him.

"You're here for entertainment."

"You want me to dance," I express with annoyance, "I get it. But she's a perfect soloist, why give her a partner?"

"Why? You assume there's a meaningful motivation for my actions."

"Isn't there?"

"Ezra," he says, "Anya is mine. She's belonged to me longer than she's been held in this manor. I claimed her a very long time ago. But even I grow weary with boredom. The drama a partner brings excites me. It's as simple as that."

As simple as that.

Our captivity is as simple as boredom.

CHAPTER 14

Anya

I WAS REQUIRED to spend two full days in Nikolai's room after he killed me—though he hadn't actually killed me this time. He told me my heart never fully stopped beating like it had the two times before, but we both know it would have given another handful of moments under the water.

There's a strange cycle I've come to expect now with Nikolai. His rage and violence slowly build over time. His frustration begins to grow when he brings me a new partner, and I think that must be the triggering event for his circular pattern of behavior.

His frustration grows into anger, anger grows into rage, rage grows into violence. All of it culminates in my punishment—whether I deserve it or not.

Once the punishment has been dealt, once his violent urges have been satiated, he finds a way to mold himself back into something that almost resembles a human being.

This is why it doesn't surprise me that Nikolai cares for me delicately in the aftermath of such a brutal punishment. I recall him doing the same before and for the life I me, I don't understand why. Part of me likes to believe its remorse that makes him behave that way, but I know it's not.

He doesn't regret hurting me.

He just knows how badly he's hurt me. He knows if he doesn't give my body the rest, care, and nourishment it needs to recover, then I won't be able to dance. That's why he insists that I stay in his room.

It hasn't been entirely awful to be held here for two days. There's a television I can watch, books to read, a small space behind the armchairs where I can do some barre work. He doesn't hurt me, he doesn't rape me, he brings me three meals a day and even sits to eat two of them with me.

It's nothing like the beginning of my captivity with Nikolai. I'm not chained to the bed. I'm not left alone and starving for days at a time. I have things to entertain me. Belonging to him is normal now, and there's a strange kind of comfort to be found in that complacency.

I hate that I think this way now.

Captivity has altered my frame of mind and being aware of that makes no difference.

By the third morning, I'm itching to get out of here, to move, to stretch my legs, to *dance*. I'm pacing the small space behind the armchairs when the door clicks open and Nikolai enters.

I spin to face him, stopping in my tracks.

Coming toward me, he asks, "How are you feeling?"

"I'm well."

He reaches for me and I step forward into his embrace as he wraps his arms around me. He strokes my hair with one hand.

Almost as if he cares about me.

"Do you wish to dance today, Anya?"

"Yes," my tone is eager, but not urgent, "please, *khozyain*."

"If I let you dance today, I expect you to keep a firm hand with Ezra. He's agitated with his concern for your condition.

He's worried."

My chest thumps unusually hard at the mention of him.

"I will, *khozyain*. I promise."

He kisses the top of my head. The foolish half of me mistakes the gesture as affection, though my wiser, hardened half knows it's nothing more than possessive posturing.

I'm his possession.

"He's in the studio. Kostya's with him. He's been practicing while you rested." He pulls back and holds me by the shoulders at arm's length. "I'm afraid to tell you that you have quite a bit of catching up to do."

I meet his gray eyes, wanting to ask a question but knowing to phrase it as a statement to keep from upsetting him. "We'll be dancing his style now. Contemporary, not ballet."

"Yes. I expect you to let him teach you, but you must not let him have control. I know this will be a challenge for you, Anya," he strokes my hair again, "but your skill will improve if you can find that balance with him. Perhaps you'll have a partner for more than one performance if you can pull this off together."

All the air leaves my body in a rush.

It's relief, but also fear.

Relief that Ezra might not be taken from me like my partners before. Fear that I won't be able to balance controlling him and learning from him...we both might see the consequences of that. Maybe it won't just be Ezra who disappears forever. Maybe I'll disappear right along with him.

But even in that way of thinking, there's an odd beat of relief.

Nikolai dismisses me and I return to my room, changing into my favorite black, spaghetti strap leotard that crisscrosses over my back and gray, cotton shorts. I throw a pink wrap sweater on, tying it at the side against my waist, and I pull my hair back into a quick, low bun.

I quickly walk to the dance studio, eager to stretch my legs and simply fall away from the world. Dance is all I have here at Mikhailov Manor. It's all I've ever had. Two days without it may as well have been a lifetime.

But there's another reason I'm eager, too.

A reason I don't want to admit.

A reason I *can't* admit.

When I reach the doorway to the studio, where Kostya gives me a nod of acknowledgement, I'm stunned into stillness by that very reason.

Ezra is spinning, flipping, turning, truly and honestly floating through the air as if gravity itself were a chain he was bursting free from with ease. I've seen so many incredible dancers in my time, but I'm simply captivated by the way he moves so effortlessly, so gracefully, so *emotionally*. I swear I can feel what he's feeling just being in the presence of his movement.

He's an artist and right now, he's painting me a picture of fear and rage and desperation.

I don't want him to stop, I want to see the rest of this routine, so instead of walking into the studio, I lean against the doorframe. The floor creaks beneath my feet as I move, and that subtle movement is enough to draw his attention. I can actually see the green of his eyes catch mine mid-leap and there's a shift.

Everything shifts.

Even I shift, as if the doorframe pushed me away from it.

He lands hard on the floor and I know it wasn't an intentional landing. I distracted him. I hate it so much when someone disturbs me in the middle of a dance, so I step inside, ready to apologize.

"I'm sorry, I didn't mean to—"

He rushes toward me, long strides bringing him swiftly into my space. He doesn't hesitate to wrap his arms around my waist and pull me into his embrace, lifting me slightly off the floor.

I'm frozen.

His touch kickstarts my heart and my pulse quickens.

My arms hang limply from my sides as he lowers me back to my feet, then holds me by the shoulders at arm's length.

"I've been so worried about you," he says frantically. "Nikolai wouldn't let me see you, he wouldn't tell he how you were, if you were okay. The last time I saw you was after you drowned and passed out in his bed. I didn't know if something had happened, if you…"

"I'm fine. I'm well. No need to worry."

"No need my *ass*. My middle name is worry these days."

My smile betrays me, slipping out though I try to hold it back. A dimple appears on his cheek as one side of his mouth curls into a half-smile.

"That's a good look on you," he says, letting me go. "The smile, I mean. I don't think I've ever seen you smile."

I swallow and purse my lips, trying to pull the happiness from my face. I'm supposed to be in control here. I can't let him charm me into taking control for himself. There will be consequences for both of us if I can't teach him what it means to be a slave of one of the four families.

But then he smiles at me full-on. It's a smile that takes over his entire face, his entire being, and it ticks inside my abdomen, coiling and tightening low in my belly.

I put my hand on my stomach and breathe out slowly to steady myself against the bizarre and unexpected attraction I have to his natural charm.

My face feels hot.

I turn and walk away from him, hoping I haven't already

begun blushing. I stride toward the stereo controls in the corner behind the grand piano to turn off his music.

"Are you really okay?" His voice is tinged with concern and now tiny wings are fluttering in my stomach.

I don't know why I'm having this reaction to him.

I don't like it.

Really, I *do* like it and that's *why* I don't like it.

I'd felt something like this toward my first partner, Jamal. It was just a simple attraction, a small spark of natural chemistry. But it had never evolved past that and I'm so glad it hadn't. If I'd allowed myself to have felt something stronger for Jamal, it would've destroyed me when he disappeared.

I try to shake off the thought of him, but it swiftly morphs into fear about Ezra's future.

No.

I can't think about this.

I shake out my arms and the feeling along with them.

"I'm really okay," I finally respond to him, though I don't turn to look. "I just need a minute, Ezra."

I'm angry at myself for using his name instead of *mal'chik*. But heaven help me, there is nothing boy-like about that man and referring to him as such just feels wrong.

I need to get out of my head.

I need to feel in control again.

I need to dance.

I spin around to face him. He's standing in the center of the dance floor, his fingers locked together, pulling down from where they're laced on the top of his head. His expression is narrowed as he studies me with concerned eyes.

This stance he's in puts his strength on display. He's not wearing a shirt and with his hands up on the top of his head this way, his torso is lengthened and lean. The lines of his dance-sculpted abs are defined and glistening from the sweat of his craft and he looks strong.

Impenetrable.

Unmovable.

Undeniably, irrefutably sexy.

Oh, shit.

He drops his hands and they land with a thud against his sides. That's when I realize I'm just standing here, staring at him, not speaking, not moving. His eyes are narrowed as they regard me with worry, but there's a hint of humor dancing behind the green of his eyes.

"Well, fuck," he says. "See? I really am gonna have to change my middle name to worry."

I lick my lips as they suddenly feel dry. "Why do you do that?"

"Do what?"

"Make everything into a joke."

"Does it bother you? I really am worried about you."

"Why?" I feel my forehead crease in curiosity.

Ezra tilts his head, looking confused. "Why wouldn't I be? Why would I feel anything but worried about you in this shit show we're living in?"

"Never mind." I shake my head. "It really doesn't matter. We should get to work. We need to learn a new routine and prepare for the performance. It's only a couple of months away."

He starts walking toward me and my shoulders tense as he nears the piano bench, stopping just on the other side of it.

"Anya, I need you to tell me what all of this is about it."

I cross my arms over my chest. "What do you want to know?"

"What's with this performance? Why are we doing it? Why does he care? It's a pretty ridiculous reason to have slaves, don't you think? Just to dance for him."

"It's not just for him. I told you, this is so much bigger than Nikolai."

He nods. "Okay, so tell me everything. I have a right to know what this is all about."

I lower my arms. "You'll be disappointed to find out why our lives were stolen from us."

He huffs out an amused sound. He steps forward, straddling the piano bench before he sits down. My mouth falls open watching him and I inhale sharply, exhale slowly.

"I have no doubt you're right. I can't imagine *any* reason being something other than disappointing. Though that's probably not a strong enough word."

"Frustrating," I offer.

He shakes his head. "Nah. Discouraging?" he counters.

"Aggravating?"

"Infuriating."

"Provocative," I say.

He smiles. "Now that's an interesting word choice."

"I don't mean in a sexual context, I—"

What am I saying?

Thankfully, he cuts me off, "Hey, I knew what you meant."

"Right," I say. "Right, I know."

I know I sound moronic and it's really unbecoming for a woman who is supposed to be in charge here.

Ezra pats the bench in front of him. "Can we just sit for a minute? Just talk to me. Tell me what's up here."

I tilt my head, looking at the bench. I'm physically drawn to him. My body wants to be close to him and he's asking me to sit and talk. I know I should remain standing, using the leverage of my height as he sits to re-establish my authority and certify my position of power over him.

But I don't.

I straddle the bench facing him. "There are four families that run a multi-billion-dollar enterprise across the globe. The O'Sheas, The Campbells, The Vittoris, and The Mikhailovs."

"Selling slaves."

"Human trafficking. Yes. It's quite the lucrative business for those involved."

"Christ," he says, shaking his head.

"You and I belong to the Mikhailovs, obviously. But the slaves belonging to any the four families are more symbolic than anything else. Our role is entertainment. Some talent slaves will belong to their family for years, decades, but when the family is no longer entertained, they might sell their slave or…"

"Or they kill them?" he finishes the thought for me.

I've been looking at my hands resting in front of me on the bench, but I lift my eyes now. I connect with his gaze and his interested stare holds me.

I nod. "I think so, yes."

"You had partners before me." He shifts, his eyes darting away then back to meet mine. "Do you know what happened to them?"

"I don't," I hesitate. "I can't think about that."

His gaze is soft and comforting as he reaches out to tap my hand between us. "I'm sorry, Anya."

I've stilled at the touch of his fingertips on the back of my hand. There's just something entirely inexplicable about the way my skin reacts to his touch. It's soothing but at the same time, stirring, fire-starting.

Provocative.

My fingers twitch and before I can stop myself, I turn my hand and open it, inviting him to take hold. I feel relief when he grips it without hesitation, holding my hand without reserve or question or expectation. He holds it confidently, in such a way that it makes my whole body tingle in light-heartedness to be so courageously touched. He's not tentative or wary or afraid that Kostya or Nikolai will see. His touch is just there, it exists for what it is, and my soul feels the vibration of it.

I feel like I've found my steadiness when I start talking again, "The four families meet quarterly to discuss business. I don't know the details. But they rotate their meeting location for each quarter, each taking a turn to host. The family who is hosting is responsible for providing entertainment before business. Once a year, it's Nikolai's turn to host, our turn to perform. The last meeting was hosted by the O'Shea family."

My eyes pinch shut for a moment as I remember being Nikolai's payment to Vigo Vittori for information at that very meeting, just after the O'Shea family talent slave performed.

"So, Nikolai owns us just so we can perform for him and his depraved colleagues once a year?"

"Yes, though it's not that simple…" I look down at our hands because I feel his thumb brush over my skin, "Or perhaps, it really is that simple and that's what makes it so demented."

"It's fucked-up. This whole thing is fucked-up."

I press my lips together. "I know."

"Tell me why I'm here. Tell me why he gives you partners to dance with just to throw them away. Does he do it to torture you?"

"I think that's part of it." I swallow and then lower my voice so Kostya can't overhear from the hallway. "Nikolai chose me a long time ago, Ezra. It's what all the families do. I first met him when I was nearly eleven years old in Moscow. He was observing a ballet class I was taking. He came every day for weeks just to watch. I don't remember much about our meeting, but I remember that he spoke to my mother. He gave her a business card and he gave me a pink rose."

Ezra reaches out and takes my other hand in his and for whatever stupid reason, I let him. The gentle contact feels nice. It feels good.

"A month later, we were moving to New York at the expense of a benefactor. That's all my mother ever told me—that there was a benefactor who funded our move. I never questioned it. I went to public school but spent all my free hours training, practicing. All my dance activities were determined by this benefactor who I knew nothing about.

"Then three years ago, just after I turned twenty-one, he came for me. It all seemed very innocent. He found me one day coming out of the studio after a long rehearsal and introduced himself as my benefactor. His face did seem familiar when I first saw him, and once he explained who he was, I was certain it was the man I had seen observing my dance classes all those years ago. He offered me an opportunity to come back to Moscow with him—a unique training opportunity which would ensure my promotion to Principal at the New York City Ballet. That was everything I'd been working toward, so I didn't even stop to think about how strange it all seemed. I went with him *willingly*.

"He took me on a private jet, won me over with his wealth and power, and I thought I was safe. It was seduction and I fell for it. He brought me here and I haven't left since, except for the quarterly meetings. I've attended all of those with Nikolai. He chose me when I was a child, Ezra. He controlled my life from the age of eleven. He trained me, groomed me. And my family never knew. He paid my mother under a false name in a secret account. There's no way anyone could track him in connection with my disappearance, though even if they could, it wouldn't matter. The four families are more powerful than any political party, than any government. I've never had a life of my own, not really."

He doesn't reply. He just watches me as if waiting for me to say more.

"I think you may be my last partner, Ezra. My last chance."

"What do you mean?"

"You said it yourself, he's impatient with me. He's always been cruel. He's always been controlling and hateful, and he's always hurt me. But he's never been so impatient with me as he has been since you arrived."

"Why is it different now?"

I sigh. "I worry...I think I'll be the next to disappear. I think that if you and I don't do well in our performance that he might get rid of me this time."

"You think he'd get rid of you and keep me instead?"

I nod and let go of one of his hands to draw circles on the bench, looking down at my fingers as if they're interesting to watch.

"I think," I begin, but hesitate, knowing I shouldn't be telling him so much of my speculation, "I think he's ashamed by his preferences. There was pressure on him to choose a beneficiary when he found me as a child. I think finding a female talent was just easier. And a female beneficiary is far and above the standard among the four families." I tilt my head. "I think my dance partners have been the only male talent slaves. I think the Vittoris have some male slaves, but they serve the lady of the house. I don't think there have ever been any other male beneficiaries."

His jaw ticks and he nods. "I get it. He doesn't just want to watch a beautiful woman dance..."

"He wants to watch a beautiful man, too," I complete the thought for him. "You're more beautiful than the others. He's been kinder to you."

He laughs. "This shit is his version of kindness?"

"Yes. This, what you've seen from him, is kindness. You have no idea what he's put me through."

His brow wrinkles. "I have a little bit of an idea. Are you telling me it's been worse than him drowning you?"

I meet his eyes and I know mine have glazed over with ice, the way they always do when thoughts of my various traumatic incidents with Nikolai jump back into my brain.

"Much worse." I sigh. "Things have been changing since his parents and his brother died a year ago. He's become arrogant, bold, self-righteous. Downright vindictive. And he takes his anger out on me."

He pauses in consideration. "I won't let him do that anymore."

"I'm afraid he will come after you, too. There will come a point when he wants you as much as he wants me. You're the first partner since his immediate family died. There's no one here to judge him, and I'm terrified of how he will use us. And when he decides he's done with one or both of us, then he's done. You see the control he has over us now? We can't escape this place. Like it or not, we are his slaves. We belong to him. Our lives are in his hands. But there is one thing we can control."

He says it so I don't have to, "Our performance."

"Yes. And it's the only thing, the only *singular* thing that makes me feel like I can wake up in the morning and go on."

My palms dampen with sweat and I immediately pull my hand away from his. I untie, adjust, and retie my wrap sweater, just to give my hands something to do.

"I shouldn't be telling you all of this. Not now. Nikolai expects us to rehearse," I stand and move to the stereo controls, "so we need to rehearse."

"Okay," he concedes with a sigh, though the tone of it is

dripping with sarcasm. "Then let's rehearse. But he wants my style, right?"

Ezra comes up behind me and reaches around me to scroll through the music options. He's looking over my shoulder to do this, his chest pressed against my back and I hold my breath. He lands on a song, starts it, then steps away, moving into the open space.

"Yes," I finally confirm once I can breathe again, "your absolutely reckless, untamed contemporary style." I roll my eyes.

I turn to face him, expecting to see him as depressed and angst-ridden as I feel, and though I can feel those emotions vibrating from him through the air, he's somehow managed to shove them down low enough for me to step over.

He gives me a charming wink. "Reckless and untamed are absolutely my style, babe."

My heart stops.

Reckless and untamed are the exact opposite of what I need for survival.

I know that.

And still, the promise lights a fire around my cold, dead heart.

CHAPTER 15
Ezra

"OH, SHIT...SHIT, I'VE got you," I grunt.

Anya reaches her arms out, ready to brace against the hardwood dance floor as she tumbles headfirst out of the lift above my head.

My arm latches around her waist and I grip her side with one hand. Her weight shifts both of us forward and I'm falling with her, though I'm determined to keep her from hitting the ground. I promised her I wouldn't let her hit the floor and I won't, but I'm going down, too.

I'm bringing her down to the floor sideways and I twist to grab her waist with both hands, rolling forward over her, and taking the fall for her. I land on my back as I twist her and bring her down on top of me, chest to chest. Thankfully, I slowed our momentum enough that it's a light landing.

She keeps rolling until she's off me and lays on her back by my side. We're both huffing and puffing because that was a fucking rush.

I turn my head to look over at her and smile. "My bad."

She turns her head to look at me, too. "You swore you wouldn't let me hit the floor," she says with all the seriousness in the world, but she can't hide the amusement that tugs at the side of her mouth.

"You didn't technically hit the floor, *I* did." I grin.

She shakes her head and looks back up at the ceiling, but I see the smile she was trying to hide, though I don't have to see it to know it's there. Every time she smiles, I feel it creep down my spine and threaten arousal that I just can't deal with in this shit storm of a situation.

We've been rehearsing a new routine for three weeks now. We've danced together nearly every day since Nikolai—in all his medical wisdom—determined Anya was recovered enough from the drowning. The more time I spent dancing with her, the more time I *wanted* to spend with her.

Something about Anya twists something inside me with every interaction.

It's a good twist.

A spine-tingling twist.

But it's a deep down, knife-in-the-gut twist, too…because we aren't living in the real world.

It's not like I can date her or something. I can build a friendship, flirt, dance with her, but that's where it all ends. Anytime I so much as think of the possibility of being anything more to her than the man who will help her survive another year in captivity, the reality of our life or death circumstance comes crashing down on my head.

It's the heaviest fucking weight in the world to carry, because honestly, I could fall for this blue-eyed girl. And it's not just that she's literally the only person around.

It's *her.*

She sits up abruptly and looks down at me. "Should we try a different lift? We've been working on this one for a week. If we can't nail it every single time in rehearsal, we can't bank on nailing it in the performance. And we have to nail our performance. You know how important this is."

I reach over and touch her arm. "Hey, I know. But we also have to push the limit a bit. You told me he wants mind-blowing talent. Well, he's not gonna get it from us wussing out for an easier lift."

Her nose wrinkles as her face scrunches. "It's not wussing out…" She tilts her head. "What does that even mean?"

I laugh. "It means giving up because of fear."

"Oh. I'm not fearful, Ezra. I just want a perfect routine."

"Perfection is boring. Besides, I really don't think Nikolai or any of these other assholes would know dance perfection if it bit them in the ass." I squeeze her wrist before letting go and I sit up, leaning back on my palms.

She sighs. "That's what I *hate* about this contemporary shit. Classical ballet has structure, form, technique that I understand. I don't understand the flexed feet and the hard mixed with the soft, and the constant shift between grace and…and…"

"And?"

Her expression ticks then falters into self-amusement, with the smallest hint of a smile. "I don't know. Don't look at me like that."

"Like what?" I'm just smiling at her.

She swallows. "Like that. Like you know something I don't. Like you know more than I do."

My eyes widen. "Well, whoa. That's definitely not true. You know way more than I do about the technique, the form, the grace."

"That's true," she agrees, and I laugh.

I hop to my feet and hold out my hand to her. "Come on."

She takes it without hesitation and shoots icy daggers of longing straight through to my heart as I pull her to stand. The song we've chosen to perform to is playing on a loop and is about mid-way through playing for the fifth time in a row.

I hold up my palms in front of her. "Okay," I tell her, "forget the routine for a minute. I wanna get you out of your head and help you understand what you're missing."

"What I'm missing?" she feigns a disheartened shock, but I know better by now.

I tilt my head at her with a grin and she mimics me to jab right back.

"Hands on mine," I tell her, smiling.

She places her palms against mine and automatically adjusts her feet to stand shoulder width apart, naturally mirroring my position.

I blow out a breath to push out the playfulness I'm feeling and take in another to center myself. "Close your eyes."

"Okay," she says easily, pressing her eyes shut, trusting me immediately.

My chest puffs out proudly at the fact that I've earned that trust from her. She doesn't give it easily and I take it seriously.

"My eyes are closed, too," I tell her and wait a beat.

She opens one eye, to see me staring and smiling at her. We both laugh and she slaps my palms.

I shut my eyes. "Okay, okay, I'm serious now. Shut your eyes."

I wait until I hear her exhale slowly, calmly, steadily.

"What you're missing is the feeling. The emotion," I tell her. "When you do the steps like you're supposed to, it's beautiful and graceful because…well, you're just naturally beautiful and graceful. But you can get so caught up in the perfection of movement that you forget about the imperfection of soul. The rawness of feeling."

I hear her sigh, but I feel it more. I feel it where my palms touch hers.

"Listen to the music. Really listen to it. And when you

start to have a real, emotional reaction to it, I want you to move, but stay connected with me. I want you to move me with you so I can feel what you're feeling."

"Okay…" I can hear the skepticism in her tone.

"Hey, just do this for me."

"I'm doing it, I'm doing it," she says.

I sneak a peek because I can hear her smiling and I can't help myself but to look. I only mean to look for a moment, but I end up lingering, watching her as she shifts into focus. I swallow, watching her breath slowly, watching her listen.

Her face holds tension as she concentrates way too hard. She's trying to think her way into feeling and it makes me want to laugh. She's not naturally stone cold, she's been hardened over time. I want nothing more than to see her crack that shell and watch it crumble beneath our feet, but I don't hold out hope that it will actually happen.

She's not safe here.

She'd need to feel safe to shed her armor.

But then I feel a twitch.

Her palms curve into mine just a little bit harder. I hold steady, giving her something strong and stable to push against. Her fingertips curl and my fingers are itching to curl right back.

I squeeze, bringing my fingers down through the spaces between hers. Her eyes snap open to meet mine and all I can see is sapphire blue. Her fingers drop slowly and now our hands are locked together.

Something inside her stirs.

I can feel it.

She can feel it.

She starts to move and soon, I'm moving with her. It's not our routine, but it's as though we've rehearsed it a thousand times.

Every movement is slow, drifting from one into the other.

We're apart at first, but gradually, she's dancing closer and closer to me. Her dancing is soft at the beginning, just fading into emotion, but it's changing, growing.

Every move she makes is sensual and my fucking heart is racing.

I need her.

The intensity I feel dancing with Anya—even just being near her—is indescribable. The way I hated her in the beginning, that powerful feeling, it's morphed and changed as we've gotten to know each other into an all new kind of intensity, a desire-fueled intensity. It's the kind of intensity I want to feel all the time.

It's the splash of cool water on a hot summer day.

It's the rush of performing for a crowd of hundreds.

It's dirty sex on a public fucking beach.

I'm just about to drag her into my arms, but the chance is taken from me. Just like everything else has been taken from me.

Nikolai gives three slow, sharp claps as he enters the dance studio. Anya jumps out of her skin with a gasp, yanking her hands free from mine and spinning to face him immediately.

He's been gone for three days on business, so his sudden appearance startles us both. I lace my fingers behind my neck and stretch as I blow out a heavy breath, watching her walk away from me to go to his side.

"I'm sorry, I didn't realize you were watching," she tells him with a bowed head.

Nikolai taps two fingers under her chin, and she lifts to meet his eyes. "I'm always watching, *moya rabynya.*"

I shudder.

"You two dance quite beautifully together," Nikolai says slowly, looking over at me. "You have chemistry."

You can't fake chemistry and he's right that we have

buckets of it. It kills me how much chemistry we have. I drop my hands to my sides, worried what he thinks he saw and what he's reading into it right now.

"It's part of the performance," I lie.

"I have something for you, Ezra. Come. Both of you," he says and exits the studio.

Anya and I share a look before we follow him. My look says, *"Well, fuck,"* and hers says, *"Just do as your told, keep your smart mouth shut, and don't make things worse."*

Yes, her eyes speak volumes.

Nikolai leads us upstairs to his bedroom and asks me to shut the door behind us. My shoulders immediately tense because this is unusual. It's unusual for us both to be invited into his room, and even more unusual for the door to be shut. If this were going to be a quick exchange, there would be no reason to shut the door. The sneer on his face tells me to be ready for an attack.

"Both of you, sit," he orders.

He gestures to the two armchairs that are angled toward each other, facing the fireplace. Anya moves immediately to do as she's told, but I'm wary, hesitant. She turns her head back to look at me after she sits.

"Mal'chik," she insists.

I move to sit, but not because he wants me to. I do it because she *needs* me to. She needs to maintain the image that she's in control of me. In reality, she is. I'd do just about anything for this girl, especially if it ensures her well-being.

Nikolai is somewhere behind us and it sounds like he's pulling open a drawer, then shuts it. He comes back around in front of us and walks over to me, handing me a plain, manila envelope.

"I do apologize we haven't been able to provide these

to you sooner. You've proven to be so detached from friends and family that it was challenging to find a suitable person for leverage. This is just the first. There will be more now that we've found her."

I look up at him. "Found who?"

His head tilts toward the envelope in my hand. "Open it."

It isn't sealed, so I lift the flap and reach inside. My fingers touch the corner of a small rectangle and I know what it is before I pull it out. Still, when I see the photograph for the first time, it's jarring.

"How the fuck did you—" I stop mid-sentence, flipping the photograph over to look at the back.

Twenty-two.

Thirty-seven.

Two numbers.

My ex-girlfriend is twenty-two years old.

Just like the numbers on Anya's photos of her sister, Lidia, I know the second number is the measurement from the rifle scope.

Thirty-seven yards.

They were thirty-seven yards away from her when they took this photo.

Every muscle in my body tightens, my pulse thumping rage through my veins.

"If you hurt her, I swear I will kill you, Nikolai."

His forehead tilts down toward me with narrowed eyes. "If you hurt me, she will die. I expect you have a good enough reason now to comply and behave."

I *have* been complying.

I *have* been behaving.

Anya's well-being is enough to keep me in line.

But this…

This is next level shit.

I finally feel the fear Anya must have been feeling all these years with her photos of Lidia. I feel Anya's eyes on me, and I turn my head to catch her curious gaze. With shaking hands, I reach over to hand her the photo.

"Who is she?" Anya asks as she pulls it from my fingers.

"My girl—" I correct myself, "My ex-girlfriend. She, uh… she left me a few days before I was taken. In Kyiv."

I really don't want to tell her this right now, but I can see the apprehension on her face. For whatever stupid reason in my illogical brain, I'm more concerned with allaying Anya's potential jealousy over a relationship that no longer exists in any sense of the word. I care about Emma a great deal. The thought of something happening to her because of my actions here threatens to unravel me entirely, and I am truly scared shitless about this photograph.

"You'll receive a new one weekly now that we know who she is and where she is."

"You're a goddamn monster," I tell him.

He shrugs. "It's business. Anya, go take a shower. Don't wash your hair, but clean thoroughly."

Jesus fucking shit.

A thick wall of tension whips up around her as she slowly rises to her feet, ready to comply. *"Da, khozyain."*

She looks at me and I see her swallow hard, worry dulling the sparkle of her eyes. If I could beat Nikolai to death right now without consequence, I would. For a million reasons, I would, but I would rip out his heart for taking away her spark.

If he even has one.

"Go," Nikolai snaps, sensing her hesitation.

She rushes off to his bathroom and a few moments later, I hear the shower water running. Nikolai moves to the bar cart next to the fireplace, pouring three glasses of what I think is whiskey. He picks up two and brings one to me, taking a seat in the armchair that Anya has vacated.

I look down at the golden-brown liquid in my glass, unsure whether I should drink it or not. I was only just barely legal to drink in the States—just a few months past my twenty-first birthday. I'd gotten drunk a few times before, just like most of the raging, rowdy teenagers I went to high school with, but this was a new drink for me.

Part of me wants to throw it back and ask for a second, just to dull the pain of knowing they're watching Emma, of being held hostage, of all this shit. The other part of me wonders if he's drugged my drink, though I watched him pour it cleanly myself.

"You make a good partner for her. I'm pleased with the progress you both are making with your routine." He sips from his glass, leaning back casually and crossing an ankle over his knee.

I scoff, "Thanks. I'm so fucking glad that our partnership entertains you, *Master*."

He smiles sideways. "I'm not as put off by your sarcasm as you think I am, Ezra. I'm actually somewhat intrigued by it."

I don't respond, instead deciding I need to partake in drink. I lift my glass to my lips and tilt it back, taking several long gulps until its emptied.

"I'd like to see you and Anya take your performance to the next level. I've been watching your lifts. The way you read each other so clearly without words. You're very in tune with each other, very in sync. I've had her try this once before, but she had no connection with her partner and it failed spectacularly. I think it will work quite well with the two of you."

"Okay," I say, setting my empty glass on the small side table between our chairs. "What is it?"

"I'm sure Anya has made you aware by now…I have a bit of a fetish for the art of bondage. I'd like you to use rope in your routine."

My jaw clenches and my shoulders tense. "I think I'd remember her telling me something like that."

He lifts an eyebrow. "Well, I'm telling you now."

I stretch my neck, tilting my head from side to side. "Okay, so what is it you want us to do?"

"I'll leave the artistic incorporation up to the two of you. But there are certain things you need to know about using rope safely, so I'm going to give you a demonstration tonight."

I laugh. I can't hold it back.

Does he really expect me to believe he gives a fuck about using rope safely?

"Why does it feel like you have more than a demonstration planned?"

He hides his secretive smile behind his glass as he takes another sip. "As I said, Ezra, it's a fetish of mine."

Fuck.

Anya's in his shower right now, *cleaning thoroughly*, as he asked her to. I feel nausea roll through my gut and a punch of adrenaline through my veins. I squeeze my eyes shut and take a deep breath. There's no sense to my sudden agitation because there's not a goddamn fucking thing I can do about this situation.

Nikolai is going to do what Nikolai is going to do, and God help the person who thought they could stop him.

Though I want to jump out of my chair, snatch him by the neck and throw him into the fucking fireplace, I know I can't. I can't if I want to keep her safe.

Anya.

And I guess Emma now, too.

The shower water clicks off and Nikolai rises from his chair. He sets his drink on the bar cart again, then heads for the bathroom door. He doesn't knock or even pause, just barges right in. I expect to hear Anya shriek in surprise, but that's real-world me. Slave-world me knows better. She's no longer surprised by Nikolai's behavior, by the way he treats her. I, on the other hand, don't think I will ever get used to it.

Anya's strength and poise through suffering are absolutely astounding, though suffering is putting it mildly. She's superhuman in her courage, a goddess of resilience. I just wish I knew those admirable traits under different circumstances.

A minute passes with them both in the bathroom and I have no idea what's going on. I stay in my seat, though I'm squirming to jump and run and fight. I'm fighting every instinct I have because I have to. I have to keep my cool to keep her safe. Not that she's ever really safe here, but I have to think in terms of relativity now. And relatively, she's better off if I do as I'm told. Nikolai is going to hurt her either way and the least I can do is not make it worse.

She exits the bathroom first and I immediately look away because she's naked.

I want to look at her.

Fuck, do I want to look at her.

But she's not walking toward me naked by choice. She's doing it because he's instructed her to. She hasn't consented to me seeing her without her clothes on, and fuck if I'm going to be a piece of shit like Nikolai.

She's still walking toward me—I can see her in my peripheral as my legs bounce in anxiety. I'm forced to shut my eyes as she gets close enough to touch. I've become so in sync with her over the last few weeks, just as Nikolai observed, and I can feel her presence all around me.

"Ezra," her voice is quiet, yet strong and insistent, "you need to shower and come back out in your underwear."

My eyes snap open and lift right up to meet hers. She looks scared, nervous, but at the same time, I see that superhuman resilience telling me that she's determined to be okay through whatever the hell is happening here.

I have to admit how glad I am to see that determination in her because I don't have it for myself. She's so much stronger than I could ever be, and I have to rely on her—I have to trust in her to get through this.

Whatever this nightmare is going to be.

My eyes linger on hers, probably longer than Nikolai is happy with, and I nearly want to smile at her when her look tells me to keep my stupid, sarcastic mouth shut and do as I'm told.

I will do as I'm told, as much as it goes against everything I am. I will do as I'm told because I know the consequence of breaking the rules here.

The least I can do is lessen Anya's suffering and I will take on mountains of my own for the blue-eyed girl I might just be falling for.

CHAPTER 16

Anya

EZRA DISAPPEARS BEHIND the bathroom door as Nikolai rounds on me. I feel a thousand different emotions right now and I'm not clear on a single one of them.

"Come here," he tells me, and I go to him without pause.

I'm standing naked in front of him and he takes every advantage, raking his eyes over my body, leering with lust and devious intent. I'm used to this with Nikolai, used to him seeing me bare. He's seen every part of me, violated every part of me. Though it never really gets better, it does become easier to accept, to become complacent.

His hands cup my cheeks and he bends, bringing his lips close to mine. "I've missed you. Kiss me, Anya."

I close my eyes first to retreat inward before he presses his mouth to mine. His lips part immediately, tongue pressing, insistent that I do the same. I open my mouth and he doesn't hesitate to taste me.

I always have a difficult time when he first starts to kiss me this way. He wants me responsive, but my initial response is always forceful rejection, though I've learned to hide it. I used to show it with pushes and shoves, kicks and shouts of protest.

I know better now.

I force my tongue to swirl back around his. It's not that Nikolai is bad at kissing—he's quite good at it. He's quite good at all of this. That's what makes it so much more disgusting, because he knows how to make me give in and want what he's doing to me.

It makes me feel disgusting for wanting anything from him, but he knows my buttons and triggers, he knows everything about me and how to make me needy for his touch in a truly shameful way.

I hear the bathroom door click open as I'm still kissing Nikolai and feel a new kind of shame…a worse kind of shame…a guilty kind of shame. It's one thing to have to endure such atrocious violations of will from Nikolai, but an entirely different matter to have a witness to it.

I had a witness once before, with Jamal, my first dance partner here at Mikhailov Manor. Jamal and I had grown close during his time here. I liked him. He liked me. Nikolai knew it and took advantage of it.

Things were far more violent in those early days, before I understood my place and my inability to escape captivity. When Nikolai raped me back then, I fought. I resisted. I screamed. I can only imagine how difficult it was for Jamal to watch.

He's been gone for a long time, and I don't want to think about him anymore.

Ezra is here to witness my shame on a whole new level, to witness my complacency to Nikolai's abusive will. I just pray that Nikolai has no intention of making me orgasm. I don't want to imagine what Ezra would think of me then.

Would he think I enjoy Nikolai and his touch just because he's capable of manipulating my senses so effectively?

Nikolai pulls away from my kiss, turning his head to look at Ezra. I don't miss the way his eyes run down over Ezra's body. I keep my eyes on Nikolai because Ezra is an unwilling participant, too, and I refuse to take advantage in that way.

Though it's hard not to look.

I see him shirtless nearly every day, as that's usually how he dances. I admire his physique nearly every day. I want him nearly every day.

But that doesn't give me a right to join in Nikola's blatant ogling in a scenario where his choices and rights are as invalid and unwanted as mine.

Still, my greedy eyes dart a glance down to Ezra's black boxer briefs before rising quickly to his face. I can't avoid meeting his eyes because his are locked on mine. It pains me to share his gaze because he's looking at me so intensely. There's fear and concern there, but I don't think it's for himself...I think it's for me.

"Stand at the foot of the bed," Nikolai says to me, turning and walking away to retrieve something from one of his dresser drawers.

I do as instructed, facing outward toward the room. Ezra is still standing just in front of the bathroom, which is around the side of the bed. From where he's standing, he has a clear view of my entire backside and I immediately feel self-conscious. I don't sense his eyes on me. Ezra is respectful, kind, a gentleman, so it doesn't surprise me to feel the absence of his gaze.

Nikolai returns with a length of coarse, beige rope and stands in front of me. "Hold still."

He begins to wrap me with rope, coiling and tying expert knots as he's done for years. The rope is rough, scratching across my skin, and I know it will burn when he pulls it tight.

He knots it behind my back in the center and wraps it around to my front, crisscrossing at my sternum. He twists the rope to form an "X" between my breasts and drapes the long ends over my shoulders. It's heavy to wear and it's already irritating my bare skin. Every movement, no matter how subtle, feels like he's trying to strike a match against my flesh.

He pulls the ends back through the knot at my back and keeps going, eventually securing my arms so they are pinned to my sides, my palms pressed firmly against my thighs. My bottom half is free and mobile, but my top half is entirely bound in the coils which are rubbing me raw.

"I'm thinking you will dance like this," Nikolai says. "Except your arms will need to be free, for safety, of course."

Ezra scoffs behind me, "Safety."

Nikolai's eyes snap over my shoulder to glare at him. "I will teach you how to bind her. In your dance, you will control her, move her with the ends of the rope. You are the puppet master and she is the puppet."

"That doesn't work with our music." Ezra's sharp tone tells me he's losing his temper.

I'm afraid for him more than I am for me, so I chance it and speak up. "Shut up, *mal'chik*," I snap at him. "We'll make it work."

Thankfully, he's quiet again and it only takes a few moments for Nikolai to turn his attention back to me. A wicked smirk tilts the side of his mouth.

"You're doing well with controlling him," Nikolai tells me. "I wonder what else you can command him to do for you."

I swallow. "There's nothing I want him to do for me."

"Nothing?" Nikolai questions. "Nothing at all?"

He snatches my chin between his fingers and thumb and pinches, lifting to tilt upward. He bends, touching the tip of his nose to mine.

"I don't believe you," he says. "I think there are things you both want to do to each other."

"I want nothing from him," I lie. "You provide me with everything I need."

Nikolai chuckles. "You're a terrible liar, Anya. Do you think I don't know you better than that by now?" He doesn't move, but his eyes leave me for a moment, glancing toward where Ezra stands, then back to me. "He wants you. And I'm nearly inclined to let him have you, only because I'm curious to watch, to see what happens. To see if he can destroy you all over again in the ways I destroyed you when I first stole you away."

That's simply not possible. No one could destroy me in all the ways Nikolai had, especially not Ezra. He couldn't and he wouldn't. Still, if anyone is able to orchestrate such destruction, it would be Nikolai.

I shiver.

Nikolai releases my chin and pushes on my shoulders with both of his large hands. "Sit."

I lower to perch on the edge of the plush, burgundy comforter. I'm forced to sit up arrow straight with the way my arms are bound tightly against my sides. I wriggle my hands, clenching and releasing my fingers. They already tingle from the restriction, and I think he's tied the ropes too tightly.

Nikolai kneels in front of me and pushes my knees apart, opening me wide for him. My thighs clench against the exposure he forces, but he's still able to spread me apart all the same. He isn't angered by the way my body reacts, and I'm thankful for that at least. I almost wonder if he mistakes the strain in my thighs as desire for him, if he thinks I clench with need rather than protest.

Surely, Nikolai can't be that delusional. Though he's had me fooled before…

"Ezra," he says, "pull the chair around, sit behind me. I'd like to give you a front row seat for Anya's performance."

"No, thanks. I'm good," Ezra replies flippantly, and I hear the edge to his tone, the crack, the pain.

I flinch as Nikolai reaches into his pocket and pulls out his switchblade, flipping it open easily with a flick of his wrist. I whimper. Every muscle in my body tenses as he presses the tip of his knife against the inside of my thigh.

"Move the chair and *sit*," Nikolai insists, "or…if you prefer to watch her bleed, I can give her yet another scar."

Ezra moves without hesitation. I'm relieved for his compliance, though the fear of pain washes over my sensibility all the same. I watch, feeling like I can't catch my breath, as Ezra drags one of the armchairs from in front of the fireplace and positions it just behind Nikolai's back. I look into his eyes as he lowers to sit. He's shaking his head with a tense jaw. He looks hopeless and I don't like the way it shadows his green eyes. I need them bright for me.

My breathing turns shallow as I feel the tip of Nikolai's blade dig into my skin. I yelp when I feel the sharp pinch of it puncturing my skin, and I look down to see a drop of blood pool and rise to force its way out. My breath catches on a gasp as I realize he's still pushing. It's not the first time he's cut me here and it won't be the last. But it hurts like new every single time he does it.

I don't dare protest. If I tell him no or stop, it will only be ignored. I know that because I'd earned harsher punishment in the past for fighting it. I know it's better to just take it, hold in my protests and tears for later, and purge them alone on my pillow. Still, fear floods through me and makes my body react. My muscles twitch, I breathe too fast, hot tears prickle at the corner of my eyes.

He's marking me with another scar. There's over twenty of them on my left thigh and his blade cuts between two of the white lines. He's looking up at me, smiling, taking such pleasure in my torment. It burns like fucking fire the way he slices into my skin, but my body remembers the feel of it. As much as it hurts, I find I can retreat from the sharp sting. I can hide from the physical pain, focus on something else, sneak my way around it. But I can't hide from the eyes that are searing hatred into Nikolai's back.

Ezra is glaring. If looks could kill, Nikolai would be sliced into pieces and scattered all around the room. Ezra looks as though he's going to pounce, and though I wish he could drag Nikolai away and save me, I know it's simply not possible.

I lock in on Ezra, staring him down until I can capture his attention. After what seems like forever, he finally tears his deadly stare from Nikolai's back and looks up at me. His eyes widen briefly before softening.

I need to hold him here, keep his attention on me. I can't risk what will happen if I lose control of him now.

In an unexpected move, Nikolai pulls his knife away and wipes the flat end of it across his slacks. He smears my blood into his clothing like it's nothing, as if painting the expensive fabric with my life force is merely a convenient way to clean off his weapon. He folds it and puts it away in his pocket. A rush of air escapes me as the tension of immediate danger lessens it hold on me. He's still dangerous, of course, but at least the blade is gone.

Nikolai bends to land a soft kiss on the top of my leg, brushing across my old scars there. He slowly works his way up to the freshly smarting wound, which is far too close to the apex of my thighs. He licks his tongue flatly across the cut, lapping up the blood as if it were some rare delicacy.

I shudder.

I shudder because it's demented.

I shudder because he's sick and twisted.

I shudder because no matter how hard I try to fight it, the heat of an attractive man so close to my sex, sensually licking the inside of my thigh, still triggers my body into reacting pleasurably.

And it makes me hate myself.

My mind and body are out of sync.

Ezra's eyes narrow on mine as he watches. I think he can see inside my soul right now. I think he knows everything I'm feeling and exactly why I'm feeling it. I expect to see judgment reflected there in the emerald green, but instead I see acceptance, perhaps even understanding. It makes me sigh from the relief of his empathy.

Nikolai is taking his liberties with me as his lips and tongue move closer and closer to my opening. My heart beats fast, both for the sensual, languid way Nikolai drifts across my skin and for the way Ezra holds me with his gaze.

I won't look away from him as long as I can help it. His stare is everything that's holding me together. It's everything that's maintaining my sanity. It gives my mind something steady to anchor to, even when my body reacts outside of my control.

My body jolts and I sigh when Nikolai licks across my folds, all the way up and over my clit. He wraps his lips around it, lightly sucking before sticking his tongue inside me.

I fight my eyelids when they threaten to close. Normally, that would be the thing that saves me—that ability to stop looking at the Devil before me and pretend that it's anyone else. But all I want is to stay locked in on Ezra's green eyes. I want to watch him watch me.

As Nikolai begins to draw unwanted pleasure from me with his skilled tongue, there's a moment. A brief, fleeting moment where I lose myself just a little, just enough that I nearly forget it's him between my legs. That moment belongs to Ezra and the way he watches me. My eyes roam over his face to see his whole expression has changed. Everything is still carved from rage, but the rage has lessened with the rise of something else.

Interest.

His curiosity is piqued, and I can't fault him for that. I won't. We're only human after all, and I'm not a complete fool to pretend he hasn't shown interest in me before. What surprises me is how it changes my emotional response.

Nikolai is raping me, for the thousandth time, touching me and trying to pleasure me without seeking or considering my consent. It's vile and filthy, and I fully expect this man to go to hell. I would send him there myself if I could.

But Ezra…

Ezra is right there and his presence changes everything. It shouldn't, but it does. And because it does, I slip.

I moan.

Unsurprisingly, Nikolai thinks I'm enjoying *him*.

"Anya," he growls against my clit as he brings two fingers in beneath his tongue.

I'm struggling to stay upright as pleasure builds within my core, intense and unwanted. Nikolai reaches up with his free hand, shoves between my breasts, and I fall backward onto the bed.

"No." I slip again, protesting the absence of Ezra's comforting face and everything stops.

Ezra pushes to his feet and I lift my head off the bed to look up at him. He takes a step forward, but Nikolai is already whirling around to stop him.

"Go and sit behind her, *mal'chik*, on the bed."

I don't want him to sit behind me.

I *do* want him to sit behind me.

I want him here, but I also want him nowhere near this sexual nightmare.

I'm more conflicted than I've ever been, and Nikolai knows it. He's done this intentionally to torture me and he's successful.

It's all so much worse that I can't move. I'm literally helpless laying on the bed right now. I could kick if I wanted to, perhaps break Nikolai's nose, if I get him just right.

But what good would that do?

Ezra sighs as he moves around to the side of the bed and I turn my head to look at him, trying to tell him I'm sorry without a word. He shakes his head and climbs onto the bed behind me.

"Pull her all the way back and sit her upright between your legs."

"No," Ezra spits out the word harshly. "No, I'm not helping you rape her."

"You will or I will make her bleed. Would you prefer that?"

"Why are you doing this? What the fuck is wrong with you?"

I'm caught between two towering infernos, blazing high and hot and completely overwhelming.

"The same thing that's wrong with you and all other men. Don't pretend you aren't hard right now. I can see it. Lay her down against you and she'll feel it," Nikolai sneers. "We're all fucking monsters. Some of us just found a way to get paid feeding the other monsters. Some of us have learned to enjoy the rewards of being a monster. Anya is my right and my reward, and I will do whatever the fuck I want to do to her. I'll do the same with you. Don't let her make you think for a second that she doesn't want this, that she doesn't enjoy this. I have the taste of her on my tongue that proves how much she wants it. In fact, why don't we let her tell you what she wants you to do? Anya…" he stands to hover above me and

I'm already shaking my head, "would you prefer that I cut you, make you bleed again? Or would you rather I fuck you?"

"What the *fuck* kind of choice is that?" Ezra shouts and I flinch at the unexpected force of his voice above my head.

It's no choice at all.

"Quiet," Nikolai broods. "Let her choose."

I press my eyes shut and shake my head, feeling the rope over my shoulders rub uncomfortably against the sides of my neck. Obviously, I want neither choice. He's a sick fuck who has given me an impossible choice to make.

He leans down over me with a sinful smile, leaning on his hands which press into the mattress on either side of my hips. "Use your words, Anya. Would you rather I cut you or fuck you?"

Both will hurt me. I'm partially tempted to tell him to cut me, but I fear he'll take it too far, that he might stab his blade into my gut to spite me and I would die right here on his bed. That doesn't sound like a half bad idea to my fucked-up sanity, but Ezra changes everything. I wouldn't want to make that choice to leave him alone here. At least with me here, I'm the buffer between them—I'm the object of Nikolai's abuses.

When did I become so willing to put myself on the line for someone else?

I suck in a quick breath, blow it out hard, swallow, and bravely dare him, "Fuck me."

"Louder, please, Anya. Convince me you'd rather be fucked."

I spit the words out with hateful passion, "I'd rather you *fuck* me, khozyain."

"Tell Ezra." Nikolai's voice is smooth and even and filled with amusement. "Tell him you want him to help me fuck you."

My eyes feel hot around the edges. "Ezra, I want you to…" I stutter as a tear slips down the side of my face, catching me off guard, "to help him fuck me."

Nikolai bends and kisses my belly button. "Good girl." He looks up at Ezra. "Pull her back and settle her between your legs."

Nikolai steps back and works his belt buckle and I hear Ezra's breath catch and stutter.

"I can't," he whispers, filled with heartache. "I can't. I can't. I *won't*."

I tilt my chin up toward the ceiling, lifting my eyes to look at Ezra as best I can from where I lay in front of him on the bed. His hands are on top of his head, fingers laced together, and his body trembles. As horrifying as this is for me, it's not a first.

But for Ezra, it is.

"*Mal'chik*," I say, "do as you're told."

I hope my calm command can ease him enough to do what has to be done.

"I can't do this," he protests.

"You can do this, and you will. Pull me back between your legs. Do it now."

There's a long pause and I hold my breath.

Ezra has to do this.

I have to do this.

Finally, he gives up, gives in, and I sigh a breath of relief that he understands.

"I'm sorry. I'm sorry, Anya. I don't know what the fuck else I'm supposed to do."

He sounds so…broken.

Oh, God.

He slides his hands beneath my back, grasping at the rope and yanking me backward along the bed.

This.

This moment.

This is my undoing.

CHAPTER 17

Anya

NEVER HAVE I ever felt so completely ripped apart. I'm struggling against every fiber in my being not to cry, not to scream, not to fight and beg Nikolai to stop.

My hands are untied. All the ropes have been pulled free from my body, though I still feel them there as a phantom scratch, the threat of dragging burns striking up again every time I move.

Nikolai has chosen to drag out our torture, taking his time fucking me every which way while Ezra is forced to hold me or move me or watch.

He has Ezra sitting in the armchair, wearing his underwear, thankfully for him. I'm on the floor in front of him, on my knees, bent forward over his lap.

I've lost all inhibition. I grip the top of Ezra's thighs at the crease where they meet his hips, unsure of whether I'm hurting him with the way I dig in my fingertips. I have to hold onto something because it hurts so much. I lean into him, letting my cheek rest against his stomach.

Nikolai thrusts into me brutally from behind, taking the part of me where his dick absolutely does *not* belong. It doesn't belong inside me in any way, but especially not there. I'm raw, dry, probably bleeding and damaged, and I just want it to stop.

I want it to stop.

I want it to stop.

I just fucking want it to stop.

The only comfort I have is Ezra. How I hate, hate, *hate* what this is doing to him. He's forced to sit there and hold me while this torture takes place in front of him.

He held me on his lap, squirming and writhing as Nikolai made me come on the bed, a real-life pornography, as twisted and fucked up as it all was. I didn't blame Ezra for being aroused by it, not one bit. But Nikolai made it all the worse knowing that what he was doing to me was affecting Ezra all the same. He used that knowledge to torture us both, by hurting me and making Ezra watch in his aroused state.

I felt horrible for the way my body shifted against Ezra's erection with every one of Nikolai's savage thrusts. Nikolai knew it was happening. He wanted to hurt Ezra in his own way, keeping him in a state of awareness and arousal throughout my torture.

"I'm sorry," I whisper into Ezra's side as I grip him tighter. "I'm sorry, I'm sorry, I'm sorry."

Ezra lifts a hand to stroke my hair, only once before it stills. His breaths are sharp and ragged. I know what he's struggling against, what he's fighting. I do everything in my power to lift my body from his lap, to limit how much I rub against him, but I can't.

I just can't.

The pain rips through me and it's all I can do to endure it.

Nikolai moves faster, with sharper thrusts, over and over. I feel his heat invade me, his sweat sliding over my backside. He gives one final razor-like thrust and grunts low and long. I feel him spill hot liquid inside me. I let myself have the satisfaction of a single, biting scream as he finally pulls out of me.

And then I start to cry.

He's hurt me like this before, but this is true hell. He's taken me to a deeper level of torment for how he's involved Ezra. Ezra was being raped as much as I was and as soon as the invasion of Nikolai's physical presence is gone, it's all I can think of.

I collapse to the floor as Nikolai puts his clothes back on, literally falling into a naked heap at Ezra's feet. He shifts forward in his seat as I sob, clinging to his ankle as I fold my body around his leg.

He clears his throat and his voice is strained. "Please, let me take her now. She needs to rest."

Nikolai laughs. "Fine. Take her and go, I've had enough of you both for one night."

I'm rising into the air a second later as Ezra scoops me from the floor and I curl into him, wrapping my arms around his neck. He's a tidal wave of calmness crashing in, washing away the debris of this hurricane.

"Oh, Ezra," Nikolai calls out as he carries me away, "don't you want your photograph of Emma?"

I'd nearly forgotten about the photograph of his ex-girlfriend.

Ezra's chest puffs higher as he sucks in a breath. "Keep it," he barks out. "I'm sure you'll be bringing me more."

"Yes, I will."

I know it the instant we're in the hallway because I feel the demon presence of Nikolai fade away. The air is immediately lighter. The smell of whiskey and cigar smoke and blood and sex fades with every step Ezra takes.

I fear someday Nikolai might try to do to Ezra what he's just done to me and the thought of it makes me ill. I know Ezra must feel ill for me now.

Ezra carries me to my room and kicks the door shut behind us. He takes me straight to the bathroom and carefully lowers me to the floor. I squeeze his arms tight, just above the elbows, as he ducks his head down to catch my eyes.

"Hey," he says softly, "I'm gonna put you in the shower, okay? Can you stand?"

I nodded slowly. Of course, I could stand. I'd had to carry myself from Nikolai's room so many times before. I'd had to clean and care for myself in the aftermath so many times before.

But then, why is it so hard to let go of him now?

Why do I feel like I simply can't survive this without him?

Have I grown weak, dependent, needy?

He reaches behind me to open the glass shower door, gripping my shoulder with one hand as if he just can't let go of me now. He turns on the water and holds his hand beneath it as my sobs slow to occasional hiccups of emotion. Then he steps inside and pulls me in with him. He puts me under the spray and closes the door behind us.

I look up at him from beneath the waterfall that runs down my hair and though the water is warm, I shiver.

There it is, finally, thankfully.

A pause.

An offbeat count in the dance of torment that has become my life...*our* lives.

It's a sigh, a breath, a brief reprieve from the pain of this night and the uncertainty of our future.

It's Ezra I share it with.

And then it's gone.

My pain comes rushing back like the volume being quickly turned up to full blast and I flinch.

"Tell me what you need me to do. How do I fix you? How

do I make the pain stop?"

I shake my head. "You can't make the pain stop."

He looks down between us and my eyes follow, drawn immediately to the red streak flowing down between my legs, swirling crimson around the drain.

"You're bleeding," he says. "I'm—"

I reach out for his fingertips with mine. "Don't you dare apologize to me for what he's done."

"Anya," he says.

I tug at his fingertips, encouraging him forward and I step into his arms, wrapping mine around his middle. He's hesitant at first, but then he does the same, squeezing and holding me tight. I'm aware of his erection still present between us, but it doesn't scare me the way it should after all I've been through. I know he doesn't want it. The fact that he still has it is a testament to the way he's been violated by Nikolai, too.

Somehow he must know I'm thinking about it. "I'm sorry. About that..." he says.

"That's not your fault," I tell him.

He kisses the top of my head, then pulls back. "If you're okay, I'll leave you alone to shower."

"No, don't go."

His green eyes flicker with gratitude. I think it seems strange at first, but really, I know he needs comfort just as much as I do. He's grateful that I've asked him to stay with me because he needs me, too. We need each other right now.

He nods. "Okay. I won't go."

I close my eyes. "Can you help me? I want to feel clean and it hurts too much to..."

"Just tell me what you need, Anya. I'll do whatever you need."

As risky as it is for my fragile sanity in the moment, I ask Ezra to clean me, I ask him to use the bath sponge to cleanse between my legs. I could do it myself, but I can feel in my gut how much he wants to help me, how much he needs to feel like he's done something to make it better.

We both need cleansing from Nikolai's assault.

He bends to one knee on the tile and starts to tentatively scrub across the tops of my thighs where Nikolai has made four small cuts—four new scars to join all the others. The soap stings, but nothing like the feeling of them being carved into my skin.

He hesitates and looks up at me. "Do you want me to..."

He doesn't finish the question because he knows that I know what he's asking.

"I just want to feel clean, Ezra. I want every trace of him wiped away."

"And you're sure you want me to?"

I nod.

Tenderly, Ezra cleans between my legs. He's soft with me, gentle. He works quickly, doing just enough to make me feel cleansed without lingering. It doesn't feel awkward and for once, I don't feel weak for asking for help. Perhaps it's just because I'm so tired and he's being so attentive, so compassionate. He stands and lightly grips my shoulders, turning me to face the spray of water.

A beat of fear tenses my shoulders. The way he grabbed me and put me under the water without warning takes my mind back to the pool. I have to remind myself that it's just a shower. I can pull my head out from under the waterfall whenever I want. Ezra's touch is light, not harsh like Nikolai's, and I know if I tell him to let me go, he will.

I breathe in courage and tilt my head toward the water, letting it run down my face. It's warm and it surprises me just how refreshing and wholly cleansing it feels. Ezra's still here with me, his hands delicate on my shoulders. He stands a step back from me and I know he's trying to give me space.

Normally it's exactly what I would need.

Nothing is the same with Ezra, though.

It never has been.

Just like I relied on his warmth, his nearness, to get through Nikolai's torment, I need him now more than I ever did. I need to be held and cared for. In truth, I always needed it. I just pretended I didn't for the last three years. I'd become so good at lying to myself that I'd convinced myself it was true.

Ezra came into my life with warmth and light and truth. Truth, even when I didn't know I was living in lies.

I cross my arms over my chest and place my hands on top of his. His fingers twitch beneath my palms and I clutch them in my grip to keep him from pulling away from me. I need him right now and I don't want him to pull away. I pull down, bringing his hands with mine until he gets the hint. He steps closer with my encouraging tug and lets his hands fall to hold my waist. He's still so tentative, so respectful, though I know it's strained. It makes me want to cry all over again.

At the same moment that I lean backward, he leans forward, giving me his chest to rest my head against. His arms finally give in, wrapping entirely around my waist to hold me, and I feel him sigh.

The coldness I've hardened my heart with over time threatens, but Ezra's warmth melts it before it can encapsulate me in ice.

"Are you okay, Ezra?"

He bends his head forward and his cheek brushes against mine. "Am I okay? Are *you*? I don't think either of us are."

"I'll survive. I've done it for three years."

"And how many years more?"

"I don't know."

"I don't want you to just survive. I want you to live, Anya. You deserve a real life. You deserve heaven and he's giving you hell."

"It doesn't help to wish for a different kind of life. This is the life he's given us, and no one is going to rescue us from it. No one."

His chest rises as he takes in a heavy breath, and I know he's nearly ready to spew a mountain of anger and frustration about our situation. But he must know that won't help me now, in this moment. He must know that will only make this hurt more for me.

Instead, he's quiet.

Instead, he's still.

Instead, he gives me peace in the chaos.

When we get out of the shower, Ezra dries me with a towel and helps me put on underwear, some looser fitting pajama pants, and a camisole tank top.

I have nothing in my room that will fit him, so he changes from his soaking wet boxer briefs and wraps a towel around his waist. I can't stand the thought of him leaving me to go to his room just for clothes, though I know it's risky that Ezra and I are alone together at all. Nikolai had drowned me before for this very reason.

His unpredictability truly is jarring.

Still, I convince myself it's okay that we're in my room together because he told Ezra to take me and go. He knew Kostya wasn't nearby. Really, I know this is a stupid thing to convince myself of, but I just need Ezra here with me. I don't understand why I feel this way and I hate that I do.

In any case, I don't want Ezra to leave me and he chooses to stay. He kneels in front of me where I'm perched on the edge of my bed. His skin shines fresh from the shower and I find that I ache with the desire to touch it, to feel the smoothness of it. I imagine it would feel soft beneath my fingertips.

"How do you go on?" he asks with curious eyes. "How do you fall asleep at night and wake up the next morning and *go on?* I think I'm going to have nightmares about this every time I close my eyes and it wasn't even me being hurt."

I speak slowly, softly, "It was every bit as much an injury to you as it was to me."

He shakes his head. "No. That's not true."

"He made you an unwilling participant, didn't he? Did you not feel violated for the way he manipulated your arousal and used it in such a way to shame you?" I sigh. "Rape is rape, Ezra…emotional or physical."

He hesitates and blinks, his brow creasing as he shakes his head. "He abuses us both. You're not wrong about that," he says. "I just don't understand how you…How many times has he done this to you?"

"Alone? More times than I care to count. With a partner? Tonight was the second time. The first wasn't nearly as awful."

I expect him to respond, but he doesn't. He just waits. He gives me the pause I need to find my words and speak them into the shared space between us. It's strange the way he brings my feelings to the surface with nothing more than a patient pause and a look.

A look that makes me feel safe, even when I'm not.

"This was the worst I've ever had it here. Not because of the vile things he did to me. He's done all of those things before…" I swallow. "It was worse because of you."

His face falls and he slumps back to sit on his heels, looking as though he's just seen a ghost. He rubs his hands on the towel straining around his strong thighs, looks down, then back up at me.

Still, he says nothing.

"I had a hard time hiding with you there in the room. I've always been able to retreat to a dark space in my mind, a corner I hide away in when he's hurting me. I've tried to hide in that dark space ever since you arrived, Ezra. I can do it when you're not near me, but when you are…" I pause. "There's just so much light in you that even if I go to that dark corner, it's not dark enough to hide in. I don't think I was ever able to hide from you, not entirely. Having you there while Nikolai hurt me, seeing how he hurt you, nearly broke me." My voice cracks and unexpected tears spill down my cheeks. "I don't know if I'm making any sense. I just…I can't let myself get attached. I can't. I know it only makes it worse, but the thought of losing you…"

I let the tears take over. He lets me cry for a few moments and then lifts back up onto his knees. He reaches for my hands, pulling them from my lap. He moves with slow intention as he puts one of my hands on his chest, over his heart, and holds the other sweetly in his palm. He licks his lips and blinks a little too long, inhaling a deep breath through his nose.

"My heart beats out of control every time I'm with you," he confesses with a gentle voice.

I force an ill-placed chuckle through my sadness, though it's entirely without feeling. "That's because torture and torment follow me like a shadow. This," I tap my hand over his heart where he placed it, "this is because of fear. Because of loneliness. Because of desperation to feel something, anything but the hopelessness for our future."

He narrows his eyes at me and shuffles closer on his knees. I feel the rough texture of the overly bleached towel rub against my shins. His nearness and touch make *my* heart beat faster, but I'm too much of a realist to think anything of it. I won't *let* myself feel anything about it, though I'm starting to wonder if maybe I should.

I want to.

"Don't do that," he says. "Don't patronize me. I know you think you know everything about me, Anya, but you don't. I know the difference between fearing and wanting. I know the difference between desperation and need. My heart beats faster for *you.*"

I try to take a breath and it catches in my throat. "Why are you telling me this?"

"I know you fear getting attached, you fear losing me. What you don't know is that I'm already attached. I'm *yours.* And I won't fucking lose you."

He squeezes both my hands tighter, holding the one over his heart and the other on my lap. He looks down and shakes his head, yet again giving me a quiet pause before looking up at me. His green eyes steal mine with life and truth and vibrancy.

Just like that, with a snap that cracks all reason, I'm stolen.

Not by a cruel master, but instead, by a brilliant man who could make me want to hope again.

This is dangerous.

But still, I want it.

I pull on our entwined hands, yanking him toward me as I lean forward and crash my lips against his. He squeezes my fingers and I can feel his restrained desperation when his pillow soft lips twitch against mine.

I feel what he's feeling.

He's aching to part them, to taste and explore me. I hesitate, but its brief. If he'd taken that liberty on his own, pressing me too hard, too fast to open for him, it would've ended right then.

But he didn't do that.

He waited.

He breathes heavy through his nose, patient in the chaste kiss, though I can feel every inch of tension in his body.

I want it because he waits.

I want it more and more with each passing second of complete respect and patience. For the first time in nearly three years, I *want* physical affection.

He is the sunshine to my wilting petals. His light gives me nourishment. Like a rose, I blossom for him, parting my lips with permission to explore this sensation with me.

Ezra's tongue slips inside and though the invasion threatens to shut me down, it's only for a moment. Then the moment passes and inexplicably, I feel free.

He makes me feel free.

I sigh into his mouth, shaking his hands from mine so I can grab his face and pull him closer. I bend over him to deepen the kiss, but he pushes back, lifting higher on his knees to meet me.

His hands fall heavy on the bed on either side of my hips. I feel it dip as he presses down and I know he's holding himself back. He's leaning into me, his tongue sweeping in and around, tasting every bit of me in a silent, desperate plea to have more of me.

I can't give him more of me, not now, and he knows it. Knowing he knows it and yet still doesn't push me sends a flurry of feeling through my stomach, tiny wings that flutter and buzz with the most pleasant sensation.

It makes me want to give him more of me.

And I know I will someday.

Because this man makes my heart beat faster in the best way I've ever known.

CHAPTER 18

Ezra

ANYA KISSED ME two nights ago, and I can't stop thinking about it.

I'm pacing inside my ugly green room after dark, too full of energy to sleep. I still get locked in at night, though I'm no longer required to wear the ankle cuff. I get to move freely—mostly—throughout the manor during the day.

Kostya follows me around more often than he follows Anya. She's proven her submission and trustworthiness over years. All I've managed to prove over months is my impatience and bad fucking attitude.

I'm wishing I could get out of here—go dance in the studio for a while or do something, *anything*, to get rid of this excess energy pulsing through my muscles—when I hear the locks turning on the door.

I wrinkle my forehead, confused because this is unusual.

It's not morning. Dinner was only a few hours ago.

Kostya always lets me out in the morning, never at night.

I move toward the door, instantly feeling defensive, because I don't know who is on the other side of it. Then someone knocks.

They *knock*.

Who the fuck is knocking on a door I don't control?

I throw my arms out, shaking my head, and they fall with a thud against my sides. "Uh, come in?"

The door swings open to reveal my blue-eyed girl standing there, holding the key.

She smiles and it hits me right in the center of my chest. "Hi."

I grin right back at her like an idiot. "What the hell did you knock for?"

She cocks her head. "To be polite. Do you wanna get out of here?"

I almost laugh. "Do you really need me to answer that?"

She rolls her eyes. "Come with me but be quiet. I want to show you something."

"A little rebellion, huh? I like it. Let's go." My heart is thudding against my ribs when I step toward her, then I stop. "Wait, where's Nikolai?"

"He just left. He'll be gone overnight."

"Kostya?"

"That's why you need to be quiet."

She's sneaking me out.

Nikolai's gone and she's sneaking me out for the night.

I feel a rush of excitement jumpstart my senses in a way I haven't felt since I was a teenager sneaking out of my foster parents' house on a school night.

My feet are moving without another thought. I meet her in the hallway, and she shuts and locks the door behind us. She wraps her fingers around my hand and squeezes, pulling me forward as she strides down the hallway.

I get this cold tingle running through my veins the moment her skin touches mine. It makes my spine prickle and rush all the good feelings I have about her low in my gut.

She stops at the end of the hallway and looks over her shoulder at me, holding up a finger to her lips, telling me to keep my mouth shut without even saying a word.

I zip my fingers across my lips and her eyes brighten, lingering on my mouth for an extra beat. I want to grab her and kiss her hard.

We move forward together, quietly rushing down the grand staircase. We turn left at the bottom and move toward the east wing. She pauses as we're about to pass the kitchen doorway and peeks her head in, pulling it right back out and jumping backward. Her backside runs right into the front of my body when she does this and I grab her just above the elbows. She turns her head to the side, and I see the blue of her eyes peeking out from the corners as she tries to look at me.

"On my cue," she whispers.

"On *my* cue," I joke, and she jabs her elbow backward into my gut.

She peeks her head back into the kitchen and gives a quick nod. We walk quickly and quietly past. As soon as we reach the garden corridor, she gives me a quick look—an almost playful look I've never seen on her before—and takes off running.

That one little lightning bolt of happiness she shows me takes on a life of its own, lassoing around me and tugging me along with her.

I run after her.

She leads us down past the pool and comes to a stop at a door to our right, opposite the cave-like alcove that leads to the pool entrance where Nikolai drowned her. She stops to unlock the door with one of the same keys she used to unlock my door.

It opens onto a hallway. I step past the entry and she joins me, shutting and locking the door behind her. It wouldn't stop Kostya or Nikolai from coming after us, but it would slow them down. I'm surprised I'm hardly thinking about what they'll do if they find us sneaking around.

I almost don't care.

We're captives whether we behave or not, so fuck the rules. Especially if this tiny little rebellion can make her look this fucking happy.

She takes my hand again and we walk side by side down the short hallway. It opens onto a foyer, reminiscent of the grand entrance, but much smaller. Same marbled floors, same ornate gold frames and crown molding, same stupid burgundy-colored walls.

Two sets of double doors sit to our left. They're dark wood, carved with intricate patterns like the doors in the grand entrance, only smaller. Anya walks us to the doors and pulls on the handle, opening it wide.

"This is Nobility Hall," she says, gesturing for me to go inside.

I grin as I walk past her and enter the large open space. It's dark, but I see what it is. This is our dance hall. It's where we'll be performing. The two aisleways that lead down to the stage are covered with plush, red carpeting, lined with rows of seats on both sides. I'd guess you could fit about a hundred people in this theater, which seems excessive given that Mikhailov Manor is so vast and empty.

I move forward as the lights come on, first in the audience, then on the stage. The stage is low, nearer to the audience than I would've expected. It's dark black wood and dark black curtains make it all perfectly, poetically haunting. It should be, given that it's tainted by the blood of slaves.

Anya's arm brushes mine as she comes up beside me and I snatch her hand in mine. I hear her take in a sharp breath and I turn my head to look at her, wanting to see the expression on her face. She tucks a strand of hair behind her ear, so demurely, so innocently, and swallows as she shifts her eyes away from my stare.

I want to hold more than her hand and she wants that, too.

I know it.

But I'm not going to push her.

She starts walking down the aisleway and I walk beside her. "This is a fairly recent addition to Mikhailov Manor."

"Oh?"

"Nikolai had it added on when I was fifteen or so, I suppose. Of course, I wouldn't have known then that he'd already had my adult years mapped out for me."

My gut rolls at the thought. "I'll never get over how sick this whole thing is."

She watches her steps, the corners of her lips tugging upward, though it's not a smile. "Neither will I."

"So, tell me what we're doing here."

We stop as we reach the stage. "I just thought we could dance."

She says it so plainly, so sweetly. It takes me back to freedom, when I could just go and do something because I wanted to, when *she* could just go and do something because *she* wanted to. It hits me then what's happening here as I watch the nervous way she shifts from one foot to the other, the way she keeps tucking that same strand of hair back behind her ear.

She just needs some normalcy and for some reason, she feels safe enough to try for it with me. Truthfully, she's risking life and limb to bring me here, and all she wants is to dance with me.

It's not all she wants, but that's all she needs.

I grin at her, nodding. "Yeah, let's do it. Let's dance."

She smiles up at me and fuck, it shoots right to my groin. I almost feel bad about that, as if I don't have a right to crave her.

But damn, do I crave her.

Her smile softens as she looks at me, fading into something even sweeter. She bites her bottom lip and lets out a heavy breath. She's giving me every signal that she'd let me kiss her if I tried.

If we were back in New York, free, just living our lives the way we wanted to, I'd already have my arms around her. I'd already be pulling her close. I'd already be kissing her the way she deserves to be kissed, with complete, reckless abandon.

But I can't do things the normal way, not with Anya. I refuse to scare or hurt her. I'll only give her what she asks me for, and I'll take nothing more.

It looks like she's about to move closer and I hold my breath. But then she slips past me, walking away from me toward the steps at the side of the stage. She jogs up them and across the hardwood floor to center stage, smiling down at me.

"Are you coming up?" she asks expectantly.

I tilt my head to the side, watching her. "Will you dance for me?"

She nods. "Only if you come up on stage with me."

"You got it," I tell her easily and jog up the five steps to meet her.

I move to sit downstage, facing where she stands in the center. I sit down on the hard wood, leaning back on my palms and crossing my legs casually at the ankles in front of me.

"All right, I'm ready," I say. "Wait. Do we have any music?"

"We can't play music. Kostya will hear it and come looking for us." She suddenly looks apprehensive at her own reminder that we're breaking the rules.

My lips curl in a smirk. "I can sing."

She raises an eyebrow. "Can you though?"

"Nah, not really." I laugh.

She shrugs with a smile. "I have music in my mind."

And in her heart and soul.

"I know you do."

With an encouraging smile, Anya dances for me.

For the past half hour, Anya's been dancing around on stage, twirling and leaping and flowing through some of the most graceful movement I've ever had the pleasure of watching.

My cheeks hurt from smiling, and I'm so fucking grateful for that ache. I don't think I've had such a long stretch of happiness since I arrived here. Anya is poised perfection and though I'm aching to touch her, I'd be plenty happy to sit and watch her dance as long as she'll let me.

She comes out of a turn, but strangely, let's it fade to a slow, unusual stop. She doesn't really finish the movement in an elegant pose the way she normally does, always the professional.

She just stops it.

Turning to face me, she touches her lips with her fingers and she lets her teeth nip at her chewed off thumbnail as her eyes shift.

She's nervous, but not in the way I've come to expect.

"What is it?" I ask her with concern.

She lets out a heavy breath and takes three quick steps toward me, stopping abruptly, just at my feet. I almost feel pushed back by the way she rushes me, but it doesn't move me away. I'm frozen to the spot by the way she looks down at me. I push up off my palms, sitting up straighter and lifting my head, making sure she knows she has my full attention.

"The night we kissed, you said you were mine," she finally says.

I somehow feel lighter to have her remember that as *the night we kissed* and not the night Nikolai cut her and raped her while forcing me to watch.

I nod once. "I said I was yours. And I meant it."

She steps over me and drops down to her knees so quickly, I hardly have time to react. In an instant, she's straddling my outstretched legs, settling her ass on my thighs, grabbing my face in her hands.

"Anya," is all I manage to say before her lips fall heavily onto mine.

I can't contain the groan of sheer relief I feel from having her body against mine, her lips on my lips. Her tongue is already fighting to get to mine and the taste of her is something other-fucking-worldly when I let her in.

She lets me taste her and enjoy her delicious mouth for several satisfying moments before she pulls her head back with a snap. Her hands slide down from my face, but drift softly to the sides of my neck. She presses her forehead to mine.

"I don't know what's wrong with me," she says softly.

I hold myself upright with one palm back on the floor, sliding the other around her waist and rubbing over the small of her back. "What do you mean?"

"There are things I want that I shouldn't want."

I lick my lips and tilt my head forward, touching my nose to hers. "And what do you want?"

Her voice is low, her hands slipping around to the back of my neck to hold me to her. "I want things from you."

I press my palm flat against her back and drag her body closer, forcing her to press in and mold against me, and she sighs. She lets me arch her back and flatten her breasts against my chest. Her curves are soft and supple against my body and I want to touch her everywhere.

I want to flip her over, lay her down, climb on top of her and make her feel everything I feel for her. I want to make her feel how desired she is, how needed she is, how loved she is.

"What do you want?" I repeat, tilting my hips to buck up into her, just for a beat, just to feel her.

Her eyes fall shut and she moans.

Like an angel chorus from the heavens, she moans.

Its pleasure filled, not fearing, and knowing that sends a rush of blood to my cock. I lick my lips and press a soft kiss to hers.

Just one.

"Please, Anya, tell me what you want."

She opens her eyes and I'm held captive by her sultry stare. She doesn't speak, but I don't think she needs to. She lets her body speak for her, just as she does with dance.

Her hips shift forward, a slow, long, experimental motion. She slides across my half-hard, denim-covered cock, pressing down and grinding into me.

"Shit," I manage, my breaths picking up their pace.

She holds steady for a few beats before rocking back, then forward again. I know what her body is telling me. She's telling me how much she wants this, how much she wants to enjoy me in the physical sense, but she doesn't know if she can, if she's ready.

I won't show it, but it actually breaks my heart. Not because I know she isn't ready for me, but because of the reason *why* she's not ready.

Nikolai.

He's abused her sexually for so long that she's probably forgotten what good, healthy sex feels like. A thought crosses my mind and now I'm wondering if she ever knew. For all I know, she was a virgin before he took her.

This train of thought alone is enough to keep my urge to whip her around and pin her beneath me in check. I'll let her decide the pace. I'll let her take whatever it is she needs from me—no matter how small—because I am beyond happy to give it.

She leans into me and her weight pushes my back down to the floor. All that worry about my urge to throw her down and she's doing it to me. My heart races and my pulse thrums a heavy beat, ticking through every muscle, as I lower to my back on the stage floor.

I toss her long hair back over her shoulder with a flick of my wrist just before she brings her lips down on mine and kisses me again. I hold her with my hand on her cheek as she moans into my mouth. The sound vibrates on my lips and makes them tingle, and I moan right back so she can feel the same.

She speaks to me between kisses, "Do you want me?"

"Yes, I want you." I lift my hips to meet hers. "Fuck, I want you."

"Would you still want me if we weren't here?"

I grab her face with both hands, her dangling hair tickling over my knuckles. "I would want you anywhere, Anya."

"How can you know that?"

"Because I know you."

She searches my eyes and I'm caught up in the blue of hers as they flicker. I know the moment she finds whatever it is she's looking for because she smiles in a way I've never seen from her before.

It's bright, happy, *free*.

It shines through her eyes and sends a shockwave of need through me, clenching low in my gut.

She knows exactly what her smile does to me because her legs are wrapped around me and I'm rock-hard beneath her. Her hips move again and it feels like heaven. It makes me want to know what it would feel like to be inside her, but I have no expectation that she'll let me find out.

Still, she's pressing and grinding against me hard and heavy now. Her cotton short-shorts leave little barrier between her and my jeans, and I crudely wonder if she'll leave a wet spot there.

Fuck, I hope she does.

"I don't think I can fuck you," she tells me, though she's grinding against my crotch.

"I don't expect you to."

"But you want me to."

"Yes, I want you to. Fuck, Anya…" I pull her down and kiss her, sloppy and wet.

She kisses my cheek, my neck, along my jawline, and my hands are all over her, touching her everywhere. I slide my heel back along the floor to lift my knee because she's pushing down on me so hard, I want to give her something to push back against.

I don't know if she can come like this with all our clothes on, but fuck, I want her to. I want that from her. I want to see her take what she needs, what she deserves, and have that fleeting moment of freedom. If all I can give her is that moment, I'll give it.

My hands slide over her back and slip down over her ass. My movements are slow because I don't know exactly how she'll react. She doesn't stop me, so gradually, I squeeze. She flips her head, tossing her silky brown hair back over her shoulder again and bites her lip, picking up her pace.

We're all but fucking with our clothes on, but somehow this all seems far more intimate.

I've already seen her naked, I've already seen her orgasm, though it was unwillingly. It actually makes me feel a little emotional to think about it because the sounds she's making now, when I *know* she wants this, are entirely different. The sounds she's making are fuel for the fire within my gut. Her sounds are fucking *magic* and before long, I'm urgently eager for relief. She's changing her angle, shifting against my jeans, rolling her hips and rocking hard.

Her long wavy hair keeps falling back down over her face and the ends tickle against my skin as she molds her hips to mine. I grip her ass and hold her against me.

"Ezra," she whispers into my neck and I shiver at the sound of my name from her sweet lips, "are you mine?"

I sigh, my answer doesn't even require a thought. "I'm yours."

She's jerking against me now, jerking and fucking and making me so hard it hurts. I lift to kiss her neck, licking across the hollow of her throat and earning a pleasure-filled gasp from her.

"I want you to come like this," I tell her, nipping my teeth across the side of her neck. "Please, Anya."

Her eyes are drifting shut, but she smiles as she bites her bottom lip. "Yes…yes…just hold still."

"Holding still, not moving." I grin at her, but she doesn't see it because her eyes are squeezed shut with tension.

It's only a few moments longer when her movements become frantic, desperate. The speed and pressure of her rubbing over my cock makes me swell. If she keeps going at that angle, right there, she's gonna make me come in my jeans.

"Jesus. Anya," I groan.

She puts her hands on my shoulders and pushes down hard, lifting her body off me just enough for her to be able to push her hips down harder, grind deeper. She's tensing and panting out these sweet little "*oh*" sounds and I know she's going to make me come.

The "*oh*" sounds hit harder and faster. She's fucking me harder and faster until suddenly, she explodes with the most incredible body trembling orgasm I've ever witnessed. The look of her letting go—of being so free with me, taking what *she* needs instead of giving under force—is so fucking hot that it pushes me right over the edge with her.

"Yes, fuck, yes," I groan as I buck up against her.

I move my hands to her back and pull her against my chest, holding her close. I can feel her heart beating fast, as if it were my own. She scoots down so she can lay her head and hand on my chest and I feel completely wrapped up in her.

We're quiet and still for minutes, just holding each other and breathing together. The hardwood floor beneath my back is starting to become uncomfortable, but the softness above me makes up for it in spades.

I'm determined to savor this moment of rare peace, holding this woman I know I'm falling hard for, but as the peaceful sound of our breathing is drowned by the open echo of the theater, I'm forced out of the moment. The echo of nothingness that surrounds us reminds me that we'll be dancing for our lives on this very stage in just a few short weeks.

I don't know what will happen then.

I don't know if I'll be killed, sold, or kept.

I don't know what fate Anya faces.

It's a thought that's too overwhelming to bear alone. I hold Anya tighter, rolling us over until I'm on top of her. I look down at my blue-eyed girl and kiss her softly, slowly.

I imagine her home with me in New York, laying comfortably in my bed with sunlight bathing her from open windows. I imagine her free and unburdened by captivity. I imagine her happy, truly, always happy.

I make a promise to myself in that moment to find a way to make that life a reality for her.

I'll find a way, even if it kills me.

CHAPTER 19

Anya

I MOAN AGAINST Ezra's lips as he kisses me for the hundredth time on the stage in Nobility Hall. He cradles me and holds me so gently in his arms, and I never want to leave this moment.

But all moments are fleeting and this one is no exception.

"We should talk about the performance," I tell him.

"Now?"

I sit up and my bones ache from lying with him on the hardwood floor. "Yes, now."

I turn to face him, crossing my legs, and he sits up to mirror my position.

"Okay, then let's talk about it." He adjusts his cock as he settles. "Christ, I still can't believe you made me come in my jeans."

I press my lips together to suppress a smile. I'm sure I'm blushing, but he just grins at me without judgment. He looks almost proud of the way he's affected me.

He should be proud.

I've never felt so…powerful.

"So, what do I need to know?" he asks.

I put my hands on my knees and straighten my spine, arching my lower back to stretch out my sore muscles.

"The four families will send representatives to stay here at Mikhailov Manor for the night of our performance. Our performance is really just an opener, entertainment for them. It's a requirement. A tradition, really. The real purpose for their presence is the quarterly meeting, as I told you before, but each family has to provide entertainment and a reception to welcome their guests when they host. That's what we exist for as talent slaves—to provide entertainment for our family once every year."

He rolls his eyes. "Right. We don't get to live our lives because we have talent. We live as slaves so Nikolai can entertain his stupid fucking guests once a year."

I sigh. "I keep forgetting how new this all is to you."

"And I hate that this seems normal to you."

"I don't think it's normal. It's just what is. This has been my life for a while. The reality is that we're not the only slaves. I can't even attempt to fathom how many people the four families have trafficked. And the other families, they have talent slaves like us, too."

"Are they all dancers? The other talent slaves?"

"No. But they're all artists, performers. The O'Sheas just acquired new talent, a singer, I think. The Campbells have a painter. The Vittoris…well, they have several."

"So, the O'Sheas and the Campbells only have one talent slave?"

"Yes. The Mikhailovs only ever had one, as I understand it, until Nikolai became the new Head of House. But the families are only allowed to be the benefactors for one talent slave at a time."

"Why be benefactors at all? Why waste the time and money?"

"It's all a grooming technique, Ezra. The four families want their talent to be…sophisticated, well-developed. The challenge lies in taking a talented person, breaking them into slavery, and seeing who can maintain their talent through turmoil."

"It's fucking sick."

I nod. "There's a bit of an unspoken competition, I think. There's a lot of pressure on the Heads of House to host an entertaining performance before they get into business."

"Nikolai is Head of House for the Mikhailovs."

"Yes, he was the oldest son, so it would have fallen to him regardless, but especially now that his family is all gone."

"What actually happened to them?"

"I think I told you, but they died in a plane crash."

"All of them?"

"His parents and his younger brother. That was over a year ago. It wasn't an accident, though."

"What do you mean?"

"The American family, the Campbells, they tampered with the plane. It's their fault it crashed."

"How do you know that?"

"Because I…I heard the phone recordings that proved it. The Head of House for the Vittori family, Vigo, he came into possession of these recordings and he made a trade with Nikolai, giving him the information at the last quarterly meeting."

I pinch my eyes shut at the memory of being shared and used by Vigo Vittori. I shudder from head to toe. Ezra sees the change in me, and of course, he asks.

"What did Nikolai trade?"

I hesitate. "He traded me. It was only for an hour. But Vigo was…he's…" I don't have the right words to describe that experience.

"What happened, Anya?" Ezra's words are so soft, tinged with care and concern.

"I don't want to tell you about it." Truly, I don't want to relive it in my mind. "I hate Vigo Vittori. I hate him as much as I hate Nikolai. I fear him, perhaps even more." I suck in a sharp breath. "I don't want to talk about it. That hour he used me nearly broke me. Please don't ask me about it again."

He watches me carefully, eyes narrowed in consideration. He swipes a hand over his mouth and swallows hard, as if physical forcing himself to digest all this new and terrible information. There's a minute of silence, of cautious understanding, and then we move forward, and I'm grateful that Ezra doesn't push me to tell him more about Vigo.

"So, Nikolai's family..." he starts carefully. "You knew them before they died?"

"Yes," I tuck a fallen strand of hair behind my ear, "I was Nikolai's responsibility, though, so we didn't interact much. They didn't interfere. His parents were as cold and callous as he is. His brother was kinder. Not *kind*, but kinder."

He nods. "So, we perform. Entertain the sick bastards. Then what happens?"

I look down. "I can only tell you what's happened here in the past." I take a deep breath. "In the past, my partner and I performed and then—"

Suddenly, I'm sucked back in time.

I look to my left, toward the center of the stage and I remember it as clearly as though it was happening right in front of me. It hasn't even been a full year since my third partner was taken from me.

Jonathan.

I'd developed a friendship with him. Of course, I had. He was kind, caring, a good person. He didn't deserve what happened to him.

After we'd performed that night, at Nikolai's quarterly meeting, Nikolai had come up on the stage as we waited to know our fate. I held Jonathan's hand because I was afraid.

Jamal and Erik had been stolen from me. I didn't know if they were dead or alive.

Nikolai didn't hesitate after the performance with Jonathan. He strode across the stage with fierce, intentional steps, a look of disappointment and rage brushing the wrinkled lines across his forehead. He ripped Jonathan from my hold. I screamed at him, begged him not to take Jonathan away, to spare him from whatever fate Nikolai had decided upon.

But it didn't matter what I wanted.

It never does.

Nikolai decided Jonathan hadn't met his excessive standards.

I couldn't help but feel it was my fault. I didn't understand, *couldn't* understand, what we'd done wrong. The performance was technically flawless. We'd worked our asses off to prepare and did everything we could.

But still, he took away my only companion.

I'd chased after them as he dragged Jonathan away, through the throng of guests waiting in the grand entrance for the reception, up the grand staircase, down the hallway, and back into Jonathan's bedroom.

Ezra's bedroom.

The door slammed shut before I could cross the threshold. I suppose I should be glad he put the door between us. I heard Jonathan scream, but after that came the silence.

The silence was so much worse than the screaming.

Kostya took me back to my room, ordered me to get ready for the reception, because I still had to greet Nikolai's guests, the four families.

I don't know what happened to Jonathan.

He might have been murdered.

He might have been injured and taken away.

All I know is that I saw Kostya bring the white comforter and bed sheets out of the room the next morning.

Except they weren't all white.

There were splashes of red.

"Anya?" Ezra says softly and I turn my head to look at him.

I don't want to see his blood on his sheets.

I launch forward, reaching for him as I climb into his lap, sitting sideways. I wrap my hands around his neck and nuzzle in close.

"He's taken all of my partners from me," I whisper, pressing a kiss to his cheek. "I don't know whether he's…whether he's killed them or sold them. But he always takes them after the performance."

He nods, pulling me closer, squeezing me tightly. "I don't know what to say."

"Don't say anything." I press my lips to his and he's ready to meet mine with a sweet, slow, passion-heated kiss.

After a minute, he pulls back slowly, just barely, his lips still brush over mine as he speaks.

"Look, I don't know what to tell you except that I'm fucking amazing. I've rocked your world and I'm gonna rock his. My dancing skills are gonna blow his fucking mind. There's no way he's getting rid of me."

Ezra smiles broadly, happily, and I see how his eyes sparkle with humor and hope.

That hope kills me.

But it also makes my heart beat faster.

CHAPTER 20

Anya

I WORK TO catch my breath after the final beat. The air is somber and still as our performance song ends. Ezra and I have just finished our final rehearsal and the knowledge that tomorrow night is our performance for the four families weighs heavy on us both.

Even so, I feel good about our routine. We've practiced and practiced and come as near to perfect as we possibly could. I know Nikolai will be pleased with this performance, and that small sliver of hope clings to me uncomfortably.

I don't know what will happen after the performance. I don't know if he will keep Ezra or take him from me. I don't know that if he does take him from me, whether he will survive or perhaps be sold as a slave commodity, a human asset.

Thinking about it is physically painful, so I try not to.

I'd rather soak in his rays of light before everything changes.

Ezra strides across the stage to me as I rise to my feet from my final position on the floor. He grabs hold of the long, dangling end of the rope that hangs free from my body, walking his hands along it as he approaches me. The rest of it is wrapped and tied around my body. We use the rope as part of our routine because Nikolai demanded it. Somehow, we'd actually managed to create a beautiful dance with it.

I shouldn't say *we*.

It was Ezra who put it all together. His talent for choreography is only outmatched by his talent for dancing.

He unties me and frees me from the binding rope. His brow is furrowed and I wonder what he's thinking.

"I think we're ready," I tell him, hoping he'll share openly with me.

I get a flicker of a smile from him, but it fades immediately. "What is it?"

He shakes his head as the last of the rope falls free. "I'm just afraid. That's all."

I want to wrap my arms around him and hold him tight, but not here. Not in the middle of the stage. This is where we will perform tomorrow, in the dance hall named Nobility Hall.

When Nikolai had chosen me as a child, he had this dance hall built just for me to perform in. It's a beautiful performance space, but it's haunting all the same.

"Come with me," I say, taking his hand and dragging him backstage.

Nikolai is wrapped up in preparing the manor for his guests who will be arriving throughout the night and tomorrow morning. Kostya is with us, sitting out in the audience, but pays little attention, always staring down at the cell phone screen in his hands.

Ezra and I have done what we need to do to prove we pose no threat of attempting escape or harm, to ourselves or to anyone else here. We've been granted the small amount of trust to do what we need to in order to prepare for our performance, so I know Kostya thinks nothing of it when we disappear behind the curtains.

The moment we are out of sight, cloaked in shadow between two curtains that hang in the wings of the stage, I reach up to put my hands on his cheeks and pull him down to me. I kiss him softly, kindly.

His arms come around me, sweeping me tightly into his embrace. I release his face to snuggle in close to him as he holds me, pressing my cheek to his strong chest.

"I'm afraid, too," I whisper.

"It's not me I'm afraid for, you know. I'm afraid for you. If he takes me away from you. What will happen to you? What will he do to you, Anya?"

I sigh. "I don't know. I don't care. I feel like I just…"

"Just what?"

"Like we just found each other." I lift my head to look up at him. His hands lift to my cheeks and he holds my face as I hold him tight around the waist.

"I want you to know…" he starts. "I *need* you to know, it's not just our circumstances that draw me to you."

I lick my bottom lip. "I know."

"It's not just our circumstances that make me *want* you."

"I know."

"I'm yours, Anya."

"Mine?"

"Yours."

He bends, lowering his face to mine. His tongue peeks out to lick his lips before he kisses me. His pillow soft mouth smothers mine with tenderness and it makes my entire body thaw to his warmth. I melt into him as he deepens the kiss. With a silent sweep of the tip of his tongue across my lips, he asks me to open for him and I do.

He tastes me with the ferocity of a man in desperate need, but holds restraint enough to do so without taking anything

I'm not willing to give. It's so strange that I don't feel like there is anything at all I'm not willing to give with him.

It's dangerous how vulnerable I am with him, how vulnerable I *want* to be.

But knowing our time may be limited, I don't want to hold anything back. I want him to know what he means to me, that I feel for him what I think he feels for me.

A part of me has feared that our captivity is the only reason we feel the way we do for each other because there is no one else. But I know that's not true by the way he's kissing me. Everything in his kiss tells me it's me he wants, and I want to tell him the same.

I let my hands drift from around his waist, roam slowly up his strong chest, fingertips graze over his neck as I wrap them around the back and hold him to me. The pull makes him groan into my mouth and the vibration of it trembles in my core.

I should be fearful of a man in lust.

But I'm not fearful of Ezra, of this.

This is not lust.

Its *more.*

His cautious need tells me he wants me, but only if I want him.

And God, how I want him.

Our kiss strengthens and grows in confidence, becoming more passionate, more urgent, more fervent in need. Deep in the pit of my stomach, I feel him. It's a soul crushing absence that insists to be filled by him.

His lips break free from mine, but move across my jawline instead, nipping and sucking delightfully, all the way back to my ear. He trails down my neck and nuzzles into the crook. We're both panting and breathless and all I can feel is *him.*

"I want everything with you," he says between kisses that

are hot against my skin. "I want time with you. I want a real life with you. I want to take care of you and make you laugh. I want to make love to you."

I whimper in both pleasure and despair. "I told you not to hope, not to plan, not to fall for me, Ezra. I told you."

His fingers skim my arms, leaving a trail of prickling flesh. His hands find mine and he lifts them away from his neck to hold them, lacing our fingers together. He brings our interlocked hands down to our sides.

"And I told you that was bullshit." He pulls back to look at me and I find him plastering a snarky smile to his face.

It's not the smile that melts that last layer of ice from around my heart. It's the tears forming a glassy sheen over his eyes.

"If there's a way…" he says to me. "If there's a way to free us from whatever fate Nikolai has planned for us, I promise you, I will find it. I will do whatever it takes. I promise you, Anya."

I let a small, sad smile tug at the corner of my mouth. "Don't make me promises you can't keep."

He presses his forehead to mine. "I wouldn't dare break a promise to you. If there's a way, I'll find it."

I wasn't afraid that he would break his promise.

I was afraid of what would become of him when he found out it was a promise he never had a chance of keeping.

CHAPTER 21
Anya

MY DRESSING ROOM door beneath the stage in Nobility Hall swings open wide. Nikolai enters as I'm sweeping an extra dust of shimmery gold eyeshadow across my lid.

I'm dressed and ready for tonight's performance, though my costume this year is rather plain as opposed to the elaborate, ornately beaded leotards and frilly tutus I'd normally wear to perform ballet. This year, I wear a nude leotard and matching boy shorts. From the audience, it mimics nudity without the crudeness of actually being naked. The rope Nikolai asked us to incorporate is the true costume, masking me in intricate binding.

Simplicity aside, theatrics are ingrained in my performer's heart. Though my hair is pulled back in a simple low bun, I've overdone it with the makeup, using gold, shimmering shadow, dark eye liner and mascara, a deep burgundy lip color, and bronzed blush which highlights my cheekbones.

"Anya," Nikolai croons as he enters the small space, "stand, let me look at you."

I set down my eye brush and turn to stand in front of him. He holds a single pink rose in his hands. It reminds me of the first day I saw him in Russia, at my childhood dance studio when I was eleven. He brings me a pink rose before every annual performance just to bring that reminder to the surface that I am his, that I have been since I was a child. I force a smile because I know he expects it.

"Beautiful as ever," he says, leaning forward to kiss my cheek. "Are you ready?"

"Almost."

"Good." He holds out the rose. "For you."

I take it with another fake smile. "Thank you, *khozyain*."

He steps forward, snaking his arms around my waist and pulls me against him. I don't hug back. I hold my arms out to my sides. He's warm—too warm—with a hint of whiskey already on his breath.

His lips move softly against my ear. "I just want to remind you that the four families will be watching tonight. I expect nothing less than brilliance…for Ezra's sake, and for yours."

He pulls away and it's not soon enough. His smile makes him look like a wolf with a rabbit trapped beneath its paw. My captivity pleases him. My internal battle with coerced compliance is a game to him. He likes to bat me between his paws sometimes, just to watch me squirm.

My gut rolls, churning a warning for me to run far and fast from the enemy who wishes to turn playful batting into painful clawing and tearing.

But the warnings are a waste of energy.

I can't run.

"I won't ruin your makeup with a kiss. You look quite stunning as you are."

I nod. I have nothing to say to him. I'd really like him to leave so that I can focus and prepare to dance for my life.

For Ezra's life.

Ezra.

"Break a leg," he says, and though it's a common

colloquialism among performers, the way he says it always sends an ice-cold breeze across my arms.

What would happen to me if I broke a leg?

Would he take me outside and shoot me?

Put the poor, useless animal out of her misery because she can no longer dance?

I've been lucky to have remained relatively uninjured in Nikolai's captivity thus far. I hate that he's just brought me such sharp awareness of the fact that I might only be one serious injury away from being completely useless to him. Another thing added to the millions I worry myself sick over, and all of that brought on by a simple phrase meant to wish performers good luck.

I'm thankful when he's gone, when I'm finally able to exhale.

Though I still have a healthy dose of fear running through my veins, the truth is that the thrill of dancing for an audience excites me. It's an excitement I've been grateful to have even in my captivity. It's something I can hold onto, some small feeling of normalcy in this nightmare.

And I don't want it ruined by Nikolai.

In this dressing room, I can fall away into my mind. I can pretend that I'm preparing to dance on stage as a soloist ballerina in New York. I can make myself believe that everyone in the audience has come here to watch me perform tonight, not because it's a tradition of sadistic slave owners, but because they yearn for the emotion of sheer artistry.

I sit at the vanity and watch myself in the mirror, keeping my eyes focused on my reflection as I turn my head slowly to the left and right. I inspect my makeup and hair for imperfections from every angle. When I'm satisfied that I look the best that I possibly can, I sigh and meet my own shrewd blue eyes in the mirror.

I wonder what Ezra sees when he looks at me.

The thought comes from nowhere, yet it seems like such an important question to ask. He looks at me differently than any other boy...

No.

Man.

He looks at me differently than any other man ever has. The thought of it sends my heart into a flurry, racing fast and fluttering. I put my hand over my chest and I can feel the *thump, thump, thump* against my palm.

If he's taken from me tonight, I don't know what I'll—

Stop.

Just stop.

I can't think about it. I narrow my eyes at my reflection, watching the ice freeze over my blue irises with a glassy sheen.

I'm hard as ice.

A glacier as thickly layered as a mountain.

Impenetrable.

At least, that's what I try to convince myself. No one has chiseled away at my icy shell so effectively as Ezra.

I close my eyes and breathe deeply, in and out, slowly, over and over. I have to focus and center myself. I have to allow myself one brief shining moment of anticipation for the thrill of performing for an audience again. I need all my attention on the dance.

Ultimately, the dance is what will decide Ezra's fate for reasons I'll never comprehend. For the sake of tradition, I suppose. For him, I will forget the rest and put everything I am and all that I have into this performance. With my eyes still shut, I review the steps in my mind, going through each count of eight in my imagination with precision.

One. Two. Three. Four. Five. Six. Seven. Eight.

One. Two. Three. Four. Five. Six. Seven. Eight.

When I finish outlining the routine in my mind, prepared for the steps that serve as the skeleton for the performance, I open my eyes. I remember how Ezra taught me what I was missing in my steps, the flesh that fattens the skeleton and makes it into something real and powerful.

Heart.

Emotion.

I need to bring that reckless abandon to the surface, but I'm afraid of losing control. I know Ezra would tell me that losing control is exactly what I need to do, but I'm afraid to do that alone. I'm not sure I can let go on my own. Perhaps it's something I can only do with Ezra.

I need him.

I need to see him, touch him, find the missing piece in him.

I stand and open the door to exit my dressing room. As if I've summoned him with my mind, he's there on the other side of the door, ready in his tan slacks that fit him like skinny jeans, barefoot, his perfect upper body exposed, shirtless.

Ezra.

He's standing, waiting there for me.

The whole world stills for a beat as I try to decide whether to crumble in sudden panic or let my heart take flight on the wings of the butterflies in my stomach.

I don't decide.

I just let the butterflies take control.

He alone is my missing piece.

He opens his arms and I step forward to hug him close.

"You look incredible," he tells me softly against my ear.

He pulls back, holding me by both shoulders and looks me square in the eye. "You ready?"

I can't help but to smile at him. His presence gives me

peace. I'm suddenly so overcome with the pleasant anticipation of performing for an audience again, that I've all but forgotten about the onrushing imminent doom.

How does he do that?

How does he make me feel this way?

I let myself forget the fear for the moment because I'll be forcefully reminded of it again too soon.

Ezra and I walk hand in hand from the dressing room beneath the dance hall, up the black staircase, and to the wings of the stage. Ezra gathers the coarse brown rope that's already coiled in a heap on the floor, waiting and ready to be used. He lifts it from the floor, shaking out the twists and turns, and begins to wrap me with it in the same way we've rehearsed over and over.

Every brush of his fingers over my barely-there leotard is electric, a static spark with every movement. He feels it, too. I know he does. I know the way he twitches with the anticipation, the way he responds to the adrenaline that spiked for the both of us the moment our feet touch the stage.

He's a performer, just as I am.

This is our happiness, however brief.

I spin around to face him as soon as the rope is tied, and bounce through my feet, hopping up and down, warming my muscles and shaking out some of the excess energy.

He smiles at me, brightly and beautifully. Ezra holds up his hands, palms facing me, and I put my hands against his.

I still.

So does he.

He captures me with the intensity of his eyes and my heart stops.

"I've got you," he says and I sigh.

"I know you do."

"We've got this."

"We've got this," I repeat.

He bends, laying his forehead against mine. We both take a deep breath in perfect sync. His touch centers me, realigns the shifting pieces of my broken soul, and with a final deep look into his emerald eyes, I'm ready to dance.

The curtain is drawn shut. The long end of the rope that binds me is draped over the pulley at center stage. Kostya raises its slowly from the wings, up, up, up above our heads. Ezra holds steady at the free end of the rope that dangles from the pulley. The other end comes out from the knot at the middle of my lower back.

Ezra pulls and I rise from the floor.

I pose in my starting position, one arm reaching behind me to grip the length of rope that suspends me as if I'm trying to pull it down, my limbs posed in a way that suggests a fight, a struggle for freedom is about to take place.

In so many ways, it is.

I nod at Ezra, who then nods at Kostya who takes the signal to pull the curtain, revealing us to the audience. As it slowly rises, Ezra pulls hard, ensuring the rope is taut, creating a striking visual angle with he and I at the ends and the pulley at the vertex, far above us, out of sight.

My pulse thrums with the exhilaration of an audience, even if it is filled with such vile creatures as the four families. I've never done a routine like this before, one that is so raw and reckless.

As the haunting melody plays, we begin with theatrics. Ezra has taught me some aerial basics, nothing that would have me starring in any circus shows, but enough to work with the concept of our dance. I struggle, I twist and turn, I climb the rope and spin to a dramatic fall, never for a second doubting that Ezra will hold steady and strong.

The more I struggle and fight against the binds that hold me, the weaker my suppressor becomes. The closer I come to reaching the floor, the weaker he becomes. It's a slow, dramatic fight until finally, my toes touch the stage.

That's when he drops the rope.

I grab it from the floor, dragging it toward me with swiftness, hand over hand, as he reaches and chases after it. When it's all bunched between my hands, he reaches me and stops. There's a beat where his solid frame looms above me, threatening to take back control. This is the beat where I finally break a sweat, though it's not because of the athletic movement—it's from the commitment in his eyes. The rawness that resembles a captor fighting his captive for ultimate power. It's so real, I can feel it in my bones. It fuels me, inspires me for our performance.

This is how we dance.

Push and pull.

Run and chase.

Fight and struggle.

Win and lose.

Ezra and I argued a lot in choreographing and practicing this dance, but there was one thing we both agreed upon without question.

I win.

Ezra's hands are on me for most of the routine. We've made it look as though I'm fighting to break free from his hold, though really his hands hold me steady, keep me balanced as I spin and twirl around him.

When I finally break free from his grip, I run to the corner of the stage, pausing through a dramatic beat to prepare for the next sequence of intricate lifts and turns. I'm about to run after him, on the attack, leap into his arms.

It's a true leap of faith.

If he doesn't do his part, I'll fall.

But I know that he *will* do his part. I trust in that.

I trust in *him*.

I stealthily ensure that the long, dangling end of the rope falls down between my legs and then I run for him. If I don't curl around the rope just right, his arms could tangle in it and restrict him from finishing the lifts. Either one of us could get injured, though worse than that would be the failure of our performance.

His arms spread wide, open to catch me as I run and when I hit my mark, I leap, forward and up, spinning through two quick, vertical rotations in mid-air before his arms close around me. He snatches me into the safety of his embrace just as gravity tugs me back down. The rope has curled perfectly around my leg.

Two counts later, I'm spinning, my head dropping toward the floor as he turns me like the hands of a clock. The moment I'm upside-down, I reach for the floor and roll my body down to meet it, chest, to stomach, to hips, then legs slithering down to the stage. I flip to my back and Ezra reaches underneath me, locking the bend of his elbows beneath my armpits. He drags me backward several steps as I let the pull lift my body from the stage, his steps picking up speed enough to raise me from the floor and he spins both of us.

I arch my back, tightening my torso to position myself properly and as one of his large hands shifts to grip the flesh of my ass, he pushes me upward. I flip as he guides me, throwing my legs backward over my head, rotating my body until I'm perched on his shoulder. I pose there, held gracefully with my hips against his shoulder, arms raised above me before twisting and rolling my body down the front of him, falling perpendicular to the floor.

He catches me just before the stage rises up to meet me, exactly the way we rehearsed. Now that we've nailed the lift, I feel the rush of emotion overwhelm me that we've done it.

There's more to our dance, and we continue spectacularly, but with that one sequence complete, I know we've just defied gravity together.

Even though the routine ends with me on the floor and Ezra reaching one last time for the dangling end of the rope, I'm crawling away, clawing my way out, fighting until the very last, ending how we began, with theatrics.

The music fades into silence.

Deafening silence.

It's just heat and sweat and the sound of our heavy breathing.

What happens now?

My mind swirls with the question, my heavy heartbeat pounding it into my brain with a steady rhythm.

What happens now?

Out of the terror of silence erupts applause. A short breath of relief and I'm brought to life again.

Not only has the familiar, beautiful sound of applause burst from the audience, but I turn my head and see that there's a standing ovation, too.

The four families are giving us a standing ovation.

The four families.

I forget how to breathe.

The four families are here.

The elation of a perfect performance doesn't fade, it falls, drops off a cliff into deep, dark depths.

Ezra is bending, holding out a hand to me to help me rise. I take it and stand slowly. As he leads me toward front and center stage, the applause echoes in my ears until it's completely overwhelming my senses.

I feel like I'm falling.

I squeeze Ezra's hand tighter as my free hand lifts to press over my erratic heart, feeling the *thump, thump, thump* through my fingertips.

We bow together and stand in waiting.

I feel Ezra look at me. I turn to look at him and that's when I feel it crack inside me, the glacier that protects my heart and soul.

It's breaking.

It's melting.

It's falling into a sea of emotions and it threatens to wash me away in a tidal wave of fear.

I rush for Ezra, crashing into him, wrapping my arms around his waist, holding him with all my might. I'm so aware that I'm still being watched. The curtain won't fall. Nikolai will remain seated, in the same spot he always sits, until every last person leaves the theater. He'll come up on stage and he'll take Ezra away from me.

Oh, God.

He can't take him.

Not Ezra.

I press my cheek to Ezra's chest as I squeeze him tighter. "I can't let him take you, I can't. Ezra, I can't. I can't. Don't let him take you."

I hear how frantic I sound, and I don't know where it's coming from. I've always been so strong, I've always been able to keep my dignity, but Ezra's changing me.

He *has* changed me.

His arms cradle me closely. He kisses my hair, then I feel his chin rest on the top of my head.

"It's okay," he says. "It's okay. I've got you."

He always says that and I know, if it were up to him, it would be true. He would have me.

I turn my head to look out into the audience. Our guests, dressed in their finest black-tie worthy attire, are exiting the theater, making their way back to the grand entrance for the reception. The side conversations and quiet chatter appears so normal from the outside.

Nothing about them is normal.

They are the wealthy elite.

Powerful.

Influential.

Buyers and sellers of human lives.

Kings and queens of the underworld.

The forty or so guests drift out from the half-full theater, but, as always, Nikolai remains in his seat, almost as if he's guarding the place where he sits. A dog marking his territory. It's not even the best seat in the house and I've never understood it.

There he sits, regarding the both of us with a look of consideration, a look that says he hasn't made up his mind yet. I tense as I get caught in Nikolai's stare and now we are connected, though I don't want to be. I feel like I have no choice but to keep my eyes steadily on his as everything and everyone else moves around us, but we three remain still.

Finally, the theater clears, and Nikolai rises to his feet. He buttons his jacket and tugs at his sleeves, adjusting his cufflinks. He looks severe in his sharp black suit. I'm sure any normal woman would find his appearance attractive tonight.

They say the Devil can charm, after all.

Nikolai runs a hand down his front to smooth out the lapels and steps out into the aisleway. Then he walks, step by careful step, over the red carpet. Coming to the end of the aisle, he turns and walks the curve along the front of the stage. My heart is ready to burst out of my chest.

It hurts.

He walks up the five steps on the side of the stage and I spin around to face him, putting my back to Ezra, putting myself between the man I'm falling for and the man who might take him from me.

Every one of Nikolai's steps resonate within me, vibrating through my muscles, aching in my bones. When Nikolai comes to a stop just in front of us, looking like the Devil himself and playing God with our lives and freedom, I hold my breath.

He exhales, tilts his head, regards us again with consideration.

Then, a nod. A simple nod.

"That performance was nothing like I expected it to be."

What does that mean?

"It was *so* much more." He claps once and grins. "Brilliant! Both of you."

Both of my hands come up to cover my mouth from the shock of his words.

I don't know what this means.

I didn't expect this reaction from him. The unexpected is nearly more panic inducing than the expected horrors I've grown accustomed to.

I don't know what this means.

That fresh panic rips through me, tearing apart my rehearsed calm and lighting a fire to an unhinged part of me I thought had died three years ago.

I throw my arms down to my sides and step forward. "You will *not* take him from me, Nikolai Mikhailov. You've taken my life, my freedom, all the best parts of me. But I won't let you take him."

He cocks his head and smiles at me, licking his lips before he says, "Come here, *rabynya.*"

My breaths quicken, but I inhale slowly to try to steady them. I can't let him see my fear, though it's there.

It's there in spades.

I step forward, one, two, three steps and I'm less than a foot in front of him. Though I would normally bow my head this close to him, I lift my chin instead.

Yes, Ezra has changed me, and I'll be damned if I'm going to lose him now. I'll go with him if Nikolai wishes to take him from me, make us both slaves to a crueler master or give us death.

"I'm going to let that outburst slide, for one reason and one reason only..." Nikolai's hands reach for my neck, sliding up either side to hold my face firmly at the jawline, "you were stunning tonight. You danced more beautifully tonight than you ever have."

He bends, pressing a soft, chaste kiss to my lips. I'm frozen in stunned silence, confused beyond belief. When Nikolai speaks again, he keeps his lips close to mine and holds my attention with his gray eyes.

"I'm going to let you keep your pet, Anya. I like that he's brought your light back, your fire. You've been so cold with me and I much prefer your warmth. So, I'll let him stay, allow him to spark that fire in you so long as he keeps it burning. But you know that if you cross a line with him, I will know. If you fuck him, I will know. You are *my* belonging and I choose what you do with your body," he lifts his head, his eyes leaving mine and he looks beyond me, over my shoulder, "and yours, *mal'chik.* Do you both understand me?"

I swallow hard and somehow manage a quick nod. "Yes. *Da, khozyain.*"

"And you?" he says to Ezra over my shoulder.

I press my eyes shut, so fearful that a sarcastic comment will shoot from between Ezra's lips

He clears his throat. "Yes. I understand."

Nikolai bares his teeth, tilting his head, squeezing my jaw too tightly. "I understand…what, *mal'chik?*"

I hold my breath for Ezra's response.

"I understand. *Master.*"

My eyes flutter shut and my shoulders relax, so thankful Ezra understands, so thankful he's behaved, so thankful that Nikolai hasn't torn him from me.

"Come, *mal'chik*. Kneel beside Anya. Show us your obedience."

Please, Ezra, please.

I feel him approach almost immediately and his heat is comforting. I see him beside me as I turn my eyes to look and Nikolai does the same. I hear him huff out a rough, agitated breath, but he lowers to his knees all the same.

"Good, *mal'chik*," Nikolai says.

His tongue runs across his bottom lip and his eyes narrow in a look I've only come to know as wanting. Only Nikolai isn't directing that look at me…he's looking at Ezra.

For today we are safe. But now I fear that the interactions to come will be more brutal, more terrifying than ever before.

Because they're going to involve Ezra more and more.

My mind is spinning, wondering if everything I thought I knew was wrong. Maybe stealing my partners from me was never about punishing me at all. Maybe it was about finding the right fit to satisfy all his needs.

I shake my head against Nikolai's grip on me, but he squeezes me, forcing me to still, forcing me to give him my complete attention.

"You have twenty minutes," Nikolai says. "Get cleaned up, get dressed, and come find me. Both of you. I expect you to remain at my side throughout the reception. After, you will have the evening to yourselves to celebrate your successful performance while I discuss business with my colleagues." He steps closer, invading my space. "Remember who you belong to. Don't make me regret giving you that freedom. If you do, I assure that both of you will have regrets of your own."

Finally, he releases me and strides away.

I burst into tears.

I'm still half-panicked, yet half-relieved.

I'm happy yet horrified.

I have no idea what just happened or why. I know I should count my blessings and be thankful that Ezra is still here beside me. Yet I can't fight the nagging feeling that something so much worse than losing Ezra is to come.

CHAPTER 22

Anya

STANDING IN FRONT of my wardrobe, I struggle to select my dress for the reception—a black-tie affair. Nikolai placed two gowns in my wardrobe to choose from for this evening.

One black.

One bright fuchsia.

He always does this. He always gives me two gowns to choose from. One was always black as night, the other bright as day.

I always chose black before.

Everything around me was black when Nikolai tormented me by stealing away my partners. Men I had grown to trust, men I had developed friendships and connections with, only to have them ripped away for no good reason other than Nikolai's incessant dissatisfaction.

There's an itch of confusion in my mind that I can't quite seem to scratch.

What was different about this performance?

Is it Ezra?

What will Nikolai do with us now that he has us both?

Will he hurt Ezra in all the ways he's hurt me?

I cross my wrists over my chest, rubbing my hands on my upper arms, adding friction to ease the chill from the foreboding shiver that refuses to let me feel okay about anything.

It all feels so wrong.

It still feels like Nikolai is going to tear Ezra from me at any moment. I know he could if he wanted to. That's all it takes with him, a simple choice and the Earth shifts beneath my feet.

I'm still standing here, staring at the two gowns as I hear a knock at the door. I know it's not Nikolai because he doesn't knock. I know it's Ezra and not Kostya alone when I hear the knock continue unnecessarily, tapping out a jaunty rhythm against the wood. It makes me smile and for that moment, I'm able to let relief wash over me that he's still alive, he's still here, and he's still mine.

I go to the door and pull it open. Ezra stands in front of me, slick and smooth in his black tuxedo, vest, and tie. The sandy blond hair that's longer on the top of his head is slicked back, styled impeccably, and his grin threatens to split his beautiful face in half.

He looks down at me and his eyes widen. "Something's missing."

My dress is missing.

I've just opened the door in my underwear and strapless bra. Not that I have any shame for being exposed in this nightmare manor. Ezra has had the misfortune of seeing me every which way from Sunday by force rather than by choice. I just hate that it's become so normal that I hardly notice it anymore when I'm bare and exposed.

"I don't know which dress to wear," I say, taking a step back.

He steps inside the room and I push the door closed behind him. Kostya is in the hallway, lurking as always, and though I used to care enough to leave the door open, *always* open, I've lost my will to try to appease Nikolai. He won't care tonight, anyway. The four families are here for the quarterly business report, so aside from the reception, he'll be otherwise occupied.

In the past, I'd spend that time crying alone in my room, grieving the loss of another partner, wallowing in my misery, pleading desperately with gods, angels, with the universe itself to take me into death along with them. With Ezra still here, the first of my partners to survive past the performance, I don't know what we will do with our time tonight.

My breath catches in my throat when it hits me that Ezra and I have time together.

Uninterrupted time.

Tonight.

"Show me what you've got," he says after I've closed the door.

My head snaps up to look at him after being so lost in thought. "What?"

"Show me the dresses. I'll help you choose."

He swallows and his eyes drift, skating over the curves of my body. That hungry look of a man in lust should set off warning bells inside me, but it doesn't with him. It clenches low and deep, and I find that I don't mind it all that much.

I might even like it.

I might even crave more of it.

I walk over to the wardrobe and grab the bottom of each gown, pulling on them so they swing out by the hanger.

"I've always worn black."

"So, wear black."

"It doesn't feel right."

"So, wear pink."

"It doesn't feel right, either."

He holds out his hands. "Okay, I'm at a loss here."

"Why are you in such a good mood?" I narrow my eyes at him, unintentionally short with him.

His forehead wrinkles as if he's confused by my question. "Because I'm not dead, Anya."

Because he's not dead.

He's not dead and he's not gone.

I exhale, slowly releasing the pettiness of such an insignificant decision as the color of my dress.

It doesn't matter.

All that matters is that we've performed, we've completed our task, I'm alive, he's alive, and we're both here, together in my room with the door shut.

We look at each other.

We breathe in at the same time.

We move at the same time.

He opens his arms for me, and I give him my body to fill them. I think he expects me to wrap my arms around his waist and hold him, but I need something more, a greater connection.

I grab his cheeks in both my hands and pull his face down to meet my lips. I rise onto my toes to press my mouth harder to his, but then he bends, pressing back, pushing me down to my flat feet. He steps forward and I step backward with him until I collide with the open door of the wardrobe, slamming it shut as he kisses me with force.

His body arches forward into mine, molding with me, as if he could move right through me. When a groan escapes through his lips—a guttural sound of need from deep within him—I feel it rattle inside me, shaking my core.

My hands slip around to the back of his neck, my fingers lacing together and holding him too tightly. I sigh into his mouth, a whisper of a plea to give me more of everything. His tongue licks mine, swirling deeper inside my mouth, tasting me with ferocity that makes dampness pool between my legs.

His hands slam against the wardrobe on either side of my head with a thud that makes my heart leap. I feel his body tremble along mine as he uses the leverage to force himself to stop.

As quickly as the kiss began, it ends. Ezra pulls his head back, though his body still pins mine to the wardrobe door.

"I'm sorry, I don't mean to be so...insistent."

"Don't apologize," I pant, putting a hand on his chest. "You don't have to stop."

He smiles, but it almost looks sad. He lets his forehead fall to rest against mine.

"When we took our final bow, I looked at you and I thought...I thought, what if this is the last time I ever get to look at her?"

"Ezra." I sigh and my body rolls forward, curling into him.

"I know I should be fearful," he goes on, "I know we're still in a shit situation, we're still slaves, I *know* all that. But fuck, Anya, I'm so grateful to be alive, to have even just one more day with you."

I feel his sincerity in my gut, and it warms me from the inside. He melts me in ways no one else ever could. Ezra is my sunshine after the snowstorm in my soul, a springtime thaw that makes the ice inside me a heavy puddle rushing desire through my veins.

My words rush out of me and I don't regret them. "I love you."

He answers me with a happy sigh. "I love you," he whispers as he places a soft kiss to my lips.

"Mine?"

"Yours."

My hands fall to his hips and now all I can think about is touching him and being touched by him. I want to feel him, keep him close, live in the reality that Ezra is still here with me.

Alive and mine.

Mine.

His hips rock forward. There's a brief flash of fear through the logical part of my brain, the part of me that fears the motivations of sexual touch. But that fear dissipates swiftly as my heart kick-starts, pulsing fire throughout my entire body, effectively shutting off the rational thought that tells me to be careful.

I pant, grinding my hips forward to meet his as I realize just how much I want him.

I need him.

I need him so much it makes me feel desperate and that scares me.

I'm almost thankful when Kostya raps loudly on the closed door to my bedroom and yells, "Five minutes."

Ezra jumps back, shaken from the reverie of being mine, and blows out a heavy breath, linking his fingers together on the top of his head.

He grins at me still standing there in my underwear and my knees go weak.

"Pink," he says with a playful look in his eyes. "Wear the pink dress. It'll go with your cheeks."

I touch my fingertips to my cheek and it's warm, surely flushed as warm as the deep fuchsia of the gown inside my wardrobe. I smile back at him and probably turn magenta for the way the heat inside me prickles like fire sparking beneath my skin.

His hands drop as I open the wardrobe to pull out the

dress. I unzip it and push my arms through the bottom of it, shimmying it down my body. The style hugs my curves almost precisely. I shake it into place and turn my head over my shoulder.

"Zip me?" I say to Ezra.

He steps up behind me and I feel his heat. His fingertips tickle my skin as he pulls the zipper up slowly.

The mermaid style dress is tight over my body until it hits my knees. There, it fans out around me, fading into a chiffon sort of fabric that layers to create the mermaid effect.

The thick straps hang intentionally off the shoulders, sweeping an elegant line across my chest, dipping into a sweetheart neckline between my breasts. I wouldn't normally have much in the way of cleavage, except for the way this dress presses everything together so tightly.

I spin to face Ezra and he gives me a once over.

"Perfect," he says, and I feel like the most wanted woman in the world for the way he stares at me with those emerald eyes.

I hurry into my shoes and take a quick look in the mirror, making sure I look perfect per Nikolai's scrutinizing standards. I place one hand over my stomach and take a deep breath, knowing that Ezra is about to see just how deep into the underworld he's been taken.

CHAPTER 23
Ezra

EYES ARE ON us as soon as we begin our descent down the grand staircase. We walk hand in hand down the marble steps, following Kostya, who leads us to the reception. There's no applause or appreciative welcome.

Just eyes.

Eerie, watching eyes amidst the quiet chatter.

It makes me feel agitated, uneasy, but I try not to care too much. I'm fucking alive and I'm still with Anya and happy for that much. I expected to be dead by now, or at the very least, on my way to a new owner without her.

I don't know how I would survive separation from my blue-eyed girl. I love her. And now that I know she loves me, too, I've vowed to myself to find a way to save us both, come hell or high water.

I lean over to her, "Did you go to your high school prom?"

She turns her head to glance at me with confusion before looking back down at the steps she treads carefully in her high-heeled shoes.

"What?" she asks.

"Prom. Did you go?"

"No," I see a hint of a smile tugging at her lips, "I had a

dress rehearsal that night. Why?"

I grin. "Figures. You were probably too cool for prom, weren't you?"

There's her smile. "And I would've been too cool for you."

I put my free hand over my heart, feigning ache. "Ouch. I'll try not to take that personally. Though it's probably true."

"Mm-hmm." She's still smiling.

"If we'd gone to school together, taking you to prom would've been a highlight for me. I'd consider myself a damn lucky man to be the arm candy for a girl that looks so hot all dressed up like this."

She looks over at me as we reach the landing. "You should consider yourself a damn lucky man to be my arm candy for this."

She meant it to be light-hearted, but she looks sad immediately after she says it.

I let go of her hand and place mine on the small of her back, leaning over to whisper close to her ear in reassurance, "I do."

She looks up at me and our eyes meet and it's soul-searing. I don't want to look away. What I want to do is kiss her. But I feel the oppressive cold of a deep winter freeze swirl around us both as Nikolai approaches. I straighten but keep my hand on the small of her back, stepping a little closer because I'm feeling fiercely protective.

"Come with me, you'll greet my colleagues with grace or suffer the consequences later," Nikolai says, looking at me when he says it.

He holds out his arm, expecting Anya to take it and fuck, if that doesn't make my blood boil. I don't want to take my hands off her. I want to keep her close. I don't know anything about these people other than the fact that they are a part of some sick slave trafficking empire. That alone makes them beyond dangerous. Because we are slaves to them, I don't know what to expect here. I don't know how we'll be treated. I don't know whether Nikolai will let them touch Anya or hurt her.

I know he shared her once with a Vittori.

Will he do it again?

The thought of it sends tension right through my shoulders and threatens to spark an adrenaline rush. But then Anya looks at me, granting me a small smile and a nod—a look that tells me we're okay right now—and I trust her. Against all reason, I trust her instinctively and it calms me. She steps forward, away from me, and slips her arm in Nikolai's.

Anya is so graceful and confident and so fucking strong I could nearly cry just watching her walk the way she does with her head held high through her pain and suffering.

I follow behind as Nikolai takes us to stand at a high table without chairs, draped in an elegant gold tablecloth that reaches all the way to the floor. A cocktail waitress walks past, as if this were some ordinary rich people party, and I wonder who she is and whether she's a slave, too.

Nikolai grabs two glasses of champagne from her tray as she walks by and she flinches as he moves, her face twitching with telltale signs of fear as she tries to remain calm and composed. Nikolai doesn't seem to notice or care and brings us the glasses as the poor girl walks away.

He sets one down in front of me and the other in front of Anya.

"Drink," he says. "Enjoy yourselves. You've done well. Tonight, you may celebrate that."

Anya lifts her glass and throws it back without hesitation. I see the tension written all over her face and I don't blame her a bit for taking the alcohol for what it is, a way to escape the reality of our situation.

I smile at her as she finishes her glass and sets it down on the table, then I drink from my own. But I'm taking it slow.

I want to be alert.

I want to be aware.

I want to be able to fight for her if some weird slave empire shit goes down.

What the fuck is this life?

Anya's eyes go wide as she looks beyond my back. At first, she looks as though she's going to retreat and hide somewhere inside her mind, but then she pulls her shoulders back, lifts her chin, brings coldness to the surface in the way she does to protect herself.

I glance over my shoulder to see what she's seeing. There's a man and a woman approaching us. They share bronzed complexions, though the woman is fairer toned with dark, jet-black hair, and dark eyes. They both have an aura that pulses severe and dangerous, like monarchs of an evil empire.

Nikolai steps out to greet the man with a handshake, the woman with a kiss to her knuckles. I want to gag over the formalities and forced politeness between slave traders.

These people are fucking sick.

Nikolai holds his arm out toward Anya, beckoning her to come to his side. I freeze watching them. She's stiffened and my hackles are up. I'm ready to pounce at the way she regards the man with fear and contempt.

"You remember Anya," Nikolai says to them as she steps into his side, his arm wrapping around her waist.

"Of course," the woman says, stepping forward to kiss Anya on the cheek. "You were lovely tonight."

Anya forces a cold smile. "Thank you."

The man rakes his eyes over Anya appraisingly.

That man is bad news.

I know it immediately.

The woman looks at me and steps closer as she speaks to Nikolai, "You've decided to keep the partner this time, I see." She smiles at me. "Wise choice, Nikolai. He is quite stunning."

I narrow my eyes at her.

"Renata Vittori," the woman introduces herself to me and I hear the accent more clearly now in her name.

Spanish? No, Italian.

She looks to be about Nikolai's age, though she's as stunningly fit as a twenty-something. She stands out from the crowd in her ivory-colored romper where all the other women wear gowns. The wide pant legs give the appearance of a gown, though, with the way they sweep together, and the V-neck cuts all the way down between her breasts. Her long, black hair tumbles in waves over her shoulders and she's tall, taller than me with her stilettos on. She's an attractive woman, oozing power, though the vileness of her intentions pulses evil.

She holds out her hand, but not for me to shake. Her fingers are curled down, knuckles presented, as if she expects me to kiss her hand the way Nikolai did.

Should I bow at your feet, dear queen of the underworld?

I swear, these fuckers.

I do what I have to do to keep the peace and keep Anya safe. I don't want to get kicked out of the party and leave her alone with these jackals. I take Renata's hand and bend to kiss her knuckles.

Wait.

Vittori.

Is that the man who…

Just as I lift my head, I see Nikolai pushing Anya toward the man. He snatches her by the wrist and drags her toward him, pulling her into a hug that's anything but friendly. Her arms dangle behind her back as she tries to avoid giving any sense that this is welcome. I see the goosebumps forming on her arms, the tremble of her hanging limbs. He kisses her cheek then releases her and she steps back immediately.

"Ezra," I'm thankful that Nikolai says my name to pull me out of my onrushing murderous rage, "this is Vigo. Head of House for the Vittori family."

I lift my head in acknowledgment but give him no more. I know now that this is the man Nikolai used Anya for as payment. This is the sick fuck he shared her with, nearly ruined her with. My hands shake with rage that threatens to explode through my fingertips.

It takes everything I've got to reign myself in, to pretend I'm an obedient and civilized slave, to stop myself from launching at him and ripping the crooked smile from his face with my bare hands.

"I don't know why you keep pretending, Nikolai. We all know about your tendencies. You should sell this one off." Vigo nods toward my blue-eyed girl and I want to strangle him. "Keep the boy for yourself. We all know that's what you really want."

Nikolai swallows and I've never seen such perfectly controlled rage. Whenever I've seen that pointed look of anger wash over his features in the past, he's taken it out full force on Anya without restraint. The same look is there now, but he controls it. Which tells me he *can*, yet he chooses not to with my girl. He *chooses* to hurt her.

"With all due respect, Vigo, I tire of your commentary on my slave choices. Perhaps you should be more concerned with your own." Nikolai looks pointedly toward a young woman I hadn't noticed before standing behind Vigo. "She looks as though she's about to faint from malnourishment. Do you care for her at all?"

He's not wrong. The young woman standing behind him with the long, blond hair wobbles, though she stands still, as though she's near fainting from exhaustion or hunger or ailment. She has dark circles under her eyes that she's tried to hide with makeup, but it only emphasizes how swollen they are from tiredness.

She's thin, too thin in her red, satin gown. A dress like that should cling to a woman's curves, but the poor girl has been flattened out, as if all the fat in her body has been sucked out with a vacuum. The girl is not well.

Vigo laughs. "I take care of myself, Nikolai. She is present to take care of me and my needs. Or have you forgotten what a slave is for?"

"I prefer my slaves to be strong enough to care for my needs. It just goes to show some people don't know how to properly break them in. Besides, she's talentless, Vigo. Her skills as a pianist are mediocre at best. You may as well have brought along one of your broken dolls in her stead. She's worth no more than any of them. You choose poorly and you train poorly."

"And I suppose you believe your Anya is worth more? A slave is a slave, Nikolai. They all become broken dolls in the end."

"As I recall it, *Vigo*," Nikolai practically spits out his name, "you rather enjoyed your time with my Anya at the third quarter meeting. We both know she's worth far more than you're willing to admit."

Anya steps sideways and bumps into the table. It lets out a sharp screech as the metal pedestal scrapes along the marble floor. I grab the edge of it as it moves toward me and settle it. She looks over at me and I catch her eyes, giving her a small smile and a nod of encouragement that says *I've got you.*

She swallows, her blue eyes telling me how fearful she

is, though I doubt anyone else can see it. She knows how to hide her fear behind the icy blue glaciers that keep her soul concealed.

"I did enjoy her," Vigo admits with a tilt of his head. "I suppose she does have a certain quality about her, doesn't she? Behaves as though she's broken, though it's clear she's not. I can imagine paying a rather large sum to be the man to watch that last bit of light fade from her eyes. It will happen one day. All little dolls break in the end."

Nikolai looks far away, far beyond Vigo. "Anya can't be broken."

"Perhaps I should purchase her from you. Prove you wrong."

"To what end, Vigo?"

Nikolai looks bored with this conversation, though the expression seems forced. He snakes his arm around my girl's tiny waist, lassoing her tight to his side.

A hand suddenly lands on my back and makes me jump. I look over to see it belongs to Renata. I shrug my shoulder to shake her off, but Anya catches my eye and subtly shakes her head.

"Oh, come now, Nikolai. I'm sure you've grown bored of Anya by now. Especially now that you've found the perfect boy for your secret fantasies, hmm?"

Anya's head bows and I see how quickly her chest rises and falls. She's upset, of course she is, this entire exchange is the stuff of nightmares.

Nikolai looks down at my blue-eyed girl. "Bored isn't the appropriate term." He regards her with some sort of twisted longing that I've never understood.

"Then what is?" Vigo asks.

Nikolai looks pointedly at him. "Exasperated."

"Well," Vigo begins with a crooked smile, "when

exasperation turns to boredom, give me a call."

"You try too hard."

"What will you do with her when she can no longer dance?"

"I will have no use for her then," he says it so coldly, so plainly, that I believe him.

"Consider that. I'll happily take your scrap now that you have a new model." Vigo glances at me.

"Boys, enough of this," Renata finally speaks. "Nikolai has finally given us the performance he's been wanting for so long. Let's celebrate that before we speak about business. This is highly undignified."

As she finishes her sentence, a young man approaches, handing her a glass of red wine. She gives him a smile of gratitude, flipping her long hair over her shoulder, and he leans in to kiss the side of her neck before moving to stand behind her.

He bows his head in servitude, but can only bow so far because a black leather collar is latched around his throat. His thick, dark hair is shaggy, unkempt in an intentional sort of way that makes him look younger than he probably is. He stands complacent, looking practically content. It's clear he's a slave, though he doesn't seem extraordinarily bothered by his circumstance.

"My apologies, Renata," Nikolai says. "As I've always said, you'd make a far more dignified Head of House than your tiresome brother."

Vigo laughs humorlessly, clapping Nikolai on the shoulder. "Let's be glad she isn't. She'd outsell your family in no time at all. She's far more ruthless than I am in her asset accrual. Then again, it's not all that difficult to outsell your family. Hardly a family anymore, is it? Quite the burden to carry it all alone."

Nikolai looks suddenly haunted, almost…human.

"Vigo," Renata chastises him, "let's not bring that up." She tilts her head with a sympathetic look at Nikolai. "I'm so sorry."

Coldness settles over him again. "It's no concern of yours, Renata. I've made a settlement with the Americans to rectify their error in judgment. I'm grateful to your brother for providing me with the evidence needed to seek justice. There is a rather large sum to be paid in reparations."

"I hope it's not purely monetary."

"Money could never be justice enough for what was done to my family."

Renata smiles, almost hopeful. The two gracefully bow out, the small, malnourished blond and the collared boy following behind them. The girl glances back at Anya and me with a look that almost resembles jealousy.

As if anyone could be jealous of our circumstances.

Unless…her circumstances are that much worse than ours.

And the man who *makes* them worse has his sight set on my blue-eyed girl.

CHAPTER 24

Anya

THE FOUR FAMILIES and their slaves traverse the steps of the grand staircase at the end of the reception. The slaves will all be shackled in the guest rooms with the same style of chain Nikolai used to chain me in my early months with him, the same chain we shackled Ezra with and all my partners before him. Then, they'll be heading to the boardroom on the third floor of the manor. It's a room that's off-limits to slaves. It's reserved only for the four families to use annually when it's Nikolai's turn to host the quarterly meeting.

Ezra and I remain with Nikolai at the bottom of the grand staircase as the guests file out. I count my heartbeats like dance steps as it thuds against my ribcage, wondering what will happen now, hoping against hope that Nikolai will be kind and grant us a reprieve tonight like he promised he would.

"You've both pleased me this evening," Nikolai says, tension clear in his voice and the way he holds his shoulders. "My colleagues are impressed by both your talent and your obedience." He looks at Ezra. "You've done especially well in dulling your impulsivity. I'll give credit to Anya for her training with you."

I exchange a glance with Ezra. He smiles through his eyes,

and though Nikolai can't see it, I can. It makes the corner of my mouth tug upward, threatening a smile I shouldn't wear in front of my master.

"I require Kostya's assistance in the boardroom tonight. This meeting is of special importance to me, and I need to focus my attention on that." He sighs. "This is probably against my better judgment, but the both of you are free for the evening. You will remain indoors. You may go wherever you like within the manor."

He takes a step toward us. "Stay *off* the third floor of the west wing where the guests and their slaves are staying. If I so much as smell the scent of you up there when I walk through later," he reaches forward and snatches my wrist with one hand, holding it up between us as he taps the top of my pinky finger with his other hand, "I will cut off your little fingers myself. Both of you. You will be quiet. You will be civilized if you run into any of our guests. Do you think you can handle yourselves?"

"*Da, khozyain,*" I say.

"Yes, Master," Ezra follows suit, though I can hear the eye roll in his tone.

I think Nikolai hears it, too. He tugs me forward by the wrist and jerks me roughly against his chest. He bends to kiss me, forcing me to open my lips to let his impatient tongue slip inside. Against my wishes, I kiss him back. Not because I want to, but because I know he demands it.

But it's strange.

The kiss is weak where it's usually strong and demanding. He releases me, looks me over with a quick flick of his eyes, a cursory glance, and then he's gone.

Nikolai strides up the grand staircase, lonely master of the manor. I almost feel sorry for him, but I don't know why because I've never felt that before. Maybe it was something in the way he kissed me, with intention but without expectation.

The fleeting moment of empathy slips from my mind swiftly. Ezra and I are left alone, watching him walk away, knowing he'll be occupied, Kostya will be with him, and we will be free together for the evening.

As free as we can be inside the home of our master with no way to escape.

Ezra looks at me and grins the widest, whitest, most perfect grin I've ever seen, and it draws some long-lost need for joy from deep within me. My heart skips a beat as Nikolai rounds the corner at the top of the staircase, the last person in the manor to disappear from our sight.

I remain still as the chatter from above fades and dissolves. I don't know what to do with myself now, but I don't have to wonder for long.

Ezra grabs my hand and we lock our fingers together as he drags me away toward the dance studio. He walks so fast and his strides are so long that I nearly have to jog to keep up with him, which is next to impossible in these heels.

"Wait," I tell him.

I pull back on his hand to free mine from his grip and stop dead in my tracks. I bend, rustling up the chiffon layers of the fanned out bottom portion of my mermaid-style gown, and wrestle with the straps of my shoes. I struggle to reach around and beneath the layers, but Ezra has already anticipated my need.

He kneels on one knee in front of me and reaches out to free me from my shoes. I put one hand on his strong shoulder to steady myself as he pulls off the first shoe, admiring the natural golden tones of his sandy blonde hair.

"I think Prince Charming is supposed to be putting the shoe *on* Cinderella's foot, not taking it off," he says with a smile, "but this is cool, too."

I bite the corner of my lip to hold back a bursting grin. "Are you comparing me to Cinderella or you to Prince Charming?"

"Both," he lifts his head to look up at me after he pulls off the other shoe and dazzles me with a pure white, sparkling smile, "obviously."

"Obviously."

He gets to his feet and holds out my shoes, which I take in my left hand as he grabs my right. We're off again, fast walking, smiling, nearly giggling like teenagers as we make our way to the dance studio.

It's as if I'm young again, home alone for the first time, my mother having decided I'm finally responsible enough to be left on my own in a big empty house.

Only I've snuck in a boy.

Ezra pulls me into the dance studio, and closes the door behind us, only he forgets to turn on the lights at first. It's dark, save for the moonlight that shines in from the high windows near the ceiling. The light reflects off the shine of the hardwood floor, flickering in a soft dance as the edge of a cloud obscures the rays.

"Turn on the lights," I whisper to him.

Alone in my favorite room at the edge of night, it feels sacred in the dark.

"Come dance with me in the moonlight," he whispers back.

I whip around because his voice is behind me. I see the outline of him moving toward the center of the room.

Wings flutter senselessly in my belly and I sigh, letting my eyes fall shut for a few blissful moments of peace, relishing the sheer joy of anticipating something good, something wanted.

I open my eyes and move toward his dark figure in the center of the room. His hand is there to meet mine as I reach out to him and he pulls me into his embrace. I throw my hands around the back of his neck, assuming the standard slow dance position of all awkward young teens falling in love at a school dance.

I don't need the lights on in this space at all. Not when I have Ezra. He is my eternal sunshine, my life force, my renewal. He refreshes my soul and makes me believe things I shouldn't. He gives me hope I don't deserve to have. He makes me want to fight again.

We sway together without music. After minutes of silence, Ezra's hands on the small of my back pull me closer until we're simply hugging one another.

"Let's say, for theory's sake, that tonight is our last chance to be free, to be together like this…" His voice is quiet, almost sad, and that alone threatens to break me. "How would you want to spend it?"

I swallow, tilting my chin up to look at him, though his face is awash with shadow. "I don't know how to answer that," I tell him honestly.

He smirks. "Oh, come on. I'm sure you've dreamed of what you would want to do if you ever got me alone."

He's being his usual charming self, flirting with me. But my response to that isn't light and teasing. It's hard hitting honesty that has to come out.

"I dream of it all the time, Ezra."

The sway stills as his emerald eyes shift along the lines of my face. The moonlight paints a bright strip right across them, as even the light is drawn to his bewitching green gaze.

"This is all I have ever wanted," I tell him in a hushed tone, "to love and be loved. To be cherished for my soul, not for my talent or my monetary worth. I think you see me."

His eyes hood, a wrinkle creasing his brow. "I do see you." He bends to press his forehead against mine. "If giving up my freedom is the price I have to pay to be yours, then I will pay it.

I don't regret a thing if it means I'm yours."

My face tenses against the beautiful soul ache, unaccustomed to these feelings of joy and wanting.

Boundless wanting.

"You're mine," I remind him—remind myself.

"I'm yours," he says, and our lips collide.

I drift against his body as his arms tighten around me. We breathe heavy through our noses, saving our mouths for the only thing they were meant for.

I feel it now.

Our mouths were made for kissing, and only for kissing each other.

My hands creep up the sides of his neck as he tilts his head, deepening our kiss. I want him against something, the wall, the floor, the piano, I don't care. I just want to press into him as closely as I possibly can and savor the sweet, sweet flavor of temporary freedom we've been granted.

Ezra must be able to read my thoughts through my moans. He moves, walking me backward until I press against the mirror that lines the wall and I know we're out of range from the security camera now. The freedom in knowing that strips away the last layer of reservation. There's no caution in this kiss now, no hesitation or fear for whether we will be found. As that realization washes over me, it bathes me in heat that melts my core.

His lips fall to my neck and he kisses me everywhere, down the sides, along my collarbone, across my jaw line. I'm breathing heavily and my hips thrust forward of their own will as my back arches, succumbing to the gravity of him.

"I'm sorry," he huffs out between hot kisses, "if I'm too rough."

I chuckle and the sound of it is hoarse, wanting. "Too rough?"

With my body molded to his, I push back and spin us both, shoving him against the mirror instead. I reach between us to unbutton his jacket and pull out his tucked in dress shirt. I slip my hands beneath the hem and feel him, really feel him for the first time.

I trace the outline of his firm stomach with my fingers. His skin is warm to touch, soft but tautly stretched over his carefully developed abdominal muscles. I can feel him flex and jolt at my touch.

"Jesus," he mutters, "I want you, Anya."

His tone is lustfully deep, sinful and sweet. The sound of it pulls at my heart but also sends a sharp bolt of desire straight through to my core, clenching low in my belly.

I pause, looking up at him. "I want you, too."

Removing my hands from beneath his shirt, I lift to my toes, holding my hands against his strong jawline and pressing the softest, most delicate, most meaningful kiss I've ever given to his soft, full lips.

My mouth brushes his as I speak in a hushed tone, "Make love to me tonight."

His eyes narrow as his head nods. "Just tell me where, tell me how you want me, and I'm yours."

I take his hand and pull him out of the dance studio, intent on taking him to any one of the random bedrooms in the manor that's not currently occupied by a guest or their slave. We leave the dance studio and practically dance down the hallway, through the grand entrance, up the stairwell, then we stop on the landing.

"I want to be in your bed." He steps closer. "I want to give you a good memory to hold onto in your room at night in case he doesn't..."

In case he doesn't keep us both here, together.

In case one of us doesn't survive.

As morbid as the train of thought is, it's reasonable. I don't have to think about it. As soon as the words come out of his mouth, I know I want that, too. I want to take him to my room, be with him in my bed. No matter what happens to us after tonight, I can always close my eyes at night and think about something good that happened there.

I can have the smell of him on my pillow.

A pleasant shudder rolls down my spine.

I nod. "Okay."

"Okay." He takes my hand and we walk together toward my bedroom.

We make the trip in silence, entering my room quietly, shutting the door behind us. The space between us is still heated, still full of need, but there's a twinge of awkwardness now that we're here, standing in the truth that something delicate and precious and meaningful is about to happen.

My heart beats for this moment, awkwardness included. It all feels so normal, so natural. The anticipation of being with someone for the first time, the curiosity over what it will be like, the subtle worry that it might not be everything you expect it to be, but knowing it could be so much greater than you ever imagined.

I've ached for this kind of normalcy for years and Ezra has given it to me. I'll be forever grateful to him for that.

Eager to have his hands on me again, I turn my back to him and glance over my shoulder. "Unzip me?"

I feel his heat swirl around me as he moves closer, sweeping me up in a summer storm. His fingers tickle my skin as he pulls the zipper down slowly. He steps in closer as I nudge the dress to fall off me to the floor, his hands falling against my sides, his lips pressing to my neck.

I moan from the softness of him, the gentle coaxing. Though I suppose he's no more or less gentle with me than Nikolai. Nikolai knew how to touch softly, how to intrigue me, how to tease my body into wanting things my heart didn't want.

But Ezra is my choice.

He could lay rough hands on me and it would still feel good because I chose it.

He's my choice.

This is my choice.

"This is my choice," I whisper, not meaning to say it out loud.

I nearly want to cry for how good that feels.

Ezra's hands still, his kissing stops. "Do you want me to stop?"

I feel the tension he holds pulse through the palms of his hands, yet he controls it.

He controls it because he's not Nikolai.

He cares about me.

He cares about what I want.

Still, I have to ask, "If I told you I didn't want to do this tonight..."

"We don't have to do anything you don't want to. I just want to be with you."

His voice sounds so sad, I can hardly bear it.

I spin to face him and his hands fall away. I reach behind me and unhook my strapless bra. I let it fall to the floor and stand in front of him, topless, exposed, waiting.

My breath catches in my chest and my heart skips a beat to see the way he looks at me. He desires me, there is no doubt about that, but it's so much more. There's a certain curiosity in his expression, the face of an explorer coming upon new land.

"I don't want you to stop, Ezra. And I don't want you to ask me again." I step toward him. "I don't need you to be careful or gentle or whatever kind of man it is you think I need you to be. I just want *you*. I want your passion, not your restraint."

I reach for his shoulders, shoving off his jacket, then I yank on his tie, dragging him down to me. He bends and kisses me, stepping forward against me and forcing me backward with his steps until the backs of my knees hit the bed behind me.

I bend to sit, looking up at him with wonder in my eyes at the way he took my permission and ran with it. I let out a sigh of relief. I don't want to be treated like a broken girl, least of all by him.

He drops to his knees in front of me and presses my thighs apart with his hands. He kisses me with passion I've never felt before and it hits me like a tidal wave. His fervor crashes into me and washes over me. It strikes in my core and my stomach clenches in pleasant need. I can feel the fabric of my underwear dampen with the evidence of how strongly I want Ezra.

I loosen the knot of his tie and he pulls it free, tossing it aside as I get started on the buttons of his vest and shirt. He stops kissing, pulls back, looks down to watch my hands work at the buttons.

My face flushes at the way he pants there on his knees. He looks at my hands as though they held the answers to all the questions in the universe. His eyes catch mine from beneath his lashes and I smile. The way he looks at me makes me feel powerful.

He makes me feel strong.

He makes me feel wanted.

When his shirt is finally on the floor where it belongs, I reach for him, pulling him in close until my breasts brush against his bare chest. His hands are still on my thighs, gliding upward, grazing the rough scars Nikolai has left there.

Ezra looks down as he rubs his thumb over the freshest

one, one he witnessed being made in Nikolai's cruelness. It's still raised, still red, still healing. Then his lips replace his thumb and I gasp at the feel of it. I run my fingers through his hair as he kisses my scars, each and every jagged line that crisscrosses my skin.

I hate them.

I think they're ugly.

But his sensuous attention almost makes me glad to have them there.

I dig into his sandy blond hair as he leaves a trail of heartfelt sensation up the inside of my thigh. I moan when he kisses over my panties, surely feeling the wet spot forming there. Before I know it, he's slipping the fabric down from my hips. I put my knees together so he can drag them from my body, and I scoot back on the bed, lowering slowly to lay in wait for him as he unbuckles his pants and kicks off his shoes.

"This feels stupid to ask given our circumstances but…" he pauses as his pants come off, leaving him standing in front of me in gray boxer briefs, "do I need to wear a condom or something?"

I smirk, shaking my head as I prop up on my elbows to look at his perfectly sculpted dancer's body. He's already hard for me, straining beneath his briefs, and I just wish he would take them off already.

"No," I tell him, "there's a private doctor that he brings in, gives me a birth control shot every three months. Nikolai doesn't have sex with anyone else and he's…he's only shared me once."

My shoulders stiffen at the unwanted memory of being used by Vigo Vittori as payment for information. The one and only time Nikolai shared me with another. Even then, my pussy was off-limits to him. Nikolai tested me for disease anyway, and I was cleared.

I hate that Nikolai is present in my mind at this moment. I want to forget about him, about Vigo, about everything that has to do with the four families.

I just need Ezra to fill me up, overwhelm my senses, take control of my mind, and make me feel something other than constant fear and terror and hopelessness.

"I don't want to talk about that," I say quickly. "I'm clean. Nothing to worry about."

I bend one knee, sliding my heel backward along the mattress and spread my legs apart, just a little farther, in invitation.

He lets out a sigh of relief at the opening I give him. "Thank God." He grins.

The underwear comes off and he practically pounces on me, climbing over my body and covering me like a warm blanket on the winter of my soul.

He kisses behind my ear. "I want to feel everything with you, Anya."

He slides down my body, lips dancing across my skin, until he finds my hardened nipple and swirls his tongue around it.

I moan when he flicks his tongue over it, teasing me into pleasure. He rubs his thumb over the other and the feeling of it is so perfect that I find myself already panting desperately in my need for him.

I've never wanted anything more than I want Ezra.

He reaches down, lower and lower until his fingers find my wetness. He slides two fingers inside me and I gasp. He stills, a look of concern mixing with the lust in his green eyes, and I worry he's going to stop.

It angers me.

If he stops, we'll regret it forever.

I narrow my eyes at him. "Don't you dare stop. Don't you *dare.*"

I don't know if it's what I say or how I say it that ignites him, but his eyes become green fire burning a hole through me. I want it to burn me hotter, brighter, faster. I want his flames to consume me entirely.

With the spark, he shoves his fingers deep inside, his fist pressing against my pussy as he stretches me roughly, reaching deep, deep within me as if he could touch my very soul that way. It's as if he needs to be buried inside me as much as I need him to be.

His mouth lands heavy on mine, devouring me with a wet, sloppy, passionate kiss. He curls his fingers over my G-spot, stroking and pressing so hotly it makes me sweat. He rests his forehead against mine and watches me as he digs into my core. With urgent need, I rock against his hand, fucking his fingers just as much as they fuck me.

Ezra has brilliantly taken a hot moment and made it hotter with the way he groans, the way his eyes sear mine with dirty intent, the way he grinds his cock against the side of my hip with every thrust of his fingers.

We rock and grind as we pant and moan together.

His voice is a deep, dirty, husky tone that threatens to undo me, to turn me into a wanton woman who actually needs sex to survive. I've wanted to *want* for so long, and Ezra has made me want everything raw and dirty he can think to do to me.

"I want you to explode," he says. "I want you to come on my hand, let my fingers feel what my cock has to look forward to."

I hiss out a breath through my teeth. "You have to work for it." Its half-dirty talk, half-truth.

He grins. "Oh, I'll work for it. Then I'll for work it again and again. I'll work all night until you tell me to stop, Anya. I don't want this to end."

"Never." I dig my fingers into his hair at the back of his

head and pull him down to me, kissing him fiercely.

His thumb slips over my clit as he curls his fingers and I gasp into his mouth. There's no rhythm to our kiss, it's just clumsy, urgent wanting.

It's reckless, just like Ezra.

He doesn't stop working me for minutes. He's as desperate as I am to get me there. I feel everything he's doing to me from the inside out. I feel raw, exposed, vulnerable, yet it's so, so, so good.

My climax claws its way out of nowhere. My body stiffens, tense against the building pleasure in my core, but Ezra keeps moving inside me, over me, all around me.

He's everywhere and everything.

But I have to stop him.

Before I tip over the edge, I have to stop him because I want to take him with me. I *need* to take him with me. I think I'll die if I don't take him with me.

I slide backward, forcing his fingers to slip out of me. "Stop, stop," I tell him. "I'm not ready yet."

He looks crestfallen, hurt, concerned. "What did I do?" He thinks it's his fault.

"Lay down," I demand, pushing at the center of his chest. "I want to make you feel what you make me feel."

He lowers to lay back on his elbows and I climb over him, straddling his hips. My hair falls around my face as I grip his jawline with both hands and bend to kiss him.

I glide slowly along the length of his cock, making him slippery with how wet he's made me.

"I want you," he breathes against my lips.

I reach between us to grasp him, guiding his tip where I need him most. He slips inside me with ease when I lower and we both groan at the feel of it.

I barely remembered what this was like—the feeling of mutual, shared pleasure.

The feeling of *wanted* pleasure.

He's buried to the hilt inside me as he kisses the side of my neck and I breathe heavily against his ear.

"Mine?" I ask.

He nips at my skin with his teeth and a shiver runs down my spine.

"Yours," he promises. "Yours, yours, yours."

I rock back and forth with him all the way inside me and he lifts his head to look at me again. I look past the green of his eyes and see his heart, his soul. Everything that he is and everything that I want is right there beneath the emerald surface.

I let my forehead rest against his as pleasure builds quickly with the slow swaying motion. I can feel tears crowding behind my eyelids when I blink.

As Ezra slips an arm around my waist to hold me close, I feel entirely overcome with emotion.

All at once, it's desire, need, longing, hoping, hating, grieving pain. The pain slices across my chest and pushes out a single gasping sob that I didn't expect. But the pain only fans the flame of the heat grinding between my legs.

I'm afraid Ezra will see my pain and try to stop this, but he surprises me. He sees my pain and feels it with me and loves me through it.

He tucks a strand of hair behind my ear and brushes a tear from my cheek. He looks as sorrowful as I feel, knowing that tomorrow we will go back to being slaves. It won't be possible to do this again because privacy will be gone. Kostya will go back to following our every move. Nikolai will go back to tormenting us with his violence.

It makes me angry.

Rage-filled lust rushes and my pussy pulses with the building need. I grind my hips harder, feeling Ezra's thick cock swelling with his quickly oncoming relief. The pulse of him against my G-spot and the stimulation of my clit as I push down hard, rubbing it frantically on the skin of his lower stomach, pushes me closer to the edge.

Where the pain fans the flame, the anger I feel pours fuel all around us. It ignites without warning, exploding into the most all-consuming orgasm I've ever felt. Just as I start to come down from the most perfect wave, Ezra thrusts up, pumping into me hard and fast, and comes with a groan, my name slipping out from between his lips in the sweetest sound.

I hate myself for doing it, but I start to cry.

I cry from relief, from anger, from overwhelming pleasure. I cry for the knowledge of what we are, what I want us to be, for where we are trapped and for the tragic hopelessness of the unknowns yet to come.

Ezra wraps both arms around me and lays back on the bed, holding me, stroking my hair, petting me, as I cry into his chest.

"I won't ever forget this," I tell him when the worst of it has passed.

"It won't be the last time," he replies with a quiet, desperate determination in his voice.

He is the strength I never knew I needed.

I know how dangerous it is to have hope.

But knowing the danger doesn't keep me from hoping when it comes to Ezra.

CHAPTER 25
NIKOLAI

"THE EVIDENCE AGAINST the Campbells is overwhelming and I demand reparations. They plotted to kill off my entire bloodline. It's only by luck I'm still standing here in front of you today. You all would have seen significant losses the last three quarters had they been successful in their plot," I speak candidly to the four families in the boardroom.

"I agree," Vigo Vittori chimes in.

He's twirling a pen in his hand as he leans back in his black leather executive chair at the boardroom table.

"Blood taken requires blood given," he says.

"I understand recourse has already been settled upon, is that correct, Nikolai?" Cordelia O'Shea, the oldest of our generation in the O'Shea family line, asks.

She isn't the Head of House because she's female, her cousin Murphy has that power. But she's allowed a seat on the board for her position as the eldest. The same is true of Vigo's older sister, Renata.

"Let us hear this settlement for a vote," Renata says.

She sits regally in her chair, pushed back from the table as if she's too good for it. Her legs are crossed, her arms intentionally placed on the arm rests, and her spine is arrow straight.

She's always had the appearance of a queen with her skin that's nearly too fair-colored to belong to a Vittori and her jet-black hair that's always perfectly styled in long waves over her shoulders. Her high heels are far too tall for practicality and she wears a perfectly tailored romper rather than an evening gown like the rest of the women.

She thinks she's above them.

It's true, she is.

"I'm curious to know what you've deemed to be a fair settlement for such a heinous act," she says with a tilt of her head.

I grin. "As your brother so shrewdly stated, blood taken requires blood given."

I've been waiting for this delicious moment for over a year, since the day my parents and my younger brother died on one of our planes that went down on its way out of Italy.

Everyone thought the Vittoris had done it.

It was their homeland.

But I knew better.

The Vittoris and the Mikhailovs haven't traditionally had the best of relationships, but that was only because both of our families fought so hard to be the best of the four. It had always been neck and neck between our two families.

But as the Campbells in the States started to increase their sales figures, they became tiresomely cutthroat. Instead of behaving like businessmen and improving their practices, they came after my family, hoping their exclusive trade line that ran through Pakistan would give them the edge on arguing for a takeover when no one was left in my family.

But I hadn't gotten on the plane that day.

I smile to myself, knowing how differently things might have gone for them had I gone down the way they wanted me to. They hadn't accounted for my obsessive and meticulous nature when it came to completing my work on travel. I needed two more days to wrap up loose ends, and I finished my work as expected before flying home to arrange the funeral for my family.

It's what my parents would have expected.

I launched my own investigation, paying vast sums to get the information I needed. The largest sum was paid to Vigo for the recorded phone conversations he'd come into possession of. I paid him by sharing Anya, something I had sworn I would never do.

But when it came down to finding out what really happened to my family and seeking vengeance on the transgressors, even she was a price I was willing to pay. She'd proven by then that she would never love me anyway, and I was drowning in my grief. The combination had been enough for me to justify handing her over to Vigo for an hour.

He'd been fucking brutal with her.

More than I'd ever been.

I'd hoped it would make her grateful for what she had with me, but instead, it made her indignant. My resentment grew daily, exponentially since that day. It compounded each time I saw her dance with Ezra.

That fucking beautiful American boy who thought he could make her love him.

None of it matters now. This is the time I've been waiting for. I'd gotten my proof that the Americans tampered with the mechanical integrity of our aircraft with the intention of bringing it down.

I've presented my evidence to the board.

I've struck a deal with the Campbells for retribution.

Now it's time for the fucking Campbells to pay.

Charles Campbell stands slowly, straightening his lapels and smoothing his jacket. His graying hair and slow movements show his age. His ever-growing gut shows his lack of care for his rapidly declining life expectancy.

He takes in a deep breath and speaks humbly to the room, "When Nikolai came to me with this news of what my son had done, I was devastated." He sniffs, his eyes glassy, but it doesn't bother me. "Blood taken requires blood given. I'm making a…a fair trade in reparations—" His voice cracks as he begins to cry like a fool and lowers back to his seat.

I take over for him. "Three of my family died. My father, my mother, and my brother. I'm taking the same from the Campbell family. He's agreed to hand over the Leblancs—his sister Fleur, her husband Gerard, and their son Leo."

Vigo slams his hand down on the table. "I object to this. What you've presented makes it clear that Chandler Campbell," Charles' son, "is directly responsible for the orchestration of your family's death. Why is he getting away without paying his debt?"

"I assure you," Charles says, "Chandler is repaying this debt to our family. He's been stripped of his place as Head of House."

"And who is taking his place, old man?" Vigo asks.

Clearing his throat, Charles replies, "I am."

Renata floats her hand up from the arm rest as if to silence them. "And who will become the Head of House when you die, Charles, hmm? I understand that Chandler is the only direct Campbell descendant remaining who carries the family name."

"My granddaughter Callista still carries the name," Charles says.

"A woman cannot be the Head of House. Do you plan to produce another heir?" Renata continues.

"Well, no…"

"Well," Renata tilts her head and speaks as calmly as a river flows, smoothly but with the power to chisel mountainsides, "I would suggest Leo Leblanc be given the title of Head of House and Chandler be handed over for execution. It seems only fair given that Chandler has masterminded the slaying of the Mikhailov family."

"Let's put it to a vote," Vigo agrees.

"But, no…you can't—" Charles attempts to interrupt and I cut him off, leaning forward and slamming my hands down on the boardroom table.

"Enough from you! You and I have come to our agreement, Charles. Three from your house for the three taken from mine. I gave you the option of selecting the three and we both knew full well the final decision would rest with the board. Now, shut your mouth and let the board vote."

Charles breaks into pathetic, sniveling sobs that I roll my eyes against.

Vigo rises from his seat, coming to stand beside me at the head of the table. "Official vote. All in favor of reparations to the Mikhailov family by the blood of Fleur and Gerard Leblanc and Charles Campbell, say aye."

A resounding agreement.

A beautifully vengeful, resounding agreement.

I straighten and smile, crossing my arms over my chest.

"All opposed," Vigo says, "say nay."

Charles shoots to his feet, his oversized gut nearly lifting the table on his way up. "Nay! We had an agreement, Nikolai."

"And the agreement is being honored by the wishes of the board," I sneer at him with a tilted head.

"It's done," Murphy O'Shea adds, "Leo Leblanc will become the Head of House for the now former Campbells. The family bloodline will continue with the Leblancs for future generations and we will no longer recognize the power of the

Campbells. Reparations should be paid immediately."

"Egan is watching over the Leblancs now. I'll go and ask him to bring them here." Cordelia stands and leaves the room.

I nod at Kostya. "Lay down the tarps."

When I say this, it sends Charles into another tailspin of useless sobbing. If I still had a heart, I might give a shit that he's about to lose his son.

But I lost my humanity two decades ago, the first time I acquired a human asset and sold her to the highest bidder when I was just nineteen years old. I signed a contract with the Devil seven years after that when I chose Anya to become my talent slave. I was twenty-six and she was just a child. The Devil came to collect on my soul the very day I collected Anya three years ago.

The empty space where my soul used to reside is now filled only with anger, mistrust, resentment, and vengeance.

There's no room for anything else.

Cordelia O'Shea returns with the Leblancs, black hoods over their heads, their arms secured behind their backs with cable ties. Their grunts and wails beneath the black hoods bring a smile to my face.

Finally.

Finally, I will get to avenge my family.

Egan O'Shea and Kostya force them down to their knees on the blue tarp that's been laid out at the front of the boardroom. I expect the blood to splatter everywhere, but at least the tarps will mostly protect my carpets from the stains. There's a reason my family chose to install red carpet here, after all.

The hoods are lifted from their faces to reveal them each gagged with black fabric they bite between their teeth. Their eyes are wide and curious as they look around the room to see that they are here with the four families. I can see the flicker of thought run across their eyes that perhaps they are safe here, they see their family member Charles, after all.

Then Cordelia ushers Chandler Campbell into the room and my face alights with sinister glee. He walks in behind her, adjusting his navy-blue suit jacket, thinking he's being called in for business.

I can't wait to blow the cocky smirk right off this bastard's face.

"I suppose you've decided to reinstate me as Head of House, then," Chandler says with an arrogant grin and a tilt of his head.

"No, dear." Cordelia taps his shoulder and gives him a crooked smile before she returns to her seat.

I pull my switchblade from my pocket and circle around to Leo Leblanc. His parents groan and attempt to shout through their gags as I approach him from behind. I bend and slice the zip ties that bind him and step back.

Leo leaps to his feet, a frightened baby bird in the eagle's nest. He pulls his fabric gag from his mouth and presses his back to the far wall, his parents crying on their knees.

I look to Chandler, who stands stoically like the callous bastard he is. I point to the spot on the tarp next to Leo's parents with the tip of my knife. It crinkles beneath my shoes as I shift my weight.

"Come. Kneel," I command.

Chandler looks dumbstruck. "Excuse me?"

"I'm sorry, son," Charles sobs like a fool, pushing his fingers beneath his glasses to pinch the bridge of his nose.

"I don't understand…"

"You laid the plans that killed my family, yes?" I say. "Blood taken requires blood given. The board has ruled. Yours is to be given as reparations along with Mr. and Mrs. Leblanc. Leo," I turn to the young man trembling against the wall, "take a breath.

You've been spared. In fact, welcome. You've been voted as the new Head of House for the Campbell family. Excuse me, now the Leblanc family."

The four families applaud in chorus.

"You may have Charles' seat. Move, Charles."

Charles rises slowly and turns away from the scene at the front of the room. Like a coward, he abandons his son in favor of cowering in the far corner. He's too weak to face his child, to tell him goodbye, to watch him die.

Leo looks to his mother and father on their knees and only begins to move as his mother nods at him eagerly, tilting her head toward the seat. At least she has the presence of mind to understand how lucky her son is to be spared, let alone to be given such a prestigious role within the four families.

Chandler still hasn't moved.

"Accept your fate, Chandler," I growl at him.

He shakes his head, backing away toward the door. "No, no, you can't do this."

Renata snaps to her feet. "Enough with the theatrics. So dramatic. Kostya, grab him and *make* him kneel. Let's get on with this. We have other business matters to attend to."

Kostya wrestles Chandler to the ground in front of me on the tarp. I haven't seen a sight so beautiful as the back of his head as he fights and screams for his life. Vigo hands me his gun—the same one he always carries in his chest holster beneath his jacket.

"Full magazine," he tells me. "One round for each of them and plenty to spare."

I cock the gun and press it to Chandler's dirty blond hair. His American arrogance and sand-colored locks flash across my vision as familiar.

Ezra Bell.

Ezra *fucking* Bell.

Ezra and that perfect golden hair and those goddamn green eyes that only look at her.

At Anya.

My Anya.

I exhale and squeeze the trigger, unloading three rounds into the back of Chandler Campbell's head. Blood sprays across my carefully tailored suit and feels warm against my cheek. I feel the liquid where it splashed onto my bottom lip and I swipe my tongue across to taste it. It's metallic, the taste of pure fucking justice.

The room is silent in waiting, only broken by the pathetic sob from Charles in the far corner of the room and a sharp cry from Mrs. Leblanc through her gag. Her sound interrupts the reverie of this satisfying moment, so I swing my arm and take her out next. Her body topples sideways onto her husband and he groans loudly as he falls to the floor. I take a step to make sure my aim is true and unload one last round into the side of his head.

Three crimson pools spill slowly out onto the tarp, puddling from beneath the three heads.

Blood taken requires blood given.

Vengeance served so sweetly.

My chest heaves with the immediate relief I feel from finally avenging my family. I reach up to swipe the blood from my cheek and swirl it between my fingers, watching the way it coats my skin in the most brilliant shade of crimson imaginable. I let out a heavy breath, letting my arms fall to my sides and tilt my head toward the ceiling. I take in a deep cleansing breath, trying to savor the moment.

But the relief is fleeting.

Now I have blood, but I still don't have my family.

I still don't have Anya's love.

I still don't have Ezra's desire.

I am still without.

And I am angrier than ever.

I hold the gun out toward Vigo, but he waves it away.

"There are plenty of rounds left for you to injure a certain dancer if you don't want a reason to torture yourself with her presence any longer."

My eyebrows slant inward as I narrow my eyes. My gut reaction is to tell him to fuck off, but there's some small part of me that hears him, a small part that feels understood in my torment over her.

That same part thinks she deserves to be one of his broken dolls.

I turn my head to glare at him. "I'm not selling you Anya." Though, for the first time, I'm not entirely sure I mean it.

I wonder if she's the reason why my relief for this moment was stolen away so swiftly. Because she torments me daily, giving her attention to Ezra, but even worse, receiving his attention in return.

I fucking hate them both for that.

The vengeance in my heart is returning anew. I don't feel satisfied that I've caused enough hurt to those who've hurt me.

For the first time, I sincerely wonder if offloading Anya to a crueler master would satisfy my obsession with hurting her and finally give my mind the reprieve it deserves.

I give Vigo another glance, a nod, then lift the back of my jacket and tuck the gun into my belt.

CHAPTER 26
Anya

MY EYES BLINK open from what was perhaps the most serene sleep I've experienced in years. I'm curled around Ezra's back where he sleeps on his side next to me.

I don't know what time it is, but I normally wake up several times during the night.

Never content.

Never feeling fully safe.

I suffer nightmares that wake me often.

But as I awaken now from a peacefully dreamless sleep, I feel refreshed in a way I've never felt before.

It's because of Ezra.

I nuzzle my nose across his spine and breathe in. I inhale the heady scent of him and kiss the center of his back tenderly.

I'm certain it must still be the middle of the night and that we probably have a few more hours of peace before I need to wake Ezra and make him leave. I don't know how Nikolai would react if he knew Ezra had been here and shared my bed. I'm risking a lot as it is not to wake him now and send him away to his room.

I roll onto my back with a yawn, my eyes drifting shut again, and I stretch my arms above my head. My bare breasts lift out from beneath the sheet and the cool air in the room brushes over my nipples, making me shiver. It's such a stark contrast to the heat of pressing them against Ezra's warm body.

I smile to myself, recalling the way he touched me last night, the way he sucked and licked and teased and made my entire body explode from pure nirvanic, *wanted* pleasure. He helped me find heaven in his arms, even if it was only for a few hours.

But then I realize those hours are done.

There's a prickle of awareness creeping over my skin.

Untangled from Ezra's overwhelming, calming aura, my heart claws its way up my throat with the swift drop-off of my sudden descent back into hell.

I can sense *him* in the room.

I hold my breath and open my eyes slowly.

Daylight peeks in from behind the closed curtains.

It's morning.

We slept all night.

And Nikolai stands beside the bed.

I swallow hard.

Inhale, exhale, inhale.

I sit up slowly, trying my best to limit my movements on the mattress. I don't want to wake Ezra. If I can just get Nikolai out of the room, let him punish me for this in whatever way he chooses, maybe I can spare Ezra the pain of having to witness it.

My pulse is pounding and I will my heart to stop beating, just until I can leave. I'm afraid Ezra knows my heart too well, that he'll feel my fear in his sleep and wake from dreamland into a nightmare.

I stand slowly. Nikolai doesn't step back, so my bare chest bumps his as I get to my feet.

"You've become an ungrateful bitch, *rabynya*," he spits the words at me, his nostrils flaring.

I whisper, "Just punish me and get it over with."

He reaches around and grabs a fistful of my hair, yanking back hard. I nearly yelp, though I try to remain quiet, as he forces my head to angle far to the side. My hands reach for his in a vain attempt to pull him off, but he holds me in place.

"Please…" I beg. "Please, please don't wake him."

I'm done for, but part of me hopes that Ezra might be spared the pain of witnessing my torment.

"Don't wake him?" he repeats with a growl. "Don't wake him?!"

"Shh, please, please…"

But it's too late.

Ezra startles. It takes a moment, but he realizes what's happening quickly enough, though Nikolai is already dragging me across the room by my hair. Ezra leaps after us, both of us clad in only our underwear.

As Nikolai pauses to pull the door open so he can drag me out into the hallway, Ezra runs for him.

"No!" I shout at Ezra because there's no point in fighting.

Ezra never touches Nikolai, never even comes close. He stops dead in his tracks, then holds his hands up in surrender before taking a slow step backward.

I glance over to see that Nikolai holds a gun in his free hand. He holds a gun and he's pulling me out to punish me. An arctic wind whips around me, a frozen brush across my skin, and my spine tingles with a rush of fear.

I scream, "No! Nikolai, please."

"I told you that you were on thin ice. I fucking *warned* you." He's come completely unhinged with the rapid way he speaks, a piece of his disheveled, ashen hair falling across his eye. "I knew you would do this, I *knew* you would. You never gave me a chance, Anya, from the moment I brought you home."

Brought me home?

"Home? You're pathetic, Nikolai. This was never my home."

"It was *always* your home. Since you were eleven years old this was your *fucking* home. You were lucky to have me as your benefactor. I paid for your talent! I own it, it belongs to *me!*"

"And I've paid my debt for it with blood, sweat, and tears."

"You've paid nothing. *Nothing.* Not so much as your gratitude. And perhaps that's why you are so ungrateful. You owe me."

"She owes you shit," Ezra interjects bravely.

Nikolai cocks the gun that's still aimed at Ezra. The sound is enough to shake my tears loose, rattling my bones into jumping at the simple yet foreboding *click.*

"No, no, Nikolai, please. I'm sorry. I'm so sorry. Just tell me what you want me to do and I'll do it. Don't hurt him, *please,* don't hurt him."

He tilts his head looking down at me and I dare to stare back. Something flashes across the gray, something desperate, something primal, something I might almost mistake as heartache if I didn't know better.

"What is it?" he snarls. "Did you fall in love with this one? You let him fuck you and now you're in love?" He laughs and it's one of the most terrifying things I've ever heard.

He swings the gun around and presses it to my temple. I whimper and flinch. Ezra is saying something frantically, but I can't make out the words.

My brain roars. It's been lit on fire by fear and it screams to escape the cage of my skull. I can't think of anything other than dousing these flames, dampening the terror.

Nikolai still holds me firmly in his grip with his fist around my hair. I sob, the cold metal reminding me of death and how close it is to becoming my reality. For the first time in so, so long, I don't secretly wish for death to take me.

I don't want to die.

I want to be with Ezra, wherever he is.

Nikolai releases my hair and I immediately step back. He moves toward me, aiming the gun at the center of my forehead with his outstretched arm.

"Walk," he says to me, holding the door open.

The fire in my head roars again, telling me to do what he says, to obey the man with the tool that could end me in less than a second.

I don't glance at Ezra.

I can't.

My eyes refuse to look away from the gun.

I don't dare turn my back to Nikolai, so I back myself out of the room, taking slow, careful steps. I creep backward down the hallway until Nikolai gets fed up with my pace.

"Turn the *fuck* around and walk, Anya," he shouts.

I jump, my bare breasts jostling, reminding me of how exposed I am. It takes all my thought and all my strength to force my body to turn, to take my eyes off the instrument of death that's threatening my very existence.

I move slowly toward the grand staircase, topless, with nothing but my panties on to cover me, knowing full well the four families are still here to watch my punishment, or perhaps even my death, in full glory.

I cross my arms over my chest, then drop them to my sides, deciding that I'd rather keep my dignity with my head held high rather than try in vain to cover myself in shame.

The only shame I feel is thinking that hope and I could reconcile our differences.

"Down," Nikolai tells me when I reach the top of the grand staircase.

I descend slowly. I felt nearly on top of the world walking down this very staircase last night in my pink gown, walking hand in hand with the boy I fell in love with. Now I descend with an ache in my chest and fear pulsing through my veins.

I'm not walking down to an empty entryway as would normally be the case. The four families mill about, crossing the space, talking to one another, some of them have their slaves with them.

Everyone turns to look as I make my way down the stairs and step down onto the marble floor.

"Kneel," Nikolai says, and the gun is against the side of my head again.

I flinch then quickly lower to my knees on the floor.

He's going to kill me here.

Everything stops.

The four families still and quieten.

I can feel every eye in Mikhailov Manor upon me.

It's a show for them, a dramatic event to entertain them. It's no different than the performances given by the talent slaves.

I feel lightheaded, sick to my stomach, and my hands are shaking with one question bouncing around inside my skull.

Am I going to die today?

Sound comes back to me in a rush as I suddenly think of Ezra, remembering he's here, he's watching this and powerless to stop it. I snap my head to look at him, just feet away, as my fire-engulfed brain explodes in pain with an all new kind of terror.

What will become of Ezra if Nikolai blows my brains out in front of him? If he's forced to see me lifeless on the floor, blood pooling around my head and staining his feet?

God, no.

I can't bear to think of it. Tears that wipe away any dignity I might have had left drip down my cheeks against my will. I sniff and tilt my chin, lifting my head a little higher, hoping it masks my fear.

It's not for me or for Nikolai.

It's for the man I fell in love with.

That man is losing his mind with worry right now. It's evident to everyone around us with the way he shouts and swears and tries to fight against Kostya. But the gun that Nikolai holds puts us both in our places.

Though I still feel Ezra's rage vibrating in my soul, Nikolai startles my attention away as he shouts to no one and everyone who will listen.

"Let this be a lesson to all of you ungrateful whores. You belong to your master. Your *body* belongs to your master. You do not get to choose who you give it to. Vicious, conniving *sluts*, the whole lot of you."

No one bats an eye at Nikolai's behavior. No one intervenes to stop him. I am nothing more than a talent slave and Nikolai can end my life right here and now if he wishes to.

He steps forward and my body jolts.

I press my eyes shut tight.

I breathe slowly.

I count.

One. Two. Three. Four. Five. Six. Seven. Eight.

One. Two. Three. Four. Five. Six—

PLAYLIST

ANYA AND EZRA'S PERFORMANCE SONG
Hallelujah by Jeff Buckley

Heart Killer by Gossling
bury a friend by Billie Eilish
Trampoline by SHAED & ZAYN
Dance Monkey by Tones And I
River by Bishop Briggs
Six Feet Under by Billie Eilish
Black Hole Sun by Nouela
Wicked Game by Chris Isaak
Iris by Kina Grannis
Unsteady by X Ambassadors
If the World Was Ending by JP Saxe & Julia Michaels
Love Me Now by John Legend
Sweet Dreams (Are Made of This) by Marilyn Manson
I Will Survive by J2 featuring Blu Holliday

The story continues in...

DANCE WITH DEATH

BRYNN FORD

AVAILABLE NOW!

ACKNOWLEDGMENTS

I've been dreaming of writing and publishing a dark romance for years—though I honestly hadn't expected this story to be the first. Anya and Ezra just kept on nudging me to tell their story and so, here we are. I'm so thankful that you decided to come along on their journey!

My beta readers—Rachel, Danielle, Carrie, and Kaylan—are nothing short of amazing! Thank you all for the helpful comments and feedback that helped me make this book the best it can be! A special thank you to Rachel for helping me catalog and keep track of all the details.

To my editor, Silvia, a huge thank you for helping me clean up my manuscript. You gave me much needed confidence in Anya and Ezra's story and I can't wait to work with you on the rest!

I'm so grateful for the amazing people at Najla Qamber Designs for making such a beautiful book cover and putting on the finishing touches with the interior formatting. You are all amazing to work with and I'm so thankful for the beauty you brought to this story!

Thank you to my husband. You've always believed in me and supported me in this crazy writing journey. I know you don't always "get it" but you're still understanding of my need to do this thing. You're the best!

To friends and family who've supported me along the way, thank you for being there for me!

Finally, a huge thank you to all you daring readers! Dark romance readers are definitely my people and I'm so happy my book made its way into your hands (and hopefully into your heart, too). I hope you enjoyed reading **Counts of Eight** as much as I enjoyed writing it—sorry for the brutal cliffhanger, but at least you've got something to look forward to, right?

ABOUT THE AUTHOR

Brynn Ford is a USA Today Bestselling Author of dark romance for daring readers. She writes emotionally heavy love stories that will twist your soul and shatter your heart before pulling you back together with a hopeful happily-ever-after.

Brynn's books are dark, sometimes disturbing, and often overwhelming. But they're always brightened by an insistent, spicy romance that will live rent-free in your head long after you've turned the final page.

When Brynn isn't obsessively writing, you may find her binge-watching favorite shows while eating far too much junk food or fanatically reading, always seeking to lose herself in the emotional roller coaster of a damn good story. She's a firm believer that her characters continue to live outside the pages in the minds of her readers. Stories don't end just because there aren't any more pages to turn.

CONNECT WITH BRYNN FORD

WEBSITE
Click "Newsletter"
to subscribe to my author newsletter!
www.brynnford.com

GOODREADS
www.goodreads.com/brynnfordauthor

AMAZON
www.amazon.com/author/brynnford

BOOKBUB
www.bookbub.com/profile/brynn-ford

INSTAGRAM
@brynnfordauthor
www.instagram.com/brynnfordauthor

FACEBOOK
www.facebook.com/brynnfordauthor

FACEBOOK GROUP
Brynn's Daring Darlings
bit.ly/brynnsdarlings

www.ingramcontent.com/pod-product-compliance
Lightning Source LLC
Chambersburg PA
CBHW020911060726
47591CB00004B/1187